THE SNOW EAGLE

by

FRANK F. BELL

-illustrated-

This book is an enhanced edition to provide larger, legible type and line spacing, plus quality white paper for better and easier reading.

To my wife Wilma for her support; my daughter
Franci Kaye whose interest and knowledge of
American Indian lore provided a most welcome
reference source, and Nuvadi, a Hopi boy.

THE SNOW EAGLE

PUBLISHED BY

WESTERN HORIZONS BOOKS
Post Office Box 4068
Helena, Montana 59604

SUN DIAL PRESS
P.O. Box 16400-141
Mesa, Arizona 85211

ISBN 0 - 934959 - 00 - 5
Printed in the United States of America
(Cover; Kiva Ceremonial Wall Painting,
Composit photo by author)

ACKNOWLEDGEMENT

This book was completed with the help of many people: attendants at museums and culture centers, folks in libraries and archives and others who helped in locating and obtaining research materials which provide a foundation for the story. Journals written by chroniclers of expeditions into the early Spanish south west named many military and government persons and others of high rank. Unflagging research provided names of obscure persons whose antecedents undoubtedly participated in events of previous centuries. The story is about these people.

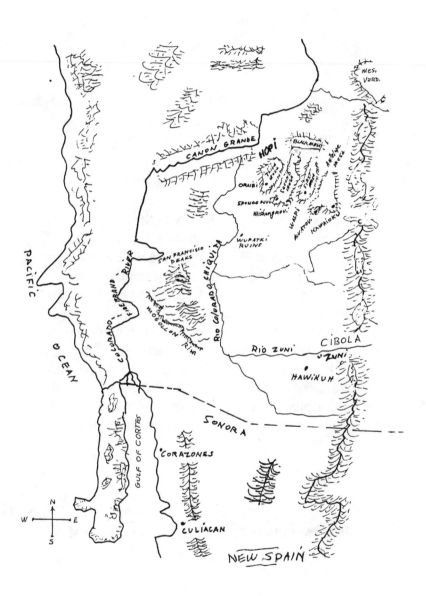

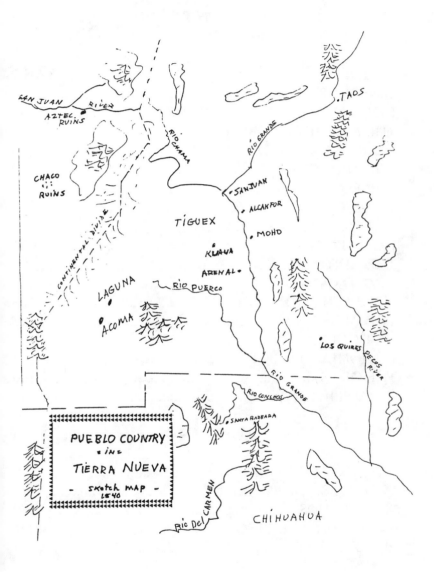

PUEBLO COUNTRY
• in •
TIERRA NUEVA
— Sketch Map —
1540

SAN JUAN RIVER

AZTEC RUINS

RIO CHAMA

RIO GRANDE

TAOS

CHACO RUINS

CONTINENTAL DIVIDE

TIGUEX

SAN JUAN

ALCANFOR

MOHO

KUAUA

ARENAL

LAGUNA

RIO PUERCO

ACOMA

LOS QUIRES

PECOS RIVER

RIO GRANDE

RIO CONCHOS

SANTA BARBARA

RIO DEL CARMEN

CHIHUAHUA

CONTENTS
PART ONE

PART TWO

ILLUSTRATIONS

PART ONE
THE SNOW EAGLE
Chapter One

DISCOVERY

Sam Michaelson, his wife Cindy and son Mark age ten, pulled off U. S. Highway 175 at the beckoning of a roadside sign announcing "Recreation Area". A space in the shade of a small grove of cottonwood trees provided relief from the hot Colorado sun.

"We are near the turn off for Mesa Verde National Park where the cliff dwellings are. " Cindy looked up from the perusal of a road map. Sam was sprawled on the camper's back seat, a can of pop in one hand.

"I would just as soon stay here for the night and go in tomorrow," Sam offered.

Mark, meanwhile, explored an adjacent area which had been bulldozed for an expanded parking zone. Heaps of dirt lay along the perimeter. He kicked into the sandy soil as he walked. "Ow". His foot connected with something solid just below the surface. The dislodged metallic-like object appeared to be a small urn or container, dark gray in color.

"Look what I found, Dad!" Mark's voice filled with excitement as he bounded up the two steps into the camper.

"Bring me a damp cloth. " Sam turned the object over in his hands.

Cindy squeezed water from the end of a towel and handed it to Mark who passed it on to his father. Particles of earth and a layer of corroded metallic substance rubbed off as Sam washed and buffed the surface. The near shapeless glob slowly changed into something recognizable in the shape of a vase or other vessel with a small pedestal emerging at one end.

"It's rather small but it looks like an urn. Here on the bottom is the faint imprint of letters and numerals!" Sam gave it to Cindy and Mark for them to see.

Cindy's examination was thorough, corroborating Sam's identification. "It does appear to be an old pewter urn but it could be some other combination of metals. See that number 1540? If it is a date, the metal has withstood over 400 years of corrosion pretty well. Some of the numbers and letters are cut quite deep while others look like they were scratched on. Mark, I think you have found something here!"

The next day the family became completely enamored and fascinated by the sight of the time worn cliff dwellings nestled in crevices and open caves, of the steep walls of Mesa Verde's deep canyons. The ancient housing projects of multi-story construction, passageways and circular ceremonial rooms depicted the reality of Indian life terminated seven centuries previous.

In the southwestern Colorado city of Cortez, Cindy visited the public library to investigate the origins of Spanish metallurgy and metal working. Her hunch was right. She found that Iberian craftsmen excelled in metal-work particularly in the forging of weapons during the fifteenth and sixteenth centuries.

Silversmiths of the time produced silver and combined with other metals, alloys, for the molding of various vessels, vases and cinerary jarrons (urns)! These artisans were also adept at installing locking mechanisms of secret design and methods of unfastening through interlinking.

That evening Sam cleaned the stem and sides of the vessel with a toothbrush and alcohol combined with applications of silver cream purchased by Cindy.

"Write down these numbers and letters Mark," Sam called out excitedly.

      lb - C-R-N-DO   —1540

      T - VA - -   -O-QI   H-OM- - A

"Look at this Cindy." Sam held out the paper indicating the markings recorded. They looked them over intently.

"I have an idea," Sam shouted as he ran out the door of the van and across a gravel pathway to the office of the vehicle park. He soon returned with a large magnifying glass borrowed from the proprietor. Held to the surface of the urn, the glass brought out the engravings and etchings for better visibility. The markings could now be combined into words and symbols.

      Ib III   CORONADO   JUNIO 1540

      TOVAR—   MOQUI   HONMANA

Cindy, peered at the two men in her family. "From my intense research at the library, I would say that Ib III is a craft mark from Iberian metal-workers, Coronado is self explanatory and of course the date is June, 1540. Iberia is part of Spain, Mark."

"Wow, The Coronado Expedition!. We can keep it, can't we?" Mark danced around the small area waving the vessel.

Cindy answered. "I don't see why not, but we should find out more about it. The other names seem to be similar to those in some of the travel folders for this area. Our next stop should be an Indian reservation. How about the Navajo?"

"I'd like to see the Aztec Ruins National Monument. It is only a few extra miles to Aztec, New Mexico." Mark was now holding a road map.

Early the following day the Michaelsons visited the colorful site of the early pueblo dwellers and proceeded on through Farmington and Shiprock, New Mexico to Teec Nos Pos, Arizona in the Four Corners area bringing together the boundaries of Colorado, Utah, Arizona and New Mexico. Here Highway 160 was rejoined, routed through Navajo country. Very rewarding was the trip through Monument Valley which had all the earmarks of a romantic land rich in Indian legends and located in the region of current and ancient villages of various tribes. Sam Michaelson, an assistant professor of Biology at the University of Denver, decided that they should seek out a knowledgeable person familiar with tribal history who could provide valuable information.

At Kayenta, Arizona a young man selling Navajo turquoise jewelry at a stand outside a pueblo-type building, provided a brief history of local Indian customs and a schedule of forthcoming dances and events. Sam delved deeper, asking for the where-abouts of an older person, a tribal spokesman perhaps, that would know about the tribe's ancient history. The accommodating young man stepped to oneside and extended an arm to nudge an old Indian sitting in an alcove in the wall of the adobe structure. Before the hand touched him, the man looked up, peering from beneath a western style black hat revealing a thatch of white hair atop a deeply lined face and forehead.

"I heard you, Pablo." A crackling voice echoed in the niche. The old man directed his gaze at Sam.

"The history of the Pueblo tribes can go back to the days of the white man's horse soldiers, the Spanish or way beyond to ancient days. Which is your interest?"

Sam produced a slip of paper containing the name Honmana obtained from the urn. "I thank you for giving of your time. The name on this paper interests me. Will you tell me if the name is one of your tribe, or possibly another"

The old man took the paper and scrutinized the words, separating groups of letters with a finger and studying the parts. "Do you have another word or name associated with this?"

"Well, yes, I guess that these words would go with it." Sam printed TOVAR and MOQUI on the paper.

Another assessment of the words was made. "These are not of our tribe or people." I am Zuni, here on a visit with relatives. You must take this to the Hopi. The Spanish called them MOQUI. HONMANA is a name for a Hopi girl."

Sam looked at the Zuni man with great respect. "Your help to me is very much appreciated. Whom do you suggest I see at the Hopi village?"

The old man peered unseeing at Sam. He did not hear the question. After a few moments he muttered. "I see the Spanish, shining metal on their chests and heads, big animals carrying them on their backs. They were a small band and they were welcome at our village. In their midst was a person in long brown robes. He placed a wooden cross at the base of a cliff. Our pueblo was high above the desert terrain.

"The leader was TOVAR, el Capitan. He inquired about a city of gold. Our Chief told him about a large pueblo that existed farther north and to the west. It was a Hopi village. The Spaniards went to that place after a few days. We heard of a great leader, Coronado, TOVAR was in his army. This was many years ago."

Sam tried to question further but turned away, observing that the Zuni had fallen asleep, his chin resting on brown arms folded across his chest.

CHAPTER TWO

HOPIS MEET CONQUISTADORES

Heading for the Hopi reservation in northern Arizona the Michaelsons traversed the Painted Desert, an area richly endowed by nature in colorful desert flatland, volcanic islands with mineret-like towers reaching upward to the blue sky and desert plateaus continually changing shades of color.

Cindy pointed to an exceptional redstone monument towering above the desert floor. "Sam, turn off at the sign ahead so we can get closer to that pillar of red rock." The road led to a parking area providing a view of several monoliths, monuments to the ancient past. With the doors of the camper opened wide, all three enjoyed a cold can of pop obtained from their cooler.

"This view is awesome. I've read that these battered relics are older than the Rocky Mountains! Many are old volcano funnels of hardened layers of lava which have withstood hundreds of thousands of years, right here in the desert. The elements, sun and wind have worn them down but their individual mystery and majesty are sealed in each one." Cindy was inspired.

"I agree with all that you have said. What amazing stories must be locked up in these ancient artifacts of nature. It would be a tremendous revelation of animals, people and flora as well as the archaeology involved." Within himself, Sam vowed to start an investigation into some of these secrets. Meantime, Mark read information panels in the shade of a shingled lean-to.

Sitting with Sam on a visitor bench, Cindy peered thoughtfully at the desert panorama. "You know, I have made several searches of family lineage which led its way back to sixteenth century Spain. Such names as Diego Lopez, Rodrigo Maldonado, Alonzo del Moral and de Guzman surfaced, many from Castile. Records indicate that a large representation of that region were involved in the exploration and conquest of the New World by the Spanish. When the opportunity arises, I want to make some inquiries."

The topic of conversation in the Michaelson family as they continued through the Painted Desert was the contemplation of hardships that would have been encountered four centuries prior crossing the region on foot or horseback.

"Quite different compared to our camper, " declared Cindy succinctly as she peered at the rugged land.

At the Hopi culture center at Shongopavi on Second Mesa they were escorted to a well lighted room containing a hand loom fitted with an intricately patterned blanket, partly completed. An elderly Indian woman introduced as Siki, or Julia her American name, removed herself from the weaving bench and held out a hand in greeting, then graciously motioned toward a table and chairs.

Cindy described their search for information concerning the names they had listed, but did not mention the discovery of the jarron. "We were told at Kayenta about Tovar coming to the Hopis and we have come seeking their historical connection."

Siki's dark eyes twinkled brightly. "You have done well. I will tell you how the first meeting with Castillians came about."

Sam had placed a tape recorder on the table. "May I connect the recorder while you are talking?"

"It will not bother me at all." Siki pulled the microphone across the table within arm's length, where she could speak freely. Her eyes closed in a stance of meditation as she recalled the legends and historical events. The narration began.

The dust swirl, a moving speck on the hot desert plain, grew as it came nearer to Antelope Mesa. Qombitua stood on a *balcón* jutting from a small room atop a stone and clay building at cliff's edge. Squinting through the haze and reflected brilliance of the morning sun, his gaze swept the vast open country. Beside him stood Honmana, a Hopi maiden visiting the village of Kawaioku. It was her daily practice to greet the rising sun and feel the warmth that it provided her people and all living things. She followed the half-circle of his inspection- a mixture of terrain and sky undulating in ghost-like figures caused by the ever present heat waves. Her serene and beautiful face showed no change of expression as Qombitua gestured in the direction where the young Indian woman had previously spotted the small dust cloud.

"We will look at that place again, later in the day. It is far off." Honmana took the outstretched hand offered to assist her over a stone step and into the adjacent room opening into a plaza.

The *vigilante* and his companion did not know that the minuscule stirring of dust was caused by a small Spanish expeditionary contingent comprised of cavalrymen, a few foot *soldados*, Zuni Indian guides and a priest under the command of Captain Pedro de Tovar, Chief Ensign in the army of General Francisco Vasquez de Coronado.

The *conquistadores* trudged forward on foot leading their lame horses over rocky ridges, around deep scars in the earth's surface and strangely shaped mounds of volcanic rock towering from the valley floor. The ancient, weathered land had sapped the strength of man and beast after five days of struggling over the rugged terrain. They were now some twenty-five leagues, about ninety five miles, northwest of the main force headquartered on the *Rio Colorado Chiquita* at Cibola, the region embracing seven Zuni villages.

* * * * *

Barely a week had transpired since the capture of Hawikuh, the largest Zuni pueblo. The fifteen hundred mile trek by the Expedition from New Spain had exhausted the army which was very low on provisions. Captain Garcia Lopez de Cardenas and a small scouting group had been attacked by the Cibolans a few miles from the pueblo, which stood six stories high in the center portion with terraced apartments flanking the sides. Although Cardenas' approach to the citadel was met by another advance guard, his pleas for them to lay down their weapons and accept gifts peaceably were ignored and they hastened to retire to the looming structure. When Coronado arrived with a small squad ahead of the main force, he found two to three hundred defenders formed in military formation and heavily armed with bows, arrows, war clubs and protected by leather shields. Another attempt at persuasion and gifts made little inroad primarily due to lack of understanding of the language and inability of interpreters to adequately define terms. Members of Indian tribes in northern New Spain who had become dominated by the Spaniards as a result of their forays and colonization over the previous dozen years, journeyed with the expedition as interpreters and guides. In their midst were southern natives whose language bore Aztec foundations similar to Zuni and Hopi. These people were then utilized to the fullest extent in the matter of interpretation, proving to be more adaptable.

A skirmish took place when a few Zuni warriors seemed to test the soldados, but was scarcely underway before the main army came into view with banners and flags waving and columns of cavalrymen two hundred fifty strong and in formation four abreast presenting a formidable front. Following were approximately two hundred foot soldiers and about four hundred native Indians and support personnel who co-mingled with families and wives of army regulars. Stretching back for a half-mile was a herd of over one thousand horses, mules and sheep. Pack animals moved slowly, weighted by domestic stores, weapons and black powder for small cannon and arquebuses. Alarmed by this array, the Cibolan warriors broke ranks, fleeing into their quarters in the pueblo. Volleys of arrows from that direction caused the general to order the attack. His men could hardly be retained since they knew that stores of food were available in the pueblo and their force had been augmented.

Built of stone and adobe with a surrounding wall, capture of the structure was not easily attained. Warriors from other Cibola villages rallied to assist in the defense of Hawikuh pueblo increasing the number inside threefold. It was practically an impenetrable fortress since no entrances were provided at the ground floor. The roofs of lower levels were reached by ladders which could be pulled up and raised to higher levels if necessary to thwart an enemy. Breaking down a gate in the wall, the general and his party drove forward but were caught in a narrow and crooked pathway to the building by a heavy shower of rocks, arrows and other missiles discharged from above. The barrage was aimed apparently at the general's golden helmet and armor, striking in successive blows which might have killed him but for the action of two officers who threw their bodies over him for protection. As he was carried to the rear and placed in a tent, command of the troops passed to the maestro de campo, Don Pedro de Tovar. After about an hour of sporadic fighting, the Indians indicated they had enough and wished to leave the pueblo. This request was granted and they left unharmed by the Castillians. When the general regained consciousness he was relieved to learn that the pueblo was in the army's hands and that the men had feasted on large quantities of food found in storage. Native women who had remained in the stronghold came forward and aided in the preparation of the repast.

Wishing to advise Viceroy Mendoza of the situation, Coronado sent patrols to learn more about the region. Reports of these surveillances revealed the fact that Cibola did not contain the legendary Seven Cities of Gold. Frustration turned to optimism when the local Indians disclosed the existence of another province to the north. It also contained seven pueblo communities located on high promontories and populated by people whom the Spaniards called Moqui. They identified the region as Tusayan province. The general soon dispatched his able officer, Captain Tovar, heading a group with orders to report back in about a month.

* * * * * *

Patches of grass and mesquite appeared in abundance as the plateau leveled off, marked with mounds of red and gray earth seemingly left behind or dropped from the sky. The group stopped, allowing the horses to munch on the savory *hierba*. Don Pedro scanned a roughly sketched map of *Tierra Nueva*, the newly explored territory adjacent to Sonora, northern province of New Spain.

An Indian guide approached. "El Capitan, look west where the sky meets the earth." High, dark shapes of mesas loomed on the distant horizon. Don Pedro smiled amid shouts and gestures emanating from guides and soldiers. He gave the order to mount and move on. They came upon deeply cut *arroyos*, wide enough to provide cover for the animals and men. Qombitua nor Honmana sighted them again. The dust did not rise above the surface.

Captain Tovar rode at the head of his band, flanked on his right by the standard bearer flying the flag of Spain and a white Christian banner displaying a red cross. At his left rode Friar Juan de Padilla, a veteran of military action in his youth. A close friend of Coronado, Don Pedro had volunteered for the expedition at Compostela in southern Mexico (New Spain) where he joined the army muster equipped with a coat of mail, a roster of Spanish and native weapons and thirteen horses. All of these were his personal belongings. He was a Castillian, a sibling of a noble family in Spain joining a throng of *hidalgos* and *caballeros* who had come to the New World to improve their status and carve out a niche for themselves as landlords or in government service. A handsome man of twenty five years, Tovar wore a *bigote* and trimmed *barba* which matched his black, well-groomed hair atop a lithe, muscular body.

The contingent arrived at darkly looming cliffs well after nightfall, making camp apparently undetected in the dim desert light at the base of the mesa. The sounds of voices came from above.

At daybreak Qombitua resumed his post and to his horror observed huge animals tethered at the floor of the desert not far from the ancient trail leading upward to the Hopi village. He rubbed his eyes. Other beasts came into view carrying men on their backs! Honmana, who had come to stand on the balcony, stared in amazement at the awesome scene. The Hopis had never seen horses or Castillians!

The lookout leaped down from his view point running to the pueblo kiva, a partly underground ceremonial room where men had gathered for the daily ceremony and prayers to the rising sun of a new day.

"The beasts with men on their backs are here! They will kill us as they did the Zuni!"

The Indians' system of communication had carried the exploits of Coronado's expedition far and wide among the Pueblo tribes, colored by accounts describing the capture of Cibola *gentre* at Hawikuh Village by fierce attackers "who traveled on animals which ate people".

Gesturing excitedly, the head elder of the council dispatched four men to gather warriors and clan chiefs who would confront the intruders.

"Qombitua, you have seen these invaders. Go to the cliff and station yourself behind boulders about half-way down where you can more closely observe their movements. Be ready to return and notify us immediately if further action is deemed necessary!"

Hearing the chatter of the natives and realizing they had been discovered, Captain Tovar shouted *battalla posicion*! The men quickly gathered in military order on the plain bordering the mesa.

The Hopi tribesmen, equipped with wooden clubs, bows and

shields, soon appeared forming a line facing the Spaniards. Don Pedro, at the head of the *castellanos*, relaxed somewhat as he surveyed the opposing Indians. Their manner seemed friendly but with an underlying agitation. The Spaniard, as well as his men, had experienced bloody encounters on the expedition's 1500 mile trek and were wary, not ready to provoke these high mesa dwellers. Tovar knew that some of the bloodshed had occurred though misinterpretation of Indians movements and intentions. This he wished to avoid.

As the Zuni interpreter moved forward to speak to the leader, two of the Hopi group marked a line between the two forces with a parallel row of sacred corn meal. The spokesman insisted that the castellanos should not cross the line toward their village. On behalf of Don Pedro, representing the King of Spain, the interpreter made the required request of the Hopi chiefs standing in the line, demanding that they express obedience to God and King. Undaunted and displaying the obstinate and unyielding aspects of their independence, the Chiefs commanded Tovar and his men to depart immediately. To cross the lines of sacred corn meal would be to do so at their peril. Through interpreters the message was delivered verbally. Regardless of this audacious challenge, two or three of the Spaniards ventured across the line endeavoring to somehow appease the villagers through peaceful and friendly signs.

By now the adversaries were defiantly facing each other. A definite advantage of striking power lay on the side of the mounted cavalrymen. The tension proved to be too much for one of the Indians. Raising his club, he struck a horse on the side of its head hitting the leather bridle strap.

Distraught by the time being spent in talking, this abrupt action caused Friar Padilla to loudly address the captain. "To tell the truth, I do not know why we came here."

Hearing this the men shouted the battle cry, "Santiago and at them".

They charged the Hopis with lance and sword. The flashing blades were met with clubs and lances as the mesa defenders stubbornly fought with a fury and single mindedness that amazed the Castillians. Wildly rearing horses trampled some of the opposition who in turn unhorsed several caballistas who fell to the earth or landed on top of an adversary. Metal and hardened buckskin chest protectors and body armor helped the Spaniards survive the onslaught while the natives did not fare as well, unprotected as they were. Some were felled, others fled up the trail to the village in confusion.

Seeing the tide of battle, Qombitua scampered to the mesa rim where councilmen and villagers had grouped behind rock piles located along the edge. The rocks, backed by expert bowmen, were normally used to harass and pelt an attacker on the mesa slope.

"Our warriors cannot hold them! Many are mounted on the animals and are shielded from the impact of our weapons by metal coverings on their bodies!"

Word was quickly spread urging the inhabitants to go to their homes and obtain gifts to be used as a peace offering. As retreating warriors reached the mesa top, the head man of the council met them.

"We will not throw the rocks down upon our adversaries. Another way will be found to allay them. Since the Spanish have only a small contingent, they are certainly not an army of occupation."

The Castillians had dismounted to check on all personnel for wounds suffered and condition of equipment. They then re-grouped and prepared to follow in pursuit.

"These natives have a way of disappearing, rather like melting into the landscape when it comes to a retreat." Friar Padilla had removed his helmet and stood wiping his brow with a shirt sleeve. "Are you all right, el Capitan?"

"Like most of our men, I came through that fray with only a slight scratch. Never have I witnessed such lack of fear and aggressiveness demonstrated by the Indians we have encountered. We have been told that these Hopis have survived in this region for a thousand years. Now we know how it was accomplished, at least where a confrontation is concerned. They sent a small force to meet us, maybe forty or fifty warriors. Possibly, they did not anticipate much action, relying on several old men and the corn meal ritual to forestall an encounter. It provides an initial insight into how they think and plan." Don Pedro paused to check his mount's saddle straps.

The captain ordered his group to assemble. With no opposi-tion in view, they proceeded up the mesa trail in a column of two with foot soldiers to the rear. Immediately behind Tovar and Friar Padilla were two cavalrymen displaying the Christian flag and that of Spain. encountering no one as they approached the pueblo, the small band stopped at a suitable camp site and dismounted.

"We are having company, el Capitan. Look who is approach-ing from near the pueblo." The friar motioned toward the village.

Men, women and children approached peaceably, carrying gifts.

"Well, this tops anything I have seen in the way of a surrender. It is really more of a welcoming gesture and desire to be friendly." Pedro smiled broadly as he awaited the arrival of several older men, obviously elders of the tribe. He beckoned to his interpreter to come forward.

"The Hopis come in peace and wish you to be their friend. They come in submission as requested and want you and the men to accept the presents they bring." The interpreter was beaming and indicated his pleasure as he conveyed the message.

The captain responded by shaking the hands of the elders and motioning to the soldiers that the gifts were acceptable. The men were amiable, gathering in mutual harmony with the villagers and laughing heartily with the children as the objects were received accompanied by signs and gestures. Included were the tanned skins of animals, some cotton cloth, pinion nuts and native birds (very likely turkeys). Some turquoises were presented but only a few.

News of the meeting had spread, bringing together people of the whole district who also pledged obedience and invited the Castillians to visit their villages. Don Pedro accepted on behalf of his king and intended to carry out the mission in the time allotted for his excursion.

Two days later, accompanied by tribal elders, chiefs and others, Captain Tovar and his entourage of mounted and un-mounted soldiers and guides, traveled to Oraibi on Third Mesa, the largest and oldest community in the Hopi nation.

Chapter Three

THE AESTHETIC CULTURE

Fray Juan Padilla and the interpreters spent many hours with assorted clan chiefs and older men of the tribal councils. The Hopis were pleased with the non-aggressive stance of Tovar's force. After all, the soldados were not ravaging and killing as had been reported from the Zuni and other tribes. In a gesture of goodwill and peace, food and water were provided in abundance. Trying to explain to Fray Padilla that all could join in a spirit of universal brotherhood, share the riches of the land in common and join their faiths in one religion proved to be a tedious undertaking. The good friar did not understand or would not bring himself to do so.

"These natives keep telling me of brotherly love but I cannot reconcile our religion with theirs. They go off into an abstract discussion which escapes me."

"My old friend, it is possible that your experiences as a soldier and your deeply rooted Christianity cause you to close your mind. It is your duty to continue the discussions and open your eyes to their world. They are truly an ancient and honorable people." Captain Tovar made his remarks to the friar in all sincerity.

The clan chiefs met with the Spaniards to determine if this man Tovar was the Hopis' lost white brother, Pahana. His return was long anticipated in a prophecy common to many Indian nations including the Mayas and Aztecs. Siki stopped abruptly. The legends lay deep in the recesses of her mind, her eyes were closed, head erect, body relaxed. The story unfolded.

Clan chiefs sat in a row behind four lines of sacred corn meal. The Bear Clan Chief, Kikmongwi, extended his hand palm up to Don Pedro. The prophecy prescribed that the true Pahana would clasp the Chief's upturned hand with his own hand, palm down, the ancient sign of brother hood. Interpreting the action as a desire for a gift, Tovar requested one of his men to produce a present to be placed in the upturned hand. Since it was apparent Pahana had forgotten the symbol of recognition, the Hopi Chiefs were wary but determined to avoid trouble with this *Kachada*, who was now in their midst and had not tried to beset tribe members after the first day's skirmish.

The chief nodded to a beautiful Indian maiden whose shining black hair swept up in butterfly whorls over her ears was accented by a brightly colored ceremonial robe reaching to the floor. It was Honmana, who with others had returned to Third Mesa upon receiving word of a proposed meeting of clan chiefs and the Castillians. As representative of the matriarch of the Bear Clan, she stepped forward. The gift was placed in her outstretched hands as she stood straight as an arrow, lips etching a faint smile on her lightly bronzed face.

"Our Chief and our Mother thank you." Her large brown eyes met Tovar's and a message passed between them.

The interpreter translated the words for Don Pedro adding the information that Hopi society was organized under a matriarchal system wherein all buildings and property were owned by the women of the clan. The matriarch was the oldest in a long line of descendants and presided over the other women and relatives.

"It is our desire to know more about the great Moqui nation, its people and the Mother that you speak of." The captain made a sweeping bow, his silver helmet in hand. Wearing his finest dress uniform, Don Pedro made a deep impression on the girl, the chiefs and the entourage.

The girl's smile charmed him. "Moqui is your word. We are Hopitushinumu, the peaceful people, known ty the shorter word, Hopi. I am Honmana, daughter of Nuvamsa, you would be most welcome to visit our Mother's *kiiho*." Again the captain was stirred by the girl's beauty, her straightforward manner and direct, fearless gaze.

Following the verbal exchange by the interpreter, Honmana turned questioningly to Chief Kikmongwi who was looking at Tovar.

"It is good. We will meet again after you have had time to learn of some of our customs." The chief moved to take his place among the council members.

The aroma of pika rose from open ovens of flat rocks outside the matriarch's abode. The delicious odor was appreciated by Don Pedro, who with the interpreter, approached the dwellings. Honmana and an older woman, both carrying baskets, came from the doorway and walked to the baking ovens. Tovar and the interpreter followed, standing alongside as the women placed pieces of flat corn bread in the baskets.

"This pika bread must whet your appetites. Will you come inside and eat them with us?"

"The aroma is irresistable. We will be happy to accept your invitation." The captain's somewhat stern countenance was visibly softened by Honmana's twinkling eyes and broad smile. They walked side by side to the adobe and rock house.

The woman, carrying her basket of pika, tugged at the sleeve of the Indian interpreter, motioning to a small terraza adjoining the building.

Honmana led the way through the doorway. Don Pedro ducked his head to enter. For the *Castilla*, a new world opened before him, yet it was an ancient world. Thick wooden beams shaped from pine logs extended across the ceiling and out through the shale rock walls of the kiiho. Adobe clay in natural reddish tan and dyed gray or white covered the interior walls. Yucca and reed mats were strewn across the hard clay floor with vividly colored rugs and blankets placed around the perimeter and hung on the walls. Masked human figures of doll-size stood in niches and on small woven reed platforms about the room. Uncovered window openings provided light and ventilation.

In a corner to the right of the entrance an aged woman tended the *horno*, used for cooking and heating. She turned as Honmana approached to introduce the tall, lean man with trimmed barba and bigotes. He wore a long sleeved, high collared white shirt and dark pantalones with high black boots. A thin bladed sword and dagger hung from scabbards buckled to his wide leather belt.

"Grandmother, this is Pedro de Tovar, Captain of the castillas who found us in our village, here on top of the mesa" The old woman's face brightened into a smile as she placed both hands on Don Pedro's forearms while expressing her welcome. Honmana interpreted the greeting in a mixture of signs and words. Tovar indicated that he understood. The sign language was common to most Indian tribes he had encountered on the Expedition. Moreover, a few Hopi words had begun to find their way into his vocabulary.

The captain pointed to a nearby doll and asked what it represented. Honmana removed the object from the stand, placing it on a mat on the floor and motioning Don Pedro to sit.

"We will eat pika, then I will explain the Kachina."

Her grandmother came forward with a fruit similar to baked apple. Honmana described it as *pi-yo*, a purple fruit surrounded by leaves, filled with water and steamed in a fire pit. Served on flat trays with pika, the combination was very satisfying to Tovar who asked for a second helping.

Having struggled with the Hopi language and noting that two-way communicating had its pitfalls of understanding, Don Pedro pointed to the tray he held and spoke to Honmana. "Tray - to hold food." He fingered the fruit. "Food".

Honmana nodded and pointed to her helping of fruit and the tray. T-tr-r-ay, foo-ood." Her smiling face looking up at the captain, bore an expression of delight. "More, you show more." Words heard previously were catalogued in her mind. "Pika, fo-ood too?"

"Yes, yes!" Obtaining a piece of wood charcoal from the open oven nearby, the captain scratched FOOD, TRAY, HOLD, on a rabbit skin, the beginning of written language for the Hopis! After they had tried a few more words, Tovar beckoned the interpreter who was engaged in conversation with the servant woman. Coming at once, the Indian translator stood ready to receive orders.

"We are making some progress in learning Spanish and Hopi words, but I wish to speed up the process. Arrange to come here each day and spend time with Honmana teaching the language." Don Pedro asked that the message be repeated for Honmana." Ask what hours of the day would be best for her. Probably three hours a day will suffice."

Honmana listened attentively. "Right after midday would be suitable. Thank you, el capitan, for making this possible."

"All right, it will suit me too as I plan to stop by a few mornings and continue with our own sessions on word learning." As the captain's reply was interpreted, Honmana was visibly excited. As it turned out, her grandmother sat in on many of the sessions. Taking to the language readily, they were able to practice and comverse to the benefit of both, progressing rapidly.

Honmana grasped a kachina doll. "These little figures represent Kachinas, helpful spirits who bring rain, water, crops and fertility. Some bring blessings from the sun and others represent animals and birds. At certain times during the year, the men dress as Kachinas, going into the kivas to dance and perform rites. The whole village comes out to dance in the plaza with other Kachinas. These spirits are part of our religion. They help link us to the great, true Spirit." It was a laborious task for Honmana to explain but with the aid of the interpreter the captain seemed to understand.

"Friar Juan Padilla has been speaking to your people about our religion. I want him to learn about yours and about the Kachinas. Will you help him?" Tovar addressed both Honmana and her grandmother.

"We have heard of the wooden cross at Cibola. After the Hopi elders have learned about your God, they will tell us." The matriarch considered her next statement." Hopi religion and ways may not be readily understood by the kachadas. Our men in the kivas will try to explain many things while you are here among us." Don Pedro noticed for the first time a bone penant worn by the elderly woman. It was inscribed with an animal's foot and bore what appeared to be saw teeth around its circumference. He rose to his feet. "Thank you for the delicious fruit and bread. It is time that I ...."

Honmana broke in. "You must stay and see the ancient artifacts of the Honawuu Clan. My grandmother is matriarch. Also, you can see my room."

Smiling, Tovar nodded agreeably. "First, I will tell my interpreter to join Friar Padilla and the other men as they may desire his services."

He was escorted into a room decorated and filled with possessions of the clan handed down for generations. The colorful display included pottery, turquoise and bone necklaces, medallions, garments and basketry. The sun had dropped below the horizon when the Hopi girl finished relating a history of many of the items.

Passing through a doorway Don Pedro noted the red, yellow and orange rays of a rising sun painted on the east wall of Honmana's room. Designs in desert colors and the blue of the sky on other walls reflected the Indian maiden's exuberance and heritage of the land. Subdued rays of sunlight illuminated the small enclave.

"Your room is very pretty." The Captain glanced about observing several dolls dressed in various costumes." What does this Kachina represent?" He pointed to a particularly brightly dressed figure.

"It is TAWA, the spirit of the sun which brings fertility so all things will grow abundantly. This kachina standing next to TAWA is HUE-MISH, or KACHINA-MANA , wearing a special hair style. You see, my hair, too, is done up like the butterfly, which unmarried maidens wear."

Tovar took her in his arms. His lips were commanding as they pressed hard against her small mouth. Honmana struggled to push away, her emotions held in check by thoughts of a conquerer of her people taking possession of her.

His strong arms increased their pressure, then relaxed as did his lips against hers. His eyes, boring straight into hers, carried an unmistakenable appeal. She raised a hand to his face, coursing her fingers over his jaw line and cheek to his lips. Her body quivered at the touch. She returned the kiss passionately.

He pulled the ribbons from the whorls, letting the long hair caress her shoulders and back. She brushed the flowing hair from her face, again peering into his eyes. He pulled at the draw strings of her soft, antelope skin *manta* and carried her to the bed of yucca leaves and thick, woven mat of feathers and furs. He unbuckled his weapons and discarded his apparel. The room grew dark as their intense *fervoz* drew them together.

A shaft of moonlight beaming across his face from a window opening caused Don Pedro to awake and become instantly alert. This was an instinctive action. No disturbing sounds could be heard. Honmana slept quietly. Fully attired, he left the abode and went to his quarters wishing to finish the night's sleep and be ready for the early morning muster of his troops.

MAP - Enlarged Hopi Mesa Region

Chapter Four

BEAR MAIDEN AND EL CAPITAN

With no change in expression Siki rose from her chair and walked toward the loom and bench where several blankets and a leather bag lay on the floor. Cindy and Sam looked at each other in dismay, apprehensive that the interview might be over. However, the old lady wrapped a blanket about her shoulders, withdrew a small pouch from the bag and returned to the table. From the pouch she produced a necklace of bone and buckskin links which she placed around her neck. A pendant, held securely by the two ends of the neck piece, lay in one hand which was extended forward for better inspection.

"This has been in our clan for generations. It is bone, now yellowed somewhat by age. The notches around the edge portray the image of the sun. An imprint of a bear's paw, the emblem of the Hono (Bear) Clan, is carved in the center."

"Why, it is the same as the medallion worn by Honmana's grandmother, " Cindy exclaimed!

"Yes, we think it is the same."

"May I see it again?" Sam leaned forward eagerly. The pendant was held up in one brown hand to provide Sam a closer view.

"It is a real treasure and undoubtedly will become more so as it is passed from generation to generation." Sam paused thoughtfully."Over the years have Spanish blood and that of other Pueblo people been mixed with the Hopi?"

"Many mixed marriages have occurred among the various tribes and Hispanics whom themselves are a mixture of Spanish and Indians of Mexico the result of colonization over hundreds of years. In my younger days I had the pleasure of teaching languages, including Hopi and Spanish at our government school at Keams Canyon Arizona on Antelope Mesa. The study and discussion of tribal legends and the Spanish Expeditions were also part of my experience in academe at Flagstaff."

"Your insight on these categories is certainly interesting and informative. We appreciate your sharing it with us." Cindy was glad for the opportunity to express her feelings.

"Thank you. Now I will tell you more about Captain Tovar and Honmana." Siki again settled back into her chair.

A long line of Hopi women carrying empty water skins and baked clay jugs wound down a path, part natural and part hewn in the rock, to a fresh water spring near the base of the mesa. Don Pedro, who had been scanning the desert basin from the cliff's edge, saw Honmana in the descending line. He found the top of the trail near an old disintegrating stone wall extending out of the village plaza. Proceeding downward, about half-way he encountered the women returning, burdened with the water filled containers. He waited for Honmana at a wide ledge while he observed two eagles, wings outstretched to ride the air currents rising from the valley floor. An occasional screech from the soaring birds served as a reminder of the wild country about him. Yet the landscape with its changing colors and forms immersed him in a natural beauty and serenity which he had not previously felt. In some ways it reminded him of the vast ever changing ocean separating his homeland and New Spain.

"Honmana's tinkling laughter brought a wide smile to the

Castillian as she appeared around a bend in the steep path. He took the water jug, placed it on a flat rock, then turned to grasp her hands. He resisted an urge to kiss her and refrained from pulling her into his arms. The column of women continued upward apparently unconcerned, but a few giggles from the younger girls could be heard.

"You are beautiful, my *princesa*. May we sit and talk for awhile?"

"This a wonderful surprise, to meet here on the cliff." Honmana's smile was warm and penetrating.

"Please tell me about your mother and father. I have observed that you are taller than the other women and the contour of your face is different."

She turned her face northward where dark mountain ridges appeared in the distance." My mother was Hopi. Soon after I was born she was lost in a flash flood not far from here. Several of our people were drowned returning from the big canyon and river to the north. My father is Havasupai. He is tall and handsome like many of the men of that nation. His name is Nuvamsa. I hope to see him again soon but I do not know when it will be."

"Would it not be better if your father lived here or took you to his tribe?

"In our social system kinship is traced in the line of the mother who lives in the household of her deceased mother. All children belong to the mother's clan, although all siblings do not live together. A designated name giver, usually an elderly woman in the clan, gives a girl child her name within twenty days of birth. Hopi boys can be named by a man who belongs to her mother's clan. Since life in the household is so dominated by the matriarch and the women, men spend much of their time in kivas performing clan rituals as well as secret ceremonies for males only. As you can understand, some men rebel and leave the clan or the village. Others, like my father, left because they were outsiders and felt they were not accepted completely into the kiva and kachina rites and societies. My father did not want to remove me from my mother's household. That is the reason I live here and not with the Havasupai.

Tovar squeezed her hand tenderly. "I hope and will pray that you may visit your father Nuvamsa so that your love may be shared. Have you seen the northern river?"

"No, I have not been in that region. But it is true that the mighty river is a small ribbon at the bottom of the great canyon, probably four of your leagues wide."

Don Pedro's orders restricted him to the Hopi mesas. He was determined and somewhat anxious to advise the general about the river. Although his small expedition had not discovered the much sought after gold and silver, this might be the important waterway to *el Pacifico Oceano* which present unfinished maps did not portray!

The last Hopi woman laden with her water jug had passed. Honmana reached into a rabbit skin pouch hanging from a buckskin thong about her neck and produced an object vaguely familiar to the captain although he could not recall the circumstances. The object, consisting of small feathers bound to a short stick, was held before him.

"I offer this *ruego pluma* to you, to keep on your person. It will ward off evil spirits and protect you. Good fortune will come to you. It is a symbol of my love."

This young woman whose shining eyes and upturned countenance radiated absolute trust and adoration, completely captivated Don Pedro.

"I accept it." His voice was husky. Deep-set feelings stirred within him. Emotion came to the surface. "It will be our emblem of love. You see, I love you too."

Honmana fastened the fetish near the dagger sheath. The captain did not have his sword. They stood and embraced. At that moment a shrill whoop filled the air. They turned to see a grotesque figure leaping down at them from a ledge above the worn path. The kachina headpiece was a blend of wolf fangs, coyote head and black crow wings attached to the sides. Hidden behind the mask was a man brandishing a *povo* in one hand, a club in the other.

Holding tightly to Honmana, Don Pedro made a dive to the left, away from the direction of the descending body and toward the inside wall of rock. They landed with Tovar underneath and rolled to one side just as the attacker ended his leap, the club flying from his grasp. The man sprang with the agility of a mountain lion at the captain, who had barely regained his feet. He was knocked to the rock surface by the impact but an out thrust arm deflected the knife and the two struggled on the shale overhang. The captain was able to bring his legs into a jackknife position and with a mighty thrust sent his adversary rolling onto the path. The mask bounced to the ground.

Unmasked, the man stepped back then lunged forward once again. Don Pedro was ready, conditioned by many weeks on the long, hard trail of the expedition,he twisted his narrow hips to one side, maneuvering like in the bull ring as the attacker raced past. The captain now had his stiletto poised. Honmana crouched between the two adversaries against the rock wall,clutching the club at her side. As the man charged again she brought the club down hard across his knees. The blow caused him to stumble a few steps then career headlong over the cliff's edge to the rocks below.

Honmana sat with hands over her face as Tovar came to her side.

"He is Qombitua, the lookout." The words came out slowly as tears streamed down her face and the captain tried to comfort her. "He is not of this village but is well known here and throughout the mesas."

Don Pedro sheathed the daga, unused. He reflected on the encounter. Was this man an assassin? Was he driven by religious beliefs or had he been in love with the Hopi maiden? The event bothered him since it might signal an uprising against he and his men.

"These concerns were quieted over a meal prepared by grandmother for her granddaughter's return and that of Tovar. She had observed him as he found and entered the path used by the women to carry water. the old matriarch had instinctively been aware of the love between these two young people. now she noted the grave concern both reflected when they entered her *kiiki*.

"I see that the water has been left behind. But no matter, enough is on hand for our needs today. What has brought the dark clouds to your faces?"

Honmana related the episode on the cliff. The captain expressed his desire to know of any implications that might arise from the encounter.

"Only a few know the true discussions in the Kiva aside from normal religious ceremonies. The assembly of the older men and designated younger men who are appointed to attend council meetings are told what can be divulged. Our elders are satisfied that the Castillas are peaceful and so the village is peaceful also. The reason for the attack on your person, Don Pedro, is known only to the dead man. Thus the knowledge is sealed as in a vault."

Seated side by side on the floor, Honmana squeezed the captain's hand and gave him a smile relieved of concern and apprehension. Her grandmother disappeared in an adjoining room. The captain placed an arm around Honmana and turned her face to his. Their lips met as they lay back on the mat in a long kiss filled with overwhelming ecstasy.

"My service with the expedition will not last long. Will you leave Oraibi and join me in New Spain? There are many beautiful places where we could live." The picture of gaily gowned ladies of Castillian and Indian heritage, *esposas* of successful men at the social events in the capital, flashed through Tovar's mind. This Hiopi maiden was more beautiful than any woman he had seen.

"When the conquistadores' quest is fulfilled and Coronado has departed these regions, I believe the time would be right. Yes, I will join you."

* * * * *

Feeding the troops, including procurement of fodder for the horses, were chores delegated to Lieutenant Tomas Blaque. Soldados assisted the Hopis in cultivating and watering maize and corn crops with several men becoming proficient in preparing and cooking corn bread, corn soup and pika along with other roots and herbs which the natives taught them where and how to locate in the desert. Meat consisted of wild fowl, turkeys, rabbit and an occasional deer. Instructed by the pueblo inhabitants, the skinning and dressing of rabbit skins became a daily job.

With the storage of rabbit skins becoming a problem, Sergeant Jose Torres went to Lieutenant Blaque. "Lieutenant, we have so many rabbit skins hanging in every tent and storage place in the camp it has become a problem. We'll soon have to move out, or they go!"

"I agree with that, sergeant. What do you intend to do about it?"

"Sir, since we do not have knowledge of the final processing to make the furs and skins useful, we decided that they should be given to the local residents. Besides the skins we have a large quantity of turkey and wild bird feathers which we understand can be used in their ceremonies. Will you find someone suitable to take and dispose of these items which are in plentiful supply?" The sergeant shuffled from one foot to another.

"Pack the skins and feathers in baskets and place them on horses. Designate the necessary men to lead the mounts where I wish to leave their cargo. We will meet here within the hour."

The pack train wound its way through the village to the house of Honyanqua, the Bear Clan matriarch, who was sitting on the veranda when they approached. Lieutenant Blaque strode through the plaza, removing his helmet and bowing to the woman who stood to meet him.

"Good afternoon senora, I am Lieutenant Blaque. It has not

been my pleasure to meet you formally but I have been informed of your graciousness by Captain Tovar and also that you are the grandmother of Honmana."

"It is nice of you to call, my granddaughter has spoken of you." Honyanqua looked the man over intently."Why do you have all of those horses and men waiting outside the plaza?"

"As you may know, our men have been helping the local people with irrigating and cultivating crop fields as well as foraging for food items. As a result we have accumulated an oversupply of rabbit skins, turkey and wild bird feathers with no more space to store them. It is our thought that you can direct us to those residents who could finish the fur skins while they are still pliable and make use of them before they dry and crack. The feathers may also be useful."

The matriarch peered out at the loaded animals."It appears that the skins and feathers you speak of are in baskets atop the horses. Will you kindly bring a basket of each to the veranda."

"Thank you, senora." The lieutenant called to one of the men to unload the baskets and bring them forward.

Pulling out and inspecting several skins, the matriarch turned to the feathers to look them over. "The skins are in good shape. Our people can use these as well as the feathers."

Blaque was pleased. "We appreciate your making the inspection and your approval of the items. Can you now provide the names of people where they can be delivered?"

"That will not be necessary. I would rather have the people come to the plaza, look these things over and choose what they want and will be useful to them."

"I will order the baskets removed and placed in the plaza as you have requested." The lieutenant gave the orders, also dispatching the men to the camp when the chore was completed.

"Thank you for making these items available, our villagers will enjoy handling them. Come sit here on the veranda." When Blaque was seated comfortably Honyanqua remarked, "You have lighter hair, nearly red, and a light complexion compared to your men. Are your roots in the area of many different people collected in groups that look much alike?"

"That is correct senora. My Anglo-Saxon name is Thomas Blake. My home is Scotland where I was born. It is part of the northwestern region of Europe."

"You apparently came to this area in a round about way. Our know ledge of the Europeans is very slim and based on rumors and stories told by the Indians living near a wide river where it empties into a very large sea. It is far to the west of where we are." The matriarch stared off into the desert a few moments, then turned suddenly to face Blaque. "What is Aan-g-lo Sasa-ahn? These are new words to me."

The lieutenant smiled. Conversation was somewhat difficult and progressed slowly with interruptions as Honyanqua pronounced certain words and grasped their meaning, with Blaque's help. She returned the smile and said something in Hopi which he did not understand.

"Anglo-Saxon is the designation for descendants and residents of the British Isles. Scotland is adjacent to England, which might be described as the mother country. I was tutored in the Spanish language while a student. Later, my family moved to Madrid, the capital of Spain, where my father was attache, the representative of Scotland. We lived in the British embassy compound near all government offices."

"Did you have any brothers or sisters?"

"In my family were two sisters and an older brother. He returned to Scotland for his advanced studies at the university and remained there. For my part, I came to New Spain four years ago in the company of Rodrigo Maldonaldo, Hernando de Alvarado, Garcia Lopez de Cardenas and several others. They were seeking a new life away from Spain and were well equipped with military gear, weapons and a coat of Hauberk mail provided them by their families, most of whom were wealthy and some of noble lineage."

"Why would their coats have Ha-a-berk mail in them? What is that? These are words I do not understand." Honyanqua peered at Blaque's upper garment.

Lieutenant Blaque noticed that the senora was observing his jacket."Our army clothing consists of ordinary garments like I am now wearing, but when we are on the march or prepared for action our uniform includes a coat made of interlinked metal rings and fabric woven together to provide a protective armor. You have undoubtedly observed them on the men. It is called Hauberk mail because that was the type of flexible fabric available under the manufacturer's name. Sometimes a vest made of solid metal is used instead of mail. I will bring samples for your inspection, if you like."

"These items would be interesting to me. Our warriors use a vest made of layers of hardened skins which is the same material in the shields they carry when necessary. Tell me about the horses. Are they ever vicious?"

"I am glad you asked about them. Seldom are they uncontrollable once they have been trained. Horses owned by the caballeros are shipped in the same vessel if equipped to handle them. However, livestock including sheep and goats make up the entire cargo in many sailing ships converted to that use since thousands of beasts of burden and herd animals are required for the New World colonies."

Senora Honyanqua was thoroughly intrigued by Blaque's account. "The men you traveled with on the boat, how were they occupied when they arrived in New Spain? What previous experience did they bring to the New World that would help colonize?"

The lieutenant surmised that the elderly lady feared colonization or had the idea of her people being subdued by invaders on her mind. "Only a dozen years had passed since Cortes had conquered that part of New Spain which is now the capital. The need for military men had been made known in Spain which accounted for an exodus of young caballeros making their way to the new country. After reaching Mexico all of the men of my acquaintance were sworn into service under Viceroy Antonio de Mendoza who had been appointed by the King of Spain as the first viceroy of New Spain. As for myself, I went into the general merchandise and supply business. Following a year-long courtship, I married the owner's niece, Maria de Rivera, widow of one of the first Spanish settlers."

"You said that your sisters remained in Spain. I suppose that they had a merry time of it what with all the people from various countries and the court of Spain itself?"

As a matter of fact, a group of young ladies became close friends with many special events and parties planned to include them. A good friend of my elder sister was the daughter of the chief of staff of the British delegation. Her name is Glendora Burrington. In no time at all they...."

"Burrington?" Cindy Michaelson interrupted Siki's narrative. "Please excuse me for breaking in like this. Burrington is my family name.

Cindy's excitement caused a brilliant flush to mount in her countenance "I can't believe this Siki, you have uncovered a chapter in my family's history that we have spent years in our search for a pathway or connection. Records show that a Clayton Burrington served in the diplomatic corps at Spain in the 16th century!"

"It must be quite a revelation to you all right, Cindy. I am excited about it too." Siki looked at each of the group. "We have had a long session today. Let us continue our discussion in the morning. I will look through some notebooks and reference material I have. Possibly more information will turn up in the next day or two. It will certainly help to refresh my memory!"

"Thank you, Siki. I appreciate your interest in this." Cindy walked to the older woman and linked an arm as they left the room.

Chapter Five

THE ABUCTION

A young Hopi boy carrying a tray of corn biscuits and cookies entered Siki's room, placing the refreshments at the center of the table. A girl followed with cups, saucers and plates which she placed before each person. The young man returned with two silver tea pots containing hot water for instant coffee or tea, the tea bags provided in a silver dish.

"These are my great grandchildren, Cathy and Nuvati."

The Michaelsons responded, giving their names as they acknowledged the introduction. Mark left the room to look for a pop machine located in the entrance way of the building.

You wish to know more about Hopi mixing and marrying members of other Pueblos and the Spaniards? Our nation is much like America, a melting pot, but smaller and older! We are descendants of the *Hisatsinom*, the people of long ago - some say *Anasazi* - who escaped from the great volcanic eruptions in the years 1066-68. Lava flowed over the land, thick layers of cinders and dust covered the fields. Survivors of different tribes of that time joined together and fled to the canyons many miles away where dwellings were constructed in caves and crevices on the face of the cliffs. After forty or fifty years, maybe longer, a yearning in the minds of many along with common language and customs which brought members of several clans and tribes together, caused them to again seek the arid desert lands. Others remained and occupied the cliff dwellings for two centuries. The Hopis emerged as a unified people building villages atop mesas overlooking land suitable for crops and containing sources of water. I might add that eventually all of the people left the cliff dwellings.

"Intermarriage has occurred among the Pueblo Indians and Castillian blood found its way into some of our clans as early as 1540 when Captain Tovar and his soldiers discovered our society." Siki set aside her tea cup and relaxed in the chair. The legend continued.

At daybreak Homnana and a close friend, Kyaqa, stood at the edge of the mesa silently praying for the welfare of the Hopis and for sufficient rain for the corn crop. The sun's first rays darted over the desert penetrating the deepest shadows. Devotions finished, they walked down the water trail, bows in hand and a quiver of arrows hung at their backs. Both of the young women possessed excellent skill for fixed targets or on the hunt. They chatted gaily, occasionally leaping on and off boulders to limber their leg muscles.

"Two rabbit furs would finish out my robe to wear at the next meeting of the chiefs from all mesas. I hope we are lucky today." Honmana drank cool fresh water at the foot of the cliff.

"I do not need anything in particular but if my arrow pierces a rabbit it will be yours." Kyaqa stood bending her bow to attach the bow string. The tough rawhide cord twanged with a low tone as her fingers tested the tension.

They headed for a patch of yucca and mesquite trees a hundred yards distant. The base of the cliff bordered one side and disappeared in a turn to the right. Large rocks sprinkled the area, the result of centuries of weathering, splitting and finally falling from the sheer walls of the mesa. Unknown to them, the two women had been under surveillance since sunrise.

Detecting a movement ahead, Honmana selected an arrow holding the bow at ready. "I believe a rabbit scampered into the shadows at that large boulder. With a "whoosh" the arrow found its mark. But a loud human shriek filled the air as a man flung himself from behind the boulder upon the ground, writhing in pain from an arrow embedded in his thigh.

Suddenly several men leaped from surrounding rocks and encircled the women. Kyaqa let an arrow fly at one assailant but it missed, the shaft splintering against a rock. Seized from behind, the two were thrown on the course sand of the desert floor. Their hands and feet were immediately bound. Honmana recognized one of the attackers as he bent over to inspect the bonds. He was Qombitua's brother from Antelope Mesa. The man realized he had been recognized.

"You and that Spanish dog killed my brother. We will see if he comes to rescue you. If he does we will kill him." The man, Ishawuu, nodded to other men to release the leg bonds and bind the arms of their captives to their bodies, enabling them to walk under guard.

"You know the penalty for kidnapping. Our Hopi chiefs will sentence you to death - and the others too." Honmana defied Isllawuu looking fearlessly into his eyes.

"If you run away like a coyote, my family will never give up looking for you and throwing you off the cliffs." The men nervously shifted their feet at this declaration by Kyaqa.

As the young Hopi women were taken away, Ishawuu talked with two cohorts, explaining his plan. One would deliver a message to the matriarch of the Bear Clan informing her that Honmana had received word that her father had come to

Shongopovi, Second Mesa, and had departed at daybreak to meet him. She was accompanied by her friend Kyaqa. The other man would visit in Oraibi, learn of any movement or plans of the Castillians and wait for further word concerning the hostages.

"We will take the two women to First Mesa and confine them at Walpi," Ishawuu explained, "then Tovar's end comes when he tries to rescue his sweetheart." An evil grin crossed his face as he demonstrated a downward thrust with a spear.

Don Pedro, meanwhile, mustered eight mounted men, an interpreter and Fray Padilla with instructions to make ready for a four-day trip visiting villages on other mesas. While preparations were underway, he rode to the matriarch's abode inquiring for Honmana. The answer was less than satisfactory.

"Honmana and Kyaqa have gone to Shongopovi. A messenger brought word that Honmana's father was there. The girls carried their bows and arrows." An elderly woman provided the information in the absence of the matriarch.

Entering the captain's mind was the thought that Honmana should not have gone off without advising him, then he realized that where her father was concerned a loving and spirited daughter would make such a decision.

Heading back to the command headquarters he was intercepted by Fray Padilla who had followed him through the village's narrow, winding street maintaining his distance a few yards behind.

"Mi Capitan, you are taking too many chances. Many places exist in the village for assassins to hide..." Padilla came along side.

"Your concern is appreciated padre. I was told that Honmana

and a friend left early to meet her father on Second Mesa. It just happens that Mishongnovi is our first destination. "What do you make of that?"

"Possibly a coincidence, whether it is part of a plot we do not know. One thing is certain, we will know soon enough when we arrive!"

"Well, we will take precautions and try to out-manuver them, whoever they may be." The two men arrived at the military arena. Calling one of his officers aside, Tovar gave an order.

"Establish your identity at the matriarch's house and request to be informed of any information concerning Honmana or her father. Send a courier to our destination immediately if pertinent word is received." Tovar and Fray Padilla headed the column of caballeros as they rode down the mesa path on their mission.

"Maintaining a medium pace, the contingent covered the twelve miles between Mesas at mid-morning, stopping at a small pond nestled in the midst of large boulders near the base of the sloping cliffs of Second mesa. The column had been in loose formation. Tovar turned his mount and spoke to the men.

"We will rest and water our mounts then advance in a column of two following the trail leading upward. If necessary we will dismount and lead the horses to the top then break out the flags and continue on, three abreast."

One of the men, Alfredo, rode forward. "Let me precede you on the trail, mi Capitan. I am small and very good at dodging spears and arrows." The caballeros joined in laughter.

"I will back you up, Alfredo! It is time that we plant the sacred flag in their front yard!" Fray Padillo scowled as he looked at Don Pedro.

"The captain's broad grin gave way to thoughtful amusement then a stern military manner. He knew that the priest could match any soldado and was undoubtedly eager for action.

"Your eagerness is welcome and I see some benefit in the plan. Alfredo, fasten the flag and staff to your horse. You will be standard bearer and enable us to assemble at the top while awaiting the rest of the column. Now let us tend to the horses."

"Bravo, el Capitan," chorused the men.

Two Hopi men stood at the rocky table top of the mesa about one hundred yards from the entry point. The column approached. Tovar, the bearded, helmeted conquistadore, flanked by Alfredo bearing the flag of Spain and Padillo holding the staff from which the Christian flag waved, signaled for the Indian interpreter to go forward.

The castillians came to a halt a short distance from the Hopis who were in earnest conversation with the interpreter. In a few minutes he turned and motioned with a raised hand for the contingent to come forward. Unmounted, he walked a few steps to meet Tovar.

"They were aware of our presence, of course, but seem amiable and apparently no cause for alarm exists. I informed them that we come in peace. They said the small village is peaceful and a meeting with the elders and a clan chief is desired."

The group convened, entering into a spirited discussion with the Zuni interpreter in the middle. Only four elders and a Chief of the Coyote Clan comprised the governing body for the village causing Tovar to shorten the length of the gathering without appearing to be abrupt.

The captain and the priest rode side by side as the Spaniards left the pueblo.

"The Chief's sincerity and conciliatory attitude were an excellent beginning for our mission. Although many questions were raised concerning the political relationship between our mother country, New Spain and Tusayan, little irritation surfaced in regard to foreign domination or religious interference."

As the friar listened his countenance brightened from a gloomy attitude earlier in the day.

"It was surely worthwhile. We have even been invited to attend an event in their kiva to further discuss religious matters. Such discourse will be required before we can rightfully expect to raise the flag. Time is going to be a problem on that point."

"One other matter remains unresolved. The Hopis claimed to have no knowledge of the whereabouts of Honmana or her father and were positive that they were not in their village." Don Pedro's countenance indicated mixed thoughts on the subject.

The mounted men pressed on to Shipaulovi located on a tongue-like projection of rock on the eastern side of Second Mesa. Tovar signaled for the interpreter and Lieutenant Tomas Blaque.

"We can detect no movement in the village. Go in and determine if they are having a siesta or have a surprise on store for us." The two men sped forward, disappearing around a corner at the first adobe hut.

The men soon reappeared, riding at a gallop toward the column. The lieutenant reported to Tovar aided by signs and expressions from the interpreter.

"Mi Capitan, an old man hailed us in the village which is nearly deserted. He came up and touched the horses, then said he had been instructed to tell the Spaniards that the chiefs and elders of the clans, as well as many of the villages await our arrival at Mishongnovi. He described it as a large pueblo less than two leagues away and located on the edge of the precipice."

"Well done, lieutenant, the Indians seem to know well ahead of our presence here. Ride with me."

Tomas Blaque had left his wife Maria de Rivera in Mexico while he sought worthwhile reward for his services with the Coronado expedition. He was a Scottish adventurer named Thomas Blake, one of several nationalities other than Castillian of the expeditionary force; including one German, five Portuguese, two Italians and a Frenchman.

Don Pedro motioned Fray Padilla to come to the front and ordered the *columna* to move on.

"I do not like this. It is a feeling of something unknown about to happen." The lieutenant volunteered his comments as the caballeros left the strangely quiet village. The contigent moved on, their trek paralleling the sheer cliffs and fallen rubble around the mesa's perimeter. Viewing the large pueblo above, they rode up a wide pathway leading to the *tumpovi*.

A smooth flagstone surface bordered with mesquite trees and bushes separated by golden clumps of grass stretched out ahead.

"What do you think Padre? Do you share the lieutenant's feelings?"

"Very much so, Don Pedro. Since leaving the first village my mind has been churning, trying to put the pieces of the puzzle together.

"Since receiving word of Honmana early this morning, the Indians seem to be steering us into a situation of their making. It could be part of a plot to eliminate us from their land!"

Tovar studied the priest, then turned to Lieutenant Blaque." "Inform the men to be on the alert for battle and ready to take to the grass on either side. This hard flagstone provides a bad underfooting for the horses and will limit our ability to maneuver."

With ensigns waving, the caballeros rode into Mishongovi.

Chapter Six

THE PEOPLE RESPOND

Honmana, arms bound to her sides, walked with head high and body erect, determined not to betray fear or falter in the sand tugging at her feet with each step. Ishawuu, walking alongside, gave her a shove at regular intervals, more to irritate her than speed their progress.

"Lift your feet, Bear squaw, they drag like the clumsy paws of your aptly named clan."

Honmana, jaw set in a grim line, turned her head slightly toward her tormentor. "You are typical of your animal clan. The coyote slinks to one side to avoid confrontation, even when the opponent is at a disadvantage. Cut these bonds so my arms may swing freely. Are you afraid? Do you expect me to fly away like an eagle?" The words were spit out while the mind sifted through possible ways to escape.

Another push preceded release from the thongs about her body.

"You had better do the same for Kyaqa. By the direction of the trail we are following, it appears that our destination is First Mesa, still three leagues distant. Why must you behave like a torturer?"

Ishawuu sneered at the young Hopi woman, but inwardly admired her determination and awareness in a hopeless situation. Kyaqa's bonds were cut. Leaving four men behind to attend to the captives, Ishawuu left with the three remaining renegades and at a loping gait veered off the trail in a northerly direction toward Second Mesa.

* * * * * *

A gathering of townspeople bearing gifts, food and water met the Spaniards as they entered the village on Second Mesa.

"Let us determine what they expect of us." Leaving Fray Padilla astride his horse, Tovar dismounted to meet an Indian advancing with the crowd. His arm and hand gestures indicated he was a spokesman. The interpreter and Lieutenant Blaque rode up, dismounted and joined the captain. A few words were familiar to the Castillians but the interpreter repeated the message in full.

"This man says you are welcome to come into the village. An assembly of tribal representatives will meet with you tomorrow morning. Please accept our hospitality."

With gestures and a limited vocabulary in the local language, the captain responded.

"I *tuwita* (understand) your spokesman. We *kiikinumto* (come to visit) peacefully and accept your *noosiwqa* (food) which we will eat with you.

The villagers cheered this short speech sprinkled with their language and signs, which they seemed to understand!

Caballeros and Hopis were soon mingling together in the village plaza a short distance inside the pueblo. A clay and stone structure bordering the square was made available to billet the Spaniards. Horses were placed in an enclosure adjacent to the plaza fenced with logs and poles of various diameters.

Don Pedro occupied a room separated from the others by a small patio. When the men had tended their horses, he gave a word of warning and direct orders.

"We are tired from the day's ride and events. However, I caution you to be ready for action at any time. Place your weapons alongside your sleeping mats. Sentries will be posted throughout the night for the usual duty periods with the added cover of overlapping. This will indicate that we have more men than they might expect, as well as providing protection to the sentries themselves."

After much discussion of the delectable Indian food, together with shaving and bathing, lamps were turned down and the compound became quiet.

The captain awoke from a deep sleep, immediately alert for a sound or sensation of movement. Only the subtle, reflected light of the stars in the desert sky through a window opening cut the blackness of the room. His eyes focussed to his right as animal instinct detected a change. With automatic movement his arms flailed outward at an unseen adversary but instead of course skin he encountered warm flesh. He enclosed the form and drew back on the sleeping mat. A soft finger pressed against his lips.

"Do not disturb the sentries. I am Naso and wish you no harm. I only wish to share your Puumpi."

Tovar pulled his arms free, fumbled for a match on a shelf near the head of the sleeping mat and lit a candle standing in a niche in the wall. The glow flickered over a young Indian woman. Her black hair fell over bare shoulders.

"How did you enter this room?"

"The door at the back, off the terrace, can be opened from outside. Please hear me, my captain, you are my protector. I knew you were sent here to free me from this place when I first saw you at the head of the caballeros at Antelope Mesa." The girl's arms reached out for the Castillian.

The captain, wary and skeptical of the young woman's story, listened intently. The sounds of low whinnies and restless horses came from the corral. He leaped to his feet, pulled on his trousers, boots and shirt and taking sword in hand cautiously opened the door to the patio. The deep dusk of dawn pervaded the area.

Suddenly the shrill shriek of a wounded man came from the far end of the patio. Dark forms brandishing spears and long knives descended from the roof tops. A loud, "Santiago", filled the area. Tovar recognized the voice of Fray Padilla. Other human figures emerged from the military quarters and engaged the intruders in fierce hand to hand fighting. By this time twilight illuminated the small compound.

Don Pedro entered the onslaught and was soon facing two adversaries. He parried, thrust and sliced, bringing one man down but he was immediately replaced by two more. As the trio of attackers advanced with knife and spear, Lieutenant Blaque, engaged nearby ran a man through and rushed to the side of the captain. Together, they overwhelmed their opponents inflicting mortal wounds.

Bodies were strewn on the sandy ground. Individual encounters were underway as Tovar and the Scotsman hacked their way through the assailants to the end of the patio around the building to the plaza in front. There the battle raged with the caballeros outnumbered, their backs to the stone wall of the barracks. Blood stains appeared on the captain's left arm, soaking through his white shirt from several knife slashes. Lieutenant Blaque fared no better. From a corner of the plaza again came the battle cry "Santiago and at them!" Juan Padilla ran forward, his black mantle discarded and blood oozing into spots on his waistcoat. The momentum of his charge carried them into the thick of the fighting. Men fell as blades and spears found their mark.

The tide of the battle turned. Several antagonists ran for the plaza gates where they were intercepted and dispatched. Others, only four or five, threw down their weapons and were driven into a corner of the enclosure near the stone building. At this point several young men of the village scaled the gate, taking up discarded arms, menacing the attackers and threatening to kill them. With the few remaining subdued, the encounter was over. The locals inside the plaza aided the soldados in tying hands and feet of the captives.

Tovar dispatched two men to check their casualties and those of the adversaries. The count was made, five soldados killed including the two sentries and sixteen of the opposition. The Spaniards were immediately at work treating the wounds suffered by every man of the contingent. Fray Padilla assisted in rendering first aid and entreated the more sorely wounded to trust in the Almighty to pull them through. He performed last rites for those deceased. Captain Tovar, Lieutenant Blaque and the Zuni interpreter, who had not been involved in the fray, started an interrogation of the captives. They were met by grunts and sullen expressions until the tip of a sword was held to the throat of one who then identified another individual as leader of the confrontation.

Naso, who had remained in the captain's quarters, appeared around the end of the building and walked toward Tovar and the group. Mesa dwellers, roused by the yells and noise of combat, stood nervously outside of the plaza peering over stone walls and through the entrances. The young Hopi woman looked at the surly prisoner asserted to be the leader.

She pointed a finger.

"That one is Ishawuu, from Antelope Mesa, brother of Qombitua of the Coyote Clan."

An entourage of elders, clan chiefs and matriarchs crowded through the main entrance to the plaza, joining Tovar in front of the captives. One of the elders spoke to the captain in a loud voice so all could hear.

"We heard the name of that one." He pointed to Ishawuu. "Naso has truly spoken. It is our desire that you know that we in this village knew nothing of the unfortunate attack on you and the soldados who we welcomed as friends and guests of Mishongnovi.!"

The captain was somewhat irritated. "Then how did these murderers assault us without your knowledge? This disaster could be classified as a large scale attack!"

"We are a peaceful people. At night we have no guards to watch over our village. These renegades must have climbed the trails during the dark hours of night and positioned themselves. Then at dawn, which is the beginning of a new day and custom among the natives, the attack was launched before the sun rose and began its journey across the sky."

Chief Kellehunva of the Butterfly Clan of Mishongovi stepped forward. "*Haliksai* (listen), *Qoyanta* (killing) of the Pahana (white men) is not to be tolerated. We will take custody of the prisoners and drag them *tumpovage* (over the cliff). One by one they will be cast to the rocks below, beginning with Ishawuu."

Translation was made by the interpreter for Captain Tovar who briefly discussed the matter and his understanding of the statement. Although outnumbered, the captain wished to press his case.

"No, no! The atrocity was planned and inflicted upon my command. He will obtain a *wikwakna* and hang Ishawuu. The others will witness the event, then you can have them."

Ishawuu screamed. "You killed Qombitua, *i'paava*. You forced Hopi *maana* to share your sleeping mat. All caballeros deserve to die!"

Don Pedro looked at the captured man and then turned to the chief. "His brother slipped and fell to his death from the Kawaiokuh water trail. Honmana will verify that."

"Lies! Now that the girl is revealed, I can divulge that I have Honmana held hostage with a friend. You came to the wrong mesa, captain, and you will not find her." Sneering, the bound man strained at his bonds. "Release me or you will not see the whore again."

The Chief raised a hand for silence. Honmana of the Bear Clan has been known to me from a *manawya* (little girl) and now as a young woman is like *i'maana* (my daughter). Let us throw these foul men over the cliff now."

One of the captives cried out. "The woman's whereabouts is known. "But you must not throw us on the rocks. I will tell if you give us banishment - a fair exchange." A man partially dressed in warrior's garb ran from the crowd of townspeople to the prisoner kicking and stomping him until pulled away by by his compatriots.

Bursting through the onlookers and running through the plaza to kneel before the Chief, came a native courier covered in sweat and breathing heavily.

My message is from First Mesa. Two young Hopi women named Honmana and Kyaqa are held hostage at Walpi. Forty unruly followers of Isawuu, including renegades from some other tribe, are guarding the hostages at the terrace building next to the main kiva. "No one is allowed to approach."

"We must talk about this. Let us go to the far corner." The Chief motioned to Tovar and a select few of the elders and lesser chiefs. Blaque and Padilla followed the captain, as did the interpreter. The Hopi delegation first talked among themselves, paying attention to the chiefs.

"Captain Tovar, twenty warriors will be placed under your command. Although First Mesa has its own chiefs to declare proper action, the murderous group of kidnappers is also, as a consequence of being there, holding the village of Walpi in hostage. It is our duty to aid them as well as gain the freedom of the two women. The prisoners at hand will be well guarded."

The tenseness in Don Pedro eased. "We will ride with your fighting men to bring an end to this *malevolo*. Only the friar, lieutenant and myself are able to participate. The interpreter, of necessity, will also join us. Your women have already treated the injuries of the badly wounded and the others who fought valiantly. They will remain in their care until able to be moved or become active. This merciful action is deeply appreciated."

A tall muscular man stepped forward. "This is Macanoma, leader of our warriors. They will consume a light meal, then be ready to leave before midday sun. First Mesa is only a short distance more than one of your leagues. May the Great Spirit be with you." Chief Kellehunva raised his right hand and turned about so all would know of the dangerous mission.

"It is my feeling that all will go well." Tovar shook the hand of the Chief as a gesture of friendship. "Our objective is to achieve the release of the Hopi women. It is well that we leave soon. We do not know if word of Ishawuu's capture and defeat of his men is yet known at Walpi. We must face that when we arrive."

Fray Padilla stroked his bigote as he confided in Don Pedro during the short walk to their quarters. "I realize that we are here on a peaceful mission to win the Indians over to our side. These murdering renegades have decimated our small force. Thinking about the days in old Spain when the iron collar of the garrote served as an example to dissidents, I wonder if something can be said for that type of punishment in this day and age?"

Chapter Seven

THE ESCAPE

A sleeping mat in one corner and another along a wall for sitting, narrowed the small confine to a cubicle. Honmana felt caged. Kyaqa was apparently in an adjacent space although no sounds could be heard through the adobe and rock partition. A lattice work of wooden bars filled the doorway opening. Rough hewn planks closed in the upper portion. Honmana was aware that a wooden peg on the frame holding the bars was operated allowing the section to swing outward. Openings between the bars were too small to reach through. Judging by arms and hands, the person delivering food trays was of small stature or possibly a boy forced to do the bidding of the guards.

Resting on her hands and knees for sometime near the doorway, Honmana finally saw the bar grate open slowly and the food tray pushed in. She clamped both hands on the exposed wrists and leaned into the opening. A wide-eyed boy looked up into her face and eyes.

"You are Hopi woman, not man prisoner. Why are you here? Is the person in the next room a girl too?"

"Yes, she is my friend. But it is a mistake, these men should not be holding us as prisoners. We must escape. Will you help us?" Homnana released the pressure on the boy's wrists.

The boy hesitated a moment. "Yes, I will help you, but I do not know what I can do. The guards do not give me much time before looking for me."

"Is the window in the back of this room far above the ground? I cannot see the sun or the sky."

"The timbers slope from the roof above, blocking the window opening. But it is only one level to the ground which is a narrow ledge at the edge of a cliff. From there, hand and foot holds carved in the rock many years past will enable you to descend to a trail leading to the base of the mesa."

The boy's helpful and straight forward manner impressed Honmana who squeezed his hand. They were friends!. "Thank you for this information. Can you bring several short lengths of rope, hidden under your mantle, when it is time to deliver the tray? Tied together, I will have enough pieces for an escape rope."

"A small ladder is in the hallway. It will reach your window. I will slide it into your room next time I come and will bring the rope too.

"The guards are playing a peg game at the end of the corridor where a large room provides tables and chairs. They will not notice."

"Please inform Kyaqa, in the adjacent cell, about our plans and tell her to be ready to come in here when you bring the next tray. Have you seen our bows and arrows? They have the Bear Clan mark."

"Your belongings are in a storage room. When the guards think that I go for water, I will bring them to you."

Everything was in readiness when the midday tray was pushed under the bars. Honmana, kneeling near the opening, spoke to the boy in a low voice.

"Is the passageway clear? Leave the grate unbolted at Kyaqa's room and tell her to slide under it and come to my room after you deliver her tray. The rope is ready and we will escape through my window."

Honmana stood on a rung of the ladder while her friend pulled herself through the small opening and descended to the outside ledge. The cord was anchored to the ladder. Honmana pulled in the rope, tied the bows and quivers securely, lowering them to Kyaqa. She then climbed into the opening, arranged the ladder inside to span the window space and made sure the rope would be held taut. The descent was accomplished rapidly.

The two women quickly slung their gear across their shoulders and started down the sheer cliff using cup-like niches hewed in the rock centuries before. Kyaqa led the way, her feet finding the openings instinctively. The strain on legs, arms and fingers made the young women wish to cry out if only to vent their feelings, but they remained silent knowing that they might be discovered. The exertion of the descent took its toll, slowing their progress until the footholds ran out, forcing them to cling precariously to the vertical rock face of the precipice. Kyaqa peered downward, observing a trail which she judged to be about ten feet below.

"We must drop to a path. My feet are in the last openings. Our ancestors must have used a ladder for this last section."

"All right, I will follow after you are on the path and in the clear."

Both were jolted by the drop but neither suffered a sprain or twisted limb. They sat together, breathing heavily and thankful to have escaped their kidnappers thus far. Peering out from their perch on the narrow trail, they were greeted by wavering images and shimmering land as heat waves distorted the desert.

The two Hopi maanas emerged from the base of the mesa, left the trail and scanned the landscape, wondering which direction would be the safest. They needed to find food and water and a suitable resting place. Thirst and an appetite had become their primary concerns.

"A drink of water and something to eat would brighten my outlook. I did not touch that last meal brought to the cell." Honmana pulled an arrow from the quiver. "I am ready to shoot at the first rabbit that comes into view."

Kyaqa pointed in the direction of a dark cluster of mesquite and saguaro cactus which seemed to rise from numerous large boulders. "Let us try to find something over there, at least it is a green spot, hopefully with a supply of water."

At that moment a scraping sound caught Honmana's attention. She looked about to see two bowmen coming down the trail. One of their bows had apparently rubbed against the rock wall.

"The guards are coming!"

Both women snapped an arrow into their bow strings and with deadly accuracy sent the sharpened shafts through the chests of the approaching adversaries. Two more men who appeared closely behind, scampered out of sight along the trail. No further movement could be detected. Still holding her bow at ready, Kyaqa moved off the path toward large sections of rock which in ages past had peeled off the cliff.

"We had better get away from here before the whole gang shows up."

One of the fleeing renegades, however, paused at a bend in the trail to peer down among the rocks. He observed the two women and drew his bow string. Though partially hidden behind the rocks, Honmana received the arrow in the left thigh, tearing the flesh in a wide gash. "Oh, my leg!" Her loud cry caused Kyaqa to freeze momentarily, looking upward where the trail appeared and disappeared on the precipice. Half of the dark form of an assailant was visible, then the shoulders and head were in view. Kyaqa's arrow pierced the *taaqa's* neck. Shaft and feathers protruded visibly as the body fell to the rocks below. She ran to Honmana and drew the blood soaked mantle away from the wound. Tearing strips of cloth from her own garment, Kyaqa bandaged the injured limb winding several pieces tightly around the thigh to retard the bleeding. With an arm steadying her friend and Honmana grasping her shoulder, Kyaqa picked up the bows and arrow bags. Together they headed in the direction of the small oasis.

DESPERATE ENCOUNTERS

Only the subdued creaking of leather saddles and tinkling of silver bridles disturbed the desert, serene in the half-light of the hour preceding sunrise. Anticipating military action, Captain Tovar had requested eight warriors to accompany his group including Friar Padilla and Lieutenant Blaque. The Hopi fighting men had fastened prayer sticks to their clothing bearing a yellow canary feather and a brown feather of the falcon. The small contingent followed a trail to First Mesa, approaching the Walpi entrance at the southwestern tip.

The choice of trails was fortunate as the group was well hidden by large boulders strewn on the desert floor from the mesa slopes. A clump of mesquite trees with water and grass lay ahead.

Meanwhile, Chief Kellehunva had responded to a request for assistance from the clan chief at Sichumnavi, a mesa village close to Walpi. Forty warriors had been dispatched to utilize that entrance to the top of the mesa and on to Walpi in a surprise maneuver. All male members of the Kokob Clan were looked upon as *Kaklehtaka*. This select inner group used common face painting in combat, the decorations identifying them as an elite and aggressive force.

The renegades atop the mesa were desperate, realizing they had placed themselves in jeopardy by allowing the two hostages to escape. Further, they were ignorant of the leader, Ishawuu's, situation. Splitting their force, twenty of the group of exiles and outlaws filed down the cliff leaving approximately the same number at Walpi to defend their precarious position at the plaza and detention buildings.

A burning sun was half-way across the sky when the band surrounded the small green spot in the desert terrain where Honmana nursed a leg wound and Kyaqa had prepared a meal of roots and edible plants she had gathered. A poultice of mud and wet leaves had been applied to the wound and again tightly bound. They sat near the edge of a small water hole amidst tall grass which grew to the base of several large boulders forming a semi-circle at their backs.

Touching Kyaqa's arm, Honmana whispered, "I heard something snap". They moved as far as possible back to the rocks and strung arrows to their bows. Before them, fallen rocks and mesquite trees were scattered in a patch work pattern allowing a limited vision of only a few yards. Suddenly, without warning, two slim bodied desperados dropped from the rocks behind, landing squarely upon the fugitives crouched on the ground. Thrashing about to the extent possible with their arms and legs, the two Hopi women were unable to release arrows but used the bows to fight off the taaqas. Unmindful of her bound leg, Honmana stood and battered her assailant on the forehead and temples, striking a final blow that sent him reeling headlong into the boulder behind. He dropped like a log. A slip on the wet grass by the other attacker gave Kyaqa the moment needed to snatch an arrow, driving into the man's stomach. He fell into the water writhing with pain as he tried unsuccessfully to grasp and withdraw the arrow with both hands.

Four additional attackers joined in the fray, shouting with delight when they had subdued their victims and pulled them to a standing position. They ignored Honmana's wound as they prepared to lead the women back to the mesa.

Their shouting proved to be their undoing. Alert Burrowing Owl Clan warriors, hearing the shouts and scuffling of the melee, immediately turned in the direction of the patch of trees. With warriors on foot close behind, those mounted on available horses led a charge, overtaking adversaries who appeared from the rocks to assist in the escort of the captives. Spears of the warriors took their toll, dropping men disbursed by the impact of the horses and the charge. This provided the women captives the opportunity to pull away and wedge themselves between boulders at the edge of the battle arena.

From another direction, an attack by horsemen roared by including several warriors, Captain Tovar, Friar Padilla and Blaque who collided head on with the remaining force of desperados. The encounter that followed was bloody but decisive when hand to hand fighting decided the victors. Don Pedro and Blaque having had a glimpse of the women during the charge, fought through the adversaries to free them from their confining space. The battle was over. Three or four of the outlaws fled leaving behind their dead and wounded. The Captain and Honmana embraced for a moment before her leg gave out and she allowed herself to be lowered to the ground. However, Don Pedro lifted and carried her to the water's edge, followed by Kyaqa who immediately began to assemble an application for her friend's wound. Lieutenant Blacque had rescued Kyaqa in the melee, deflecting against the rocks a spear that had been thrown haphazardly. He now assisted the nearly exhausted young woman whose heroic spirit provided needed motivation to aid those suffering injury. Blacque's military field kit contained required bandages.

Friar Padillo conducted the ceremonial last rites for those who died in the battle.

"We lost two warriors. The other side fared much worse. Clan members are preparing to transport the two bodies to their mesa for the native ceremony of death. "

Six warriors came forward explaining that they would remain to help protect the Hopis women and two would accompany the bodies of the fallen comrades.

"I wonder how Macanoma and his warriors have fared. The question is: were many desperados left at Walpi or did the majority pursue Kyaqa and Honmana?" Tovar pondered the question then looked at Honmana.

"You would not know how this came about since we have not had the opportunity to discuss these events." He explained how the chief at Second Mesa had received a message stating the whereabouts of the captives and dispatched his warriors in two groups.

Honmana suggested that a warrior question one of the wounded attackers.

This produced information that about twenty men remained at the mesa after the Hopi women escaped and a contingent of the same number was sent to locate them and return with the captives again in custody.

"We need not expect another attack. Do you agree?" The lieutenant and Friar nodded in agreement with Honmana's assessment.

" Then the warriors may return the bodies of their dead and we can scout ...."

The captain stopped abruptly. His tone and countenance changed.

"Let us rest here. Honmana and Kyaqa surely need sleep as a priority the next few hours before further travel. Moreover, it will enable us to tend further to the wounded."

Friar Padilla peered at his captain appreciatively. He had hoped that events had not excessively hardened Don Pedro beyond the point where human considerations were forgotten.

Honmana gestured at Tovar to sit beside her. "Ishawuu and his followers kidnapped Kyaqa and I early one morning when we had gone out to hunt rabbits. The fur was needed to complete our ceremonial mantles. He is Qombitua's brother and cursed you in his accusation that you had deliberately killed his brother on the cliff. We were taken to Walpi on First Mesa and imprisoned as hostages."

"Hopefully the thoughts of those events can now be put aside. I have good news! Ishawuu has been captured and is held at Second Mesa. A message, was received stating that you had gone to see your father at Shongopovi. It was false, of course. Our plans to visit the Hopi communities did not include the fierce battle that occurred after we had been billeted and lights out for the night. We lost several men in our contingent. Ishawuu had planned to murder us all, but the tables were turned. After the adversaries had been defeated, the chief, who had been unaware that these desperados were well armed and had taken positions in and around the plaza, wanted to throw Ishawuu and his band down on the rocks. However, we prevailed upon him to detain them as prisoners. Our wounded are under the care of many women tending their needs, and the supervision of the chief."

Kyaqa, busy as usual in her favorite vocation- preparing delicious meals - approached with small reed mats loaded with a mixture of edible desert plants, *tuva*, water and corn provided by the clan warriors. The food was eagerly accepted and devoured by the small and greatly appreciative group. That is, except for Lieutenant Blaque who rose as Kyaqa came near and volunteered to assist.

"You have been very busy, Kyaqa, preparing this meal and acting as nurse for Honmana. I must now insist that you take this food, sit down, and eat it. Plenty is left for me, which I can obtain for myself from your outdoor *cocina*. You will need water too." He dipped his water bottle of deer skin into the cool spring and handed it to the startled girl. This was a new experience for her.

"You are very kind, Lieutenant. I will do as you say. "Kyaqa brushed her long dark hair aside revealing a beautifully rounded face and gleaming white teeth framed in a wide smile.

Blaque returned the smile, placed some of the prepared food on a mat and returned to sit alongside Kyaqa. The others observed these events, happy in the thought that new friends could be made under the circumstances.

"El Capitan, although it seems quiet, I think it would be best if we scouted the area, particularly toward the mesa. A warrior can accompany me." The Friar, first a man of God in his administering to his fellow humans, was also a consumate soldier, a veteran of many campaigns.

"You are our stalwart protector in many ways, my friend. The extra strength always seems to come to you so that you may follow your instincts. We will wait here for your return."

Signs of retreat were evident all along the trail to the mesa. Broken prayer feather sticks, fetishes, discarded bows, quivers and the blood stains of wounded men dotted the pathway. Friar Padilla and the warrior came upon a wounded, dying man. The man gasped out the information that Owl Clan warriors had killed or driven away the remaining followers of Ishawuu in a bloody battle at Walpi.

"To my knowledge, no one escaped to reach the desert floor but me. I am not a coward. My great mistake was in placing my allegiance with the wrong person who spoke of untrue grievances and insults from the Spaniards. Your testimony at Antelope, priest, was passed on by the clan elders and I wanted to know more. That is now passed. Will you perform last rites for me?"

The unfortunate man died before Friar Padilla could reply. The rites were performed as requested and the man laid to rest in a shallow grave covered with stones.

* * * * *

"Although our ancient legends and much history have been retained in my mind, many aspects such as names and events of the Spanish intrusions in Tierra Nueva must be refreshed from time to time. These notes and references I have placed on the table deal with names originating in Spain which may help to shed light on your ancestors." Siki opened a journal and beckoned to Cindy. "Will you sit here by me and read a few lines. The excerpts are from the chronicles of Pedro de Castaneda who accompanied the Coronado Expedition."

"I will happy to participate, Siki." Cindy sat as requested and read from material translated from original Spanish documents stored at the King's library and archives, circa 1540.

The muster for Coronado's Expedition occurred at Compostela. These men who had arrived from Spain at various times and voyages scheduled, included Diego Gutierres, Diego de Chevara, Juan Gallego and Diego Guzman. Most had armor, horses and weapons. Captain Arellano might have been best equipped, having eight horses, various pieces of body armor, crossbows, an arquebus, several types of swords and arms of the country for himself and servants. Much of the equipment was medieval. High ranking officers included Lope de Samaniego, campmaster and Tristan de Arellano who had led a small army on his own second in command. Captains and ensigns in the six companies listed Diego Lopez, Pablo de Melgosa, Alonzo Gomez and Juan de Villareal with chroniclers Castaneda and Pedro Mendez de Sotomayer. Ages spread between seventeen and thirty years.

Cindy explained, "I have not read every name as many have already been mentioned in Siki's narrative.

Siki responded. "By tracing names of the caballeros in other journals, we might find more information, for example, who they married, who were close friends in Spain and other significant facts. We know that marriage was important, as at the time the expedition got underway the Emperor of Guatemala issued a significant order that all landowners must marry.

The following year Pedro de Alvarado returned from Spain as custodian of 'twenty maidens, well bred, the daughters of gentlemen of good lineage', needless to say he expected them to be quickly assimilated into the life of matrimony! Will we find familiar names of these and other damsels who decided that New Spain was part of their destiny?"

Chapter Eight

HOPI MYSTIQUE

"You must be tired of so many words coming from my mouth. Rooms are available at a small motel if you wish to stay for the night. It is the adobe building next to the visitor center. " Siki rose and reached for a colorful mantle which she placed around her shoulders.

Cindy Michaelson helped arrange the shawl-like garment. "My, your retention of these historical events is amazing. We appreciate your relating them to us."

"The genes of a hundred generations live in my body and my blood. Stories and legends come from the recesses of my mind. It only needs the telling to become known. We did not have a written language, so the transmittal has been accomplished over centuries by constant repeating one to another. Much occurred in the kivas where men gathered and talked in various habitats and environments over probably thousands of years. The 'Fourth World' of the Hopis helps sort things out and provides a source."

"The Fourth World of the Hopis- it sounds mysterious, Siki. " Cindy hesitated, not wanting to pry.

"It has its own mystique, spiritual, if you wish-or a religion. It is the time we live in now and a place where we, as Hopis, remember what has happened before and discover what may happen in the future. "Siki paused for her words to sink in. "Tomorrow I would like to tell you more about Tovar and Honmana. Will you come to see me?"

"We surely will. Thank you for spending your time with us. This has been most interesting. We will be back tomorrow!" Sam conveyed the consensus for his family as they left the room to check in at the motel.

Once inside, Sam inspected the urn. "This piece of metal must surely be a part of the local history. Do you suppose that we should show it to Julia-Siki tomorrow." He ran his fingers over the engraved letters on the vessel.

"I think Siki should continue her narrative as she indicated. The urn and its etchings might cause her to change and lead off in another direction. We can wait to see what develops tomorrow. It is all right with me if we stay here an extra day or two." Cindy looked at Sam and Mark. They nodded their approval.

"I'd like to take a side trip tomorrow with a group of young people coming in from Tuba City. The man in the visitor center said they are visiting some ruins near the next mesa and I could go along. Mark produced a folder describing points of interest and locations.

"No problem. It would be a fine excursion for you. You might even discover another historical object!" Sam winked at his son.

Using his sharpest tool at hand, a steel finger-nail file, Sam probed and scraped indented rings circling the metal object in the upper half near the rounded top. The lower half was flat at the base. Washing the rings clean with alcohol, he looked for marks or depressions which might indicate a joint or joining point. He twisted the upper and lower sections applying all the strength of his hands to no avail. The probing uncovered several notches spaced between two rings but no visible indication of a junction or fitting. "We'll take this to the archaeological department at the university when we return. They undoubtedly have methods which will divulge the hidden secrets in such things. In other words- open it." Sam caressed the corroded jarron as if expecting something to happen.

Cindy took it onto her hands. "It seems light enough to be hollow. Let's stop at a library and see if information is available on metals and metal working in Spain and that area back in the sixteenth century. It might have originated there."

"Good idea. " Sam agreed.

Siki was busy at her loom when the Michaelsons arrived the next morning. Her greeting was cheerful and pleasant.

"Your sleeping time gave you a peaceful rest? I hope so, my sleep contained dreams of many years ago and things that happened came clear in my mind." The elderly lady placed the customary shawl about her shoulders as she seated herself across the table. Her narrative continued.

Friar Padilla and his Owl Clan warrior returned and ate heartily of the food offered by Kyaqa. The priest eyed Captain Tovar.

"El Capitan, this excursion has not been a glorious success. I have not planted a cross or converted anyone to our Christian beliefs. " He related his encounter with the dying man.

"The Indians in their kivas conduct rituals and speak of their origins in a way that escapes me. I want to understand them better."

Honmana looked at Tovar, then Friar Padilla. "It is true that many of our own people have difficulty comprehending abstruse Hopi teachings and ceremonies. The meanings of certain rituals are understood by those initiated into a special coterie. These rites tell of our creation and the existence and emergences from prior worlds. It is a view of life very religious in nature, patterned upon a universal plan of creation of all things and their progress in the evolutionary process of life.

"An understanding, from their abstract beginnings, is impressed upon all Hopis. This has been accomplished through the centuries by ceremonies, rituals, dances, songs and recitations throughout the year. The people are members of clans having animal or plant names, for example; Coyote Clan and Yucca Clan. This is an obvious example of harmony within the universe. It is the purpose of our religion to maintain this harmony. Another example is the large variation in Kachina costuming and dancing representing many aspects of nature as well as our kinship with other living things. Our very existence depends on and relates to an understanding of a universal environment."

Friar Padilla's countenance expressed a mixture of contemplation, concern and finally a deeper understanding of what he had witnessed in the Kivas. Honmana is really part of the mystique, he thought.

"But the people on all the mesas have declared themselves to be in submission to our coming and therefore to our control and way of religion. Is that not true?"

"Submission is not to be construed as subservient. Hopi prayers and ceremonies as well as our way of life are deeply embedded through countless generations of involvement and belief. This will not change overnight - it may never change. "A sternness passed across Honmana's face then passed into serenity as she continued her observance of the Friar and Captain Tovar.

"You have interpreted many things to us Honmana, truly, the most informative of any session in which I have been privileged to attend. On our first morning, at the base of Antelope Mesa, our initial meeting turned into a skirmish in which the Hopi warriors scrambled up the trail into the village area. By the time our soldados arrived at the top and regrouped, the village people were coming forward peacefully, bringing gifts and declaring themselves in submission. You, of course already know of these events. The question is: was this superficial, a charade perhaps?" Tovar paused, but Honmana did not answer. He then continued.

"Since we have fought side by side with the Hopis to rid the villages of these bandidos who held you and Kyaqa hostage, I believe we are truly at peace but they are not to be considered a conquered people."

"Honmana, are you now able to travel? We must leave for Walpi *estar al vivaque*."

Kyaqa stood beside Honmana who pulled herself to a standing position. A few steps tested the leg to her satisfaction. Kyaqa had bound the wound with cotton strips and the bleeding had stopped.

Glancing at Tovar, Honmana had an impulse to throw her arms about the captain and depend upon him for support. However, she knew this open display of affection would not be welcome in front of the men. Instead, she took Kyaqa's arm.

"I am ready."

"You are no *servienta*. My horse is yours to ride." Lieutenant Blaque led his mount forward. "Kyaqa will ride double with you and I will share a steed with the warriors."

This spontaneous act of chivalry was approved by everyone and the group was soon on its way.

Macanoma, the Owl Clan leader of the warriors, rode down the trail to meet the battered group as it arrived at the base of First Mesa.

Honmana and Kyaqa were immediately taken to the clan chief's residence where the women administered to the wounds and gave them baths. Many wounded warriors had been billeted in the building and adjacent plaza. Tovar's men rejoined their own contingent. The captain, Blaque, Fray Padilla and the interpreter shared available space.

Prior to supper, prepared as a special feast by the women, Tovar visited Honmana in a small room near the treatment area. In the few moments of privacy available they embraced and declared their love for each other.

"Rest and favor your leg so the wound will heal." The captain spoke huskily. He did not wish to leave this beautiful woman. "I am departing in the morning for Second Mesa to check on our wounded there. Then on to Oraibi to inspect that area and re-visit the Chief. Upon our return we shall all proceed to Antelope Mesa." Honmana kissed him passionately.

Up with the sun, Captain Tovar summoned Lieutenant Blaque, Friar Padilla and the remaining men, advising them to be alert for the possibility of opposition on the trail to Second Mesa. Upon arrival they were informed that Ishawuu and most of his followers had been put to death or banned from the Hopi nation.

Captain Tovar was momentarily disappointed by the actions of the clan chief and elders but he realized that punishment was in their domain and not with an outsider. He ordered a junior officer to prepare the wounded soldados for transfer to Antelope Mesa and confided in the Friar and Lieutenant Blaque.

"Third Mesa remains a mystery. To avoid an unnecessary show of force, we will approach with only a few mounted men. Oraibi, the oldest of the Hopi villages in Tusayan, is also represented as the largest community of the Hopis. The possibility remains that secret caches of gold and other riches are stored there. Lieutenant, muster cavalrymen. We will leave following the midday *comida*."

The Friar watched Blaque as he left to complete his orders.

"There goes a fine soldado and a fine young man. Maybe he can be promoted, aye El Capitan?"

"You may be right about the riches. The Hopis, however, seem to dwell more in their religion and ceremonials than in a quest for gold and precious stones. This region seems empty of such things, as is Cibola and its seven cities. The opportunity may arise at Oraibi to discuss our Christian religion at length and plant a cross on the mesa!"

Tovar smiled as he considered the eager Friar's statement.

"Years may required to include these people in a province of New Spain. Certainly the existence of vast riches is remote. But we could establish a foothold for Christian understanding if an open mindedness exists, even a small indication. Success rests mainly on your shoulders and is a great challenge, Friar. You may wish to discuss Honmana's statements with the interpreter, he has proven himself to be a knowledgeable and practical man. Such background information might be helpful when you are in sessions with the elders in their kiva."

The captain stood erect, buttoning a fresh tunic. "I will talk to Chief Kikmonguui, leader of the Bear Clan in Oraibi. It is time now to determine if a friendship can be welded. Surely our fighting side by side with the Hopi warriors against the renegades is meaningful and demonstrates our honorable intentions!"

"They have declared their submission. Can more be done that that?"

"I suppose that is enough, but I do not feel an atmosphere of real cordiality and acceptance of all our views, although they are friendly and hospitable. Too much should not be expected of them at this time. After all, the shock of seeing their first white men, horses and our peculiar retinue, must still be a cause for unidentified emotions."

On the ride to Oraibi Captain Tovar continued his discussion with Friar Padilla. "A sense of mystery, distinctive I believe to the Hopis, envelopes this vast dry land. These rocky promontories, four of them jutting skyward in the desert, house the Indians in little stone villages mounted like miniature fortresses on the apexes of stone masses. The people must have come from distant places centuries past, seeking asylum from the depredations of warlike tribes. They eluded their enemies and found sanctuary in these lofty mesas and the desert itself, which proved to be an ally. The migration or trek across these sun scorched waterless regions was undoubtedly *una journada de muerte* for many."

"I agree with your observations, mi Capitan. The isolation of this place makes me wonder if it was decreed by God or another deity that they come here."

"Friar, take notice of the small fields of corn which the locals cultivate with no visible running water but only rains which come sparingly maybe two or three months during the year. It was apparently determined by the tribesmen that the springs of fresh water located around the perimeter at the base of the mesas were derived from pockets of water stored in seams and cavities in the rocks. The water drains slowly, lasting throughout the year. The women can be seen at each village toiling down trails on the cliffs and returning with the life sustaining water. The men till the soil laboriously endeavoring to prevent its burial under the constantly shifting sands.

"In my view, these people have scored a victory over the adverse and difficult skirmishes devised by nature. They exist above the usual human exploits of war against other peoples. In fact, Honmana has pointed out that the word Hopi means peaceful, or the peaceful people. We must keep that in mind if we are to co-exist with them."

At Oraibi, Friar Padilla fared no better in his zeal to "plant a cross" than at his original meetings. In the kiva, surrounded by artifacts and wall paintings depicting centuries of deeply embedded rituals, the chosen men espoused their religion at length. The very culture and waking hours of the Hopi comprised their religion. The Friar did not did not grasp, or possibly understand, enough of these discussions to open a breach and put forward his own doctrine of Christianity. He decided that many years would pass before the Hopis would change.

Chief Kikmonguui, hosting a group of the oldest men representing all villages on the mesas, allowed Captain Tovar to address the assembly. The captain found that it was the governing body for Tusayan which listened intensely to his statements delivered with the aid of the interpreter. They accepted the desire of the Castillians to be peaceful friends and declared that their intentions were the same. At this meeting the Captain was informed of a very large river to the north, a distance of about three days travel. Down the river lived people with "very large bodies".

Kuaua kiva underground wall painting. (Bell-photo)

Chapter Nine

THE PARTING

Vicious encounters and heavy fighting on First and Second Mesas had gained mutual respect of the Castillian and Indian warriors. Beset by ambush and devious night attacks, the loyal followers of the clan chiefs as well as Tovar's men had defeated and routed the desperados. Kyaqa and Honmana, hopping about with a single crutch, had joined the Hopi women in treating the wounded men. Some of the cavalrymen and foot soldiers had recovered from their disabilities and were able to prepare those still bed-ridden for transfer to Antelope Mesa under orders of Lieutenant Blaque. Horses at hand plus two extras brought on the expedition's forage into Hopi country, were utilized to move the men in hammock-like mats with cords at the middle and each end slung over the animals for transporting.

Ample facilities at Walpi and the nursing skills of the women made possible the rapid recovery and preparation of the men for the trip to Antelope Mesa. The logistics had been carefully planned by Lieutenant Blaque.

Kyaqa, seeing the lieutenant in the open plaza, approached him with new confidence gained in working with Honmana and the Hopi women in the native infirmary.

"Lieutenant Blaque, some of the women wish to give you useful gifts which they have made. Will you come to the building at the north end of the plaza and see what they have?"

"The pleasure will be mine, Kyaqa. Will you lead the way?"

Military responsibilities had prevented him from seeking out Kyaqa. This was an opportunity to be with her that he would not miss!

They entered a large room where several women were working with clay pottery. This was unusual since in most villages clay utensils were fashioned in family dwellings where the women could also mind the children or tend to baking. Kyaqa proceeded to one end where vessels of many shapes lined the floor or stood in recesses built into the mud and stone walls. She nodded to nearby craftswomen-experts at clay pottery artistry- to come forward to describe their works. They peered at Blaque with shy modesty.

The clay forms were mostly wide mouth water jars of various shapes and sizes, small canteens; low, flat bowls and plain cooking vessels designed for various functions. Many large and extra large size water jugs were in evidence. Some of the pieces were adorned with designs related to kachina religious ceremonies, animals, birds and mystic designs handed down in the clans from mother to daughter for generations.

Kyaqa pointed to a wall where vessels protruded from recesses. "This ware is different from that on the floor."

Lieutenant Blaque stepped forward as a vase was removed for his perusal. A variety of colors brightly portrayed kachina masks and figures glowing on a cream exterior. Other vessels were adorned against a red or orange exterior. He rubbed a bowl with the sleeve of his tunic.

"This pottery is glazed. No wonder that the colors are so vivid!"

"The art of glazing has been forgotten over the years. Our ancient ancestors were part of the Anazazi who produced these beautiful specimens many centuries past. We want to give you whatever you like." Kyaqa beamed prettily as a ray of the outside sun shown through an opening, framing her face.

The lieutenant pondered his decision, finally speaking so all could hear. "This is your heritage, the gift to you from your ancestors of a prehistoric time. I will not accept such a priceless gift." He stood with the gleaming bowl in his hands. Slowly, he turned and placed the vessel in its slot in the wall. Dismay crossed the upturned faces.

"However, I will not disappoint you. One of these canteens on the floor will be very suitable for my needs."

Relief registered as Kyaqa reached for the pottery and handed it to the lieutenant.

Harsh voices of men in the plaza preceded the appearance of three Indians at the entrance of the pottery room. The lead man pointed a finger at Blaque.

"Hah! Our information was correct. The soldier is here. Kill him first, then we will help ourselves to the Hopi treasure." The apparel and language were unfamiliar to the lieutenant.

Kyaqa shouted at Blaque as two of the men sprang forward. "They are not Hopi. They mean to kill you!"

The lieutenant, who had not understood the Indian's words, reacted quickly to Kyaqa's shrill warning bringing up the canteen to smash the face of one assailant who stumbled on by. The broken pottery served as a deadly weapon as Blaque swung again, this time opening the face and neck of second man in bloody wounds.

The third of the trio lunged toward the lieutenant's back, an *obelisco* in one hand. Kyaqa, screaming, threw herself across the man's legs. As he fell and struck the floor, the dagger still clutched in his hand pierced his mid-section. He made an effort to clear the woman's weight from his legs before rolling over on his back, sightless eyes peering at the ceiling. Only seconds had passed. The lieutenant turned to face his adversary and witnessed the struggle. He scrambled over the fallen man's body to reach Kyaqa, who lay still, a large dark circle of blood forming at her side. He took her head and shoulders up into his arms, pressing his lips to her forehead.

The wounded girl's eyes fluttered open as she endeavored to focus on the lieutenant's face. Their eyes met.

"Since the days at the spring beneath the large rocks of the mesa, my heart has been full as my love for you surged through my body. Not since I was a small girl, learning things from my father, have I felt such love. His strength was my strength. Real love does not come very often, that I have come to understand." Her eyes drooped as the effort to talk taxed her vitality.

"I love you, Kyaqa. It must not end this way. We have a whole life to share together."

Her body slumped as the blood drained life away and the breathing stopped.

The pottery artisans, mostly old women and men on hand at this period of the day, had grouped in one corner clutching their work pieces to make space available for the lieutenant. Meanwhile, the urge to continue the fight had gone out of the remaining two assailants who lay moaning on the floor. One of the pottery workers slipped through the door, hurrying to the nearest kiva to get help. Several local men soon arrived, binding the hands and feet of the trespassers and dragging them away. Upon surveying the scene, one of the men clutched Blaque's arm in a sympathetic and friendly gesture, urging him to release his grasp on the Indian maiden. Aware that Kyaqa had saved his life, the lieutenant held the lifeless form, reluctant to release the person whose living countenance was forever emblazoned on his mind through such a short but everlasting time together.

The soft voice of an Indian woman penetrated his mind. "It is very difficult for you but you must allow the men to take Kyaqa's body and prepare for the death ritual."

Lieutenant Blaque looked up into Honmana's beautiful face, lined with sadness. "She saved my life, but lost her own. If only some way was possible to change these things. It was a most unnecessary reward for such a brave and beautiful young woman."

"It is truly impossible to alter such events after they have happened. The memory is all that we have, but not all that is left. Her face will appear before you many times and then will fade as the mind absorbs other things over periods of time and life continues. " Honmana's words were comforting to the young officer.

A touch of lips was the lieutenant's parting act of affection as Kyaqa's body was covered in a white manta and carried away.

"Has your wound healed? Do you feel able to travel?" The lieutenant rose to stand beside Honmana.

"I feel strong now and my leg wound does not bother as before. Where do you wish to go?"

"The intruders may be part of a large band. I wish to notify Captain Tovar of this event. When they appeared, the leader of the desperados shouted that they would kill me then help themselves to the Hopi treasure. Is such treasure in a cache somewhere?"

"We have no treasure of gold and precious stones. These

marauders have thought wrongly of that for many years. I have heard the Spaniards found such riches and took them from the Aztecs. If that is the ploy here, they will be deservedly disappointed." The words came bitterly from Honmana's lips as she looked challengly at Blaque.

"It was not my intention to upset you, Honmana. We would be in a position to aid the Hopis if a raid came about from these outsiders. The knowledge of such treasure, or the lack of it, does not mean our intention would be to carry it away. Our aim is to determine what this land holds and provides for the possibility of future settlement. This includes such resources as water, productive soil, minerals and the people them selves. The expedition has found that these northern provinces are not comparable in many ways to the southern regions of New Spain. I doubt that El Capitan expects to find a huge bounty of riches. You should know by now what his inner feelings are."

"Sometimes my tongue races ahead of my brain. Your words have calmed me. Hopefully, you too are aware that our great riches are in our minds. These are the treasures that our ancestors brought forward to us including close co-habitation with the Earth and Sun in our way of life."

Lieutenant Blaque was impressed by the wisdom and understanding of this young Hopi woman. His broad smile reassured Honmana.

"Will you be ready to leave within the hour? I will arrange for horses and two or three caballeros to accompany us. Let us meet at the plaza."

Honmana expressed her approval and left to gather her few traveling necessities and her bow and quiver.

Don Pedro listened attentively to Lieutenant Blaque's details of events at Second Mesa. Orders were issued immediately to his *escuadron* to be on twenty-four hour alert for the possibility of assassins or strangers in the area. Chest armor would be worn when outside their bivouac. The information was also passed on to the local chief.

"Lieutenant, you were to see that the troops were billeted at Antelope Mesa. The time for us to return to General Coronado's headquarters will soon be here."

"El Capitan, the wounded are gaining back their strength and the caballera are ready to move. An officer is temporarily in charge as I plan to return at sun-up to the encampment. In view of Kyaqa's unfortunate death, I brought Honmana on this trip and saw that she was safely at her grandmother's abode in compliance with her request. She does not complain about her wound."

"You have handled this very well, lieutenant." Tovar placed both hands upon the man's shoulders. "I am happy that you survived the attempt on your life. The demise of Kyaqa was extremely unfortunate. Her name will live forever in the annals of our *destacamiento!*"

Honmana's grandmother greeted the captain as he entered the small patio at her household.

"My granddaughter related her numerous experiences to me since she and Kyaqa left to hunt rabbits. Some of them were like nightmares, very difficult to believe that such conflicts can arise within our own people. Poor Kyaqa, it saddens me to know that she will not return. My heartfelt thanks go to you for rescuing Honmana and keeping her safe from further harm." The old woman's face wrinkled even more as she smiled at the captain.

"Please come inside."

The tall conquistador bent forward to clear the doorway. He removed the helmet, allowing a thick thatch of black curly hair to spring forth, reaching the nape of his neck. Once inside he stood erect, clean shaven and wearing a flawless white blouse, black trousers and shining boots with a wide mid-belt supported the sword. He placed the helmet on a bench, withdrew his sword and laid it alongside.

Honmana appeared, her hair freshly groomed and fashioned into butterfly whorls. She wore a white deer skin manta. Tovar stepped to meet her outstretched arms. As they embraced she spoke softly.

"It is so wonderful to be together again in this place. El Capitan, your body feels like a pottery jug!" Her fingers found the buttons of his shirt to reveal the chest armor underneath. It was not metal but hardened animal skin shaped as a vest which the natives of New Spain had provided Coronado's officers and men. Leather thongs were unbuckled leaving the captain bare chested. The embrace was much more gratifying. Hand in hand they walked into the adjacent room.

"These Kachina friends of yours intrigue me. This one seems to be smiling and its gaze always meets our own from any direction." The captain removed the figure from its alcove and settled back to a sitting position on the matted floor.

"It represents goodness, bountiful corn crops and fertility to continue such things year after year. It's image was in my mind as we sat near the spring following that terrible encounter below Second Mesa. Then the fighting was over, looking into the cool sparkling water removed the thoughts of confrontation and killing.

The new thoughts coming to mind included you, mi Capitan!"

The captain placed an arm around Honmana's shoulders. "Telling me these things makes me wish to be able to think like a Hopi and to gain some of the wisdom and peace of mind that you have. My troops and I must soon depart from your mesas and return to the main expedition's encampment at Cibola. That, unfortunately, limits the time left to absorb your traditions, values and teachings. Your love is already in my blood stream and my love for you grows by the day."

Honmana pressed her lips against his, expressing her love. He held the kiss, his arms entwined with hers to bring their bodies closer. The bonds of love were compelling but thoughts of Tovar leaving caused the Indian maiden to release her lips and peer deeply into the captain's eyes. "I will tell you now that I have made inquiries and have had discussions with the elders in the kivas concerning the relationship between Hopis and white people. Can we live side by side? May we marry and have children?" Tovar's solemn expression indicated a need for answers. Honmana continued. "They say we, the Hopis, are fortunate to have met with a force of soldiers led by a man of open mind and understanding of the consequences of native people being squashed by conquerors and the differences in their being treated as fellow human beings. They believe that we are capable of-living side by side as long as we trust each other and communicate our true thoughts, one to the other. The meetings and discourse with Fray Padilla have revealed major differences in religious concepts. Primarily, the Spaniards want us to immediately assume another mantle - that of the Christian. Our ancestral beliefs and rituals are so firmly based in our minds that probably many years or generations may pass before acceptance. On the other hand, the white people have not indicated or demonstrated that they understand much of our religion.

"Our way of life, living each day as nature permits on these high mesas, is another point of concern. Would the Spaniards be content to live as we do?"

"The Hopi view of living and of spiritual conciliation with natural things is truly remarkable". The captain searched for the right words. "The Pueblo tribes undoubtedly have heard all of the horror stories associated with their meetings with the Spanish, several of which resulted in confrontations disastrous to both.

"The area to the south, now called New Spain, was discovered then taken by force when the rulers opposed all offers of peaceful coexistence. Moreover, the treatment of the people by these rulers was outrageous and outside the realm of normal human behavior, as well as the basic teachings of Christianity. I am willing to admit that chicanery and dreadful atrocities were credited to both sides. Sincerely, I hope that such events will not occur again." He drew Honmana close. "I have been unable to tell you before because my thoughts have been running in many directions. Our stay here is nearly over. Time and army orders have the knack of catching up to each other."

Honmana placed her arms around the captain. "Then must you leave? This was not unexpected as the thought of it lurked in the shadows of my mind."

"In a day or two. Most of the preparation has been completed with our men assembling at Antelope Mesa."

"Antelope Mesa, how I remember the specks of dust far off on the horizon, then your appearance the next morning. at the foot of the cliffs. The span of time seems so short since then, even though so much has happened."

"I have loved you since I first saw you." Tovar, breathing heavily, pulled Honmana down beside him on the mat.

"My love for you has grown and filled me with much happiness," She whispered.

"We must continue to share our love and live our lives together. This will be our dream and our goal. A courier will come with my message when I learn of the direction the expedition will take."

The fire of their love consumed them as the day waned and shadows lengthened across the room.

****

Friar Padilla rode alongside Captain Tovar as the small contingent headed toward the rising sun. Skirting a chimney-like rocky knoll, each man turned to look back at the receding mesas. The outline of stone and mud dwellings atop the steep cliffs were barely visible.

"Will our joining with the main force take us forever away from these people, or do you expect that we will see the Hopis again?" The Friar's countenance was solemn as he peered at the captain.

"Our next assignment will undoubtedly take us east into a region known as Kansas. Where the trail leads from there, I do not know. We could possibly swing southward then back to New Spain I suppose, or return by the routes already traveled and muster again at Cibola."

"Do not think it presumptuous of me, el Capitan, but other thoughts seem to be in your mind, the Hopi maiden, Honmana, perhaps?"

The captain scowled at Padilla, then his countenance cleared. "You are right, my friend, thoughts of the past few weeks are in my mind. Honmana's face keeps appearing, blocking out the future whatever it may be, and occupying most of my thinking about how our friendship can be continued."

****

"You have something on your mind Honmana?" The old grandmother looked up from her baking as her granddaughter walked across the room and stood peering out through the patio into the vast arid land.

Honmana turned and walked slowly toward her grandmother. "I would like to be sitting at the grinding stones crushing the white meal and blue corn in preparation for my wedding. But it is my fate that the captain, who I love with all my being, is out there beyond the mesas and I do not know when we will be together again. He has shared my bed and spoken of his deep love for me."

"You should not spend your days contemplating the time when a message will be received from Captain Tovar or an exact week or month when he will return to you. We have learned from the Zunis that the expedition is very large and cumbersome, moving slowly along the trails. Therefore it is unlikely that the army will move like the road-runner birds of the Rio Grande region. No, the Castillians will investigate all pueblos large and small, and survey the land in order to prepare their maps which the white men depend on to see where they have been."

Honyanqua looked at her granddaughter closely, but received no response.

"If the Spaniards have their way, life as we know it in our province and others might find profound changes in the future. With the Cibolans subdued and at peace, the general has asked them to talk to friends and neighbors in other pueblos and tell them that Christians had come to the country. The strangers only desire is to be their friends, to find good lands to live in and for them to come and visit the newcomers when possible. In other words, they wish to know more about the Pueblo people. Only time will tell how long the conquistadors will stay and whether they will settle in our domain."

Chapter Ten

G R A N D   C A N Y O N   D I S C O V E R E D

The Michaelsons enjoyed a hearty breakfast at a small restaurant adjoining their motel before taking a short walk around the area, breathing the clear, high mesa air. Entering the information center, they were met by Siki who took them to a room near artifact displays. It was furnished with a settee, table and chairs used as a lounge and for other purposes by employees.

Sam set up his tape recorder then crossed over to Siki. "Before we continue this morning, we want to show you something." He produced a small, soft leather bag and pulled out the challice. Cindy placed it in the Indian woman's hands.

"It is a jarron or some type of vessel that Mark kicked up from the dirt in a camping area on the road to Mesa Verde. We have cleaned and polished it." Cindy stood as the object was turned over and over then kneeled down and pointed to markings on the surface.

"It has the words CORONADO JUNE 1540 on this side and the letters Ib III. On the other side are the words TOVAR, MOQUI, HONMANA. Some are barely visible or legible."

Siki looked at Cindy. "These words indicate that this urn was used to carry a message. It surely belonged to General Coronado and was sent by Tovar to Honmana in a Hopi settlement."

"We have tried without success to open it." Sam described some of the attempts they had made.

"Artifacts such as this can be studied carefully and possibly separated into its parts by the research laboratory at the Northern

Arizona Museum located near Flagstaff. Could it be that the vessel was never delivered?" Siki paused as the significance of her question penetrated. Hesitating occasionally as if to collect her thoughts, she continued her narrative.

"No message had been received from Captain Tovar who had told the general what he had learned about a great river located northwest of the Hopis. Coronado was much impressed by Tovar's report and within a month or so a small contingent was dispatched, apparently about a dozen soldados headed by Don Garcia Lopez de Cardenas. Honmana's life changed with the arrival of Captain Cardenas and his party of explorers. Don Garcia was received and well accepted by the Hopis. He outlined his quest to see the river and requested the services of Hopi guides for the journey north, asking for the proper provisions and supplies necessary for that region. Six guides volunteered as did Honmana. She explained to Cardenas that her father resided at a northern river village and that she was acquainted with the route having traveled it several times. The Captain accepted the volunteers as a group and since he proved to be easy to talk with, Honmana asked about Captain Tovar. Cardenas would not give any information since movements of officers and men were kept within the top command and all had taken oaths of silence.

Honmana had another reason for wishing to depart from Oraibi. She confided in her grandmother.

"Grandmother, I nave been accepted as a guide to go with the Spaniards and our men who volunteered for the journey into northern regions. I wish to visit my father but I have another reason."

"Your old grandmother probably knows the reason my dear, you are pregnant, is that not so?"

Honmana nodded her head. "It is so grandmother. I should have realized that you would know! Without a husband I will not feel comfortable here. I expected to receive a message from Captain Tovar but none has come."

"It is correct that you should leave this village. Your father's home would be an acceptable place to give birth when the time comes."

"Thank you, grandmother." Honmana embraced the older woman, aware that considerable time would pass before they could be together again.

* * * * * * * *

As the eager group plodded through desert country, Honmana turned to look back at the Hopi mesas, wondering when, if ever, she would again join her grandmother and friends there. At second night's encampment the guides discussed their slow progress saying, "we could travel in one day what it takes the Spaniards two days to accomplish". Their displeasure was not brought to the captain's attention, however, and twenty days elapsed before the river was sighted.

They had reached a high *barranca* from which the river below appeared to be about six feet wide. It was half a league wide according to the Indians, who pointed to the other bank. One of the men, schooled in surveying, reckoned the *abismo* at approximately three leagues across on an air line. Three days were spent on this high promontory searching for a path or trail down to the river. A descent appeared to be impossible. They had discovered the Grand Canyon! Named the Tison (Firebrand) River by the Spaniards and downstream Indians, the great river which had cut the magnificent gorge was later named the Rio Colorado.

* * * * * * * *

Pausing to reach for a journal in a stack before her, Siki explained. "I am sure you are interested in more than Hopi legends concerning el Canon Grande. Sam, will you please read from this section. It is taken from documents by Pedro de Castaneda writing on the discovery of the canyon by Cardenas.

Sam, deeply engrossed, read eagerly from the bound volume. Captain Pablos de Melgosa, Juan Galeras and another companion found it impossible to descend to the canyon bottom on account of great difficulties. Returning from their final attempt about 4 P.M. in the afternoon, they had found that what seemed to be easy from above was not so, but instead very hard and difficult. Those who stayed above had estimated that some huge rocks on the sides of the cliffs seemed to be about as tall as a man, but those who went down swore that when they reached these rocks they were bigger than the great tower of Seville.

Heeding the guides' statement that no water was available within three or four days travel, they did not go farther up the river. Water was obtained by excursions inland from the gorge each day. They came back from this location and the expedition did not have any further result. The villages of the province remained peaceful since they were never visited again, nor was any attempt made to find peoples in that direction. The general received a written account of what they had seen because one Pedro de Sotomayer had gone with Don Garcia Lopez Cardenas as chronicler.

"That is most interesting. It was nice of Castaneda to give credit to Sotomayer for the report of the discovery, it earned Don Pedro a place in history! Isn't it wonderful that we have in our hands the very words written by those who participated in the events. How were they to know that four hundred years later thousands of Americans would come at various times and stand in awe at the spectacular sight!" Sam was visibly moved.

"Some of the names mentioned in the journal are on a list I have prepared which can possibly help reveal connections with the Spanish court and embassies which were undoubtedly the scene of turmoil and intrigue in those explosive years. Captain Melgosa, for example, was a native of Burgos. He was not present when the army mustered at Compostela, but arrived in Mexico later, coming to Culiacan as captain of infantry. Juan Galeros was born at Almendralijo, a town undoubtedly named after an Arab incursion into Spain. He was equipped with three horses, native weapons and a coat of mail. Pedro de Sotomayer, a young man designated as official historian of the expedition, was apparently a man of letters and high recommendation from Spanish officialdom.

"With your permission, Siki, I will continue to search these transcripts for a tie-in with Cindy's family." Sam passed the bound pages back to Siki.

"You surely have my consent on the matter of further research and use of these journals. In my opinion, further investigation is the only way available to ascertain events concerning the Burrington kin, particularly in the far distant past. My help is accessible at any time. Now, I have a little more to add to that chronicle. "Siki continued her narrative.

Dwarfed, twisted pines populated this high country which had no inhabitants in the area. The Spaniards decided that no one could live there due to the cold at this time of the year. They were frustrated over the difficulty encountered in obtaining water. Guides explained that on past such excursions in this region the Indians had women with them who carried extra water supplies in gourds. The gourds were buried along the way for use on the return trip.

With the mission of discovery completed, further exploration was deemed unnecessary and Captain Cardenas decided to return from that location. Thereupon, Honmana and two of the Hopi guides took their leave from the small expedition, heading down river to locate a Havasupai village where her father resided.

DEATH AND NEW LIFE

After following the canyon rim for five days, the adventurers came upon a pile of stones formed into a small tower eight to ten feet high, located at the brink of a steep precipice. The guides knew this to be the marker for a trail. About fifty feet away they found the start of a pathway behind a large boulder balanced precariously on the rim. The river lay below, only a small section visible from their observation point. The trail twisted and turned down the canyon wall between boulders and outcroppings, eventually leading into a meadow lined with bushes and the Indian village. A lookout of The Havasupais had signaled the coming of someone on the trail and a delegation was waiting as Honmana and her guides emerged.

A friendly welcome was received by the newcomers and greetings were exchanged in a mixture of Hopi and Havasupai language and expressions. Honmana took the initiative.

"I am Honmana, daughter of Nuvamsa. My friends and guides are Quitoya and Yutanuu. We are pleased with your warm welcome. We have been traveling for many days and wish to stay for a rest and visit. Is my father now in the village?"

"Yes, your father is here and he is well. We will take you to him."

Upon learning that the Hopis had accompanied white men, who were called Castillanos, to the rim of the gorge where they had observed the great river for the first time, the Havasupais excitedly asked many questions and discussed what they had heard. The moccasin grapevine had spread the word of a Spanish Expedition in the region!

The sounds of voices brought Nuvamsa to the doorway of his *hawa*, a domicile constructed of slim cottonwood poles, bent and covered with willows, reeds and brush.

"Honmana!" The tall, erect man came toward to embrace the daughter he had not seen for three years. "You have grown into a beautiful young woman!"

"I am glad to see you looking so well, father." Honmana held on to her father lovingly, not wanting to break the embrace.

"Your daughter and these men were guides for an expedition from the far south seeking the great river. Others remained with the white men who turned back after reaching the canyon but were unable to descend to the river." A spokesman related all that he knew about the newcomers.

"Thank you for bringing them to my hawa. They must rest now, later they will tell us more about the strangers."

As the local welcoming group dispersed, Nuvamsa spoke gratefully to the Hopi guides whom Honmana had introduced to her father with much respect and humility. "I thank you from deep in my heart for bringing my daughter over the long and hostile terrain from the village of Oraibi." The men acknowledged the compliment. "Please go to my second hawa and make yourselves comfortable. Take this large vessel full of water to help cleanse yourselves of the dust of the trail." He gestured to a nearby structure.

Honmana was delighted with her room in which brightly colored mats lay on the floor and blankets hung on the walls. It was adjacent to the main entry room of the well maintained home.

Her father was pleased. "As you can see, I have occupied only this room. A little voice told me that you would someday come to our home again. That is why the other room, your room, has been kept in readiness." Nuvamsa and Honmana laughed and embraced again in a long awaited reunion.

"How is your grandmother, Honyanqua? In the years that have passed no word has been received of events at Third Mesa, or for that matter, any of the Hopi pueblos. After the death of your mother, it was a hard decision to make, leaving you there in Oraibi. Although we have had several meetings, the long intervals and not having you at my side have caused me to regret bringing about our separation. It would have been better if I had remained with you." Nuvamsa's love for his daughter shone through a lined countenance.

"Grandmother is in good health and is busy in her home. A good friend provides the extra help she needs. As matriarch, it seems that a constant flow of Bear Clan members call on her for counseling. Life goes on!"

"I will provide an extra blanket or two, as you may remember that the nights are sometimes very cold in this canyon." A small circle of stones at one side of the larger room contained sticks and small logs when needed for heat. Cooking was done outside in the open, weather permitting.

Nuvamsa left the dwelling, going to the home of a close friend, who, as had most of the villagers, heard about the arrival of his daughter. After a short discussion, the proud father suggested that a special feast would be a good thing to have in honor of Honmana and her Hopi friends. Before sundown, the entire village had gathered to partake of the supper prepared by the Havasupai women. Groups of men and women gathered about Honmana, Yutanuu and Quitoya who answered many questions concerning the soldiers; where they were from, how big were the horses and would the white men return?

The shrill cries and laughing of children greeted Honmana when she awoke the next morning. Dressing and stepping outside, she observed games and antics of children at play. The memories of her childhood participation in such things had faded after she had moved to the Hopi mesas.

Sticks clicked as a ball was whacked from one child to another amid much screaming and hilarity. In this game the boys mixed their playing sticks with the girls. The sport, tha-se-vi-ga (skinny), had the objective of scoring a goal after working the ball through the opposite side. Tossing the ball demonstrated the dexterity of the children in juggling three or four small melons, the objective being to maintain them all in the air in a rotating fashion.

More voices filled the air from nearby ponds and clear reservoirs where the warm sands of beaches attracted many children. A closer inspection convinced Honmana that wading, swimming and diving were still main ingredients of youthful activities.

In the afternoon Honmana observed a group of women, some tending babies, actively engaged in gambling games continuing for hours. Simple games of chance, using smooth pebbles for counting, also involved children with the girl winners receiving pendants or bracelets and the boys trading arrow heads and spear tips. Thoughts of her childhood in this canyon coursed through the mind of the young woman, half Hopi, half Havasupai, who despite an undercurrent of mixed feelings, now dwelled in the present and the lighthearted happiness she felt. This had been her life before her mother died and she was taken to her Hopi grandmother at Oraibi.

Spring passed and the summer months came indicating changes in Honmana's appearance. Inside the hawa she sat down with her father, telling him about her pregnancy, her love for Captain Tovar and events which occurred involving his presence and many confrontations.

"I made a decision to accompany the Spaniards to the great river after the captain had returned to his headquarters and no word was heard from him. Grandmother agreed that it would best that I leave."

Nuvamsa listened attentively. "We must not repeat this to anyone or speak of it again."

"But father, I wish to have my baby here where you are and among old friends."

"My daughter, you are not aware of the tribal beliefs that strongly oppose marriage or association of our women with the pahanas. This also affects other members of the family. It goes back many generations in tribal history, although I think that few, if any of this clan has even seen a white man."

Unknown to them, an informer outside the entrance had listened and overheard the conversation. He ran quickly, reporting what he had heard to a member of the tribal council. This man, who was a friend of Nuvamsa, immediately went to him warning of possible action by certain tribe members. Moreover, he suggested that Nuvamsa, his daughter and the guides leave without delay for their own safety since the informer would undoubtedly tell others.

"Honmana, a friend has advised that our conversation was overheard and insisted that the only way we can be safe is to leave quickly. Gather a few belongings and place corn and pieces of squash in pouches. I will notify the guides that we must depart." Nuvamsa walked swiftly to the adjacent hawa and informed the two Hopis.

Armed with bows and arrows and carrying light items for travel, the guides arrived within minutes. The four left on the run disappearing in the brush at the edge of the village. Nuvamsa turned for a last look at his domiciles as they started up a trail leading to the top rim of the canyon. At a turn in the path Quitoya and Yutanuu paused to release a large boulder, loose rock and gravel which dropped to the trail below. Shouts were heard indicating their pursuers were on the trail.

Fleeing up the winding path, Honmana and the three men were weaving between large boulders, twisted trees and bushes that somehow had rooted on the walls and in crevices of the precipice. Voices carried up from below. The chase was closing! The guides and Honmana had disappeared around a protruding rock ledge after passing a point on the trail visible from another turn below, when an arrow whizzed through the air into her father's chest. Clutching the protruding arrow, he twisted and fell headlong down the cliff, landing on a jutting rock ledge. His body lay still. With yells and cheers filling the air, the three fugitives looked downward where Nuvamsa's body lay with an arrow extending outward and dark patches forming on the rocky shelf. The lifeblood poured from the wound. Honmana suppressed a scream, covering her face with her hands.

Horrified by the scene, the trio realized it would be impossible to stand and face the oncoming warriors. The two guides, one on each side, practically carried Honmana upward to the canyon rim. At this point the two men dug furiously at the base of a large, old juniper tree which stood precariously at the canyon edge with most of its roots exposed. Grasping larger lengths of branches laying over the ground, they were able to push the tree slowly until it toppled over into the trail loosening large boulders as it crashed down the precipice coming to rest where it effectively blocked further advance by the Indians. The onrushing rocks and debris showered the trail as Honmana stood ready with her bow, on the lookout for any signs of the antagonists.

With the ensuing dust cloud providing added cover, the group started eastward, running as far as possible before resting and pacing themselves thereafter until nightfall. In a short time they stopped at a small fresh water spring surrounded by lush grass in which they gratefully lay down to sleep.

At daylight, Quitoya spoke to Honmana expressing his sorrow over the death of her father. The three ate small amounts from their supply of provisions and started on the long trek to Oraibi. Yutanuu had expressed his condolences to Honmana and offered to carry her bow and quiver. She let him have them seeing that the bronzed, handsome young man was eager to help her. The pace was slower now as the men reduced their usual gait-somewhere between walking and running- in deference to Honmana who could feel the signs of life in her pregnancy.

Three days later severe winds reaching high velocity swept in from the distant mountains driving face searing sand raising dust squalls which impeded the progress of the small group, awash in the solitude of the desert terrain. The men noted the dark skies to the west, indicating rain had fallen or was headed their way with the wind as a fore-runner. Half way across a wide, dry river bed they were engulfed in a torrent of raging water cascading down from an narrow cut in the plateau. Locking arms with Honmana in the middle they attempted to stay together but her two male companions, knocked off their feet by the current and unstable under footing, were unable to hold on to Honmana who was swept toward the opposite bank. Wet and cold, she dragged herself onto a sand bar near the edge of the floodwaters. Making his way to the same side of the river, Quitoya found Honmana, picked her up in his arms and carried her to safety well above the swirling water.

"Take me to the juniper trees." Honmana's voice was barely a whisper.

"Thank you. Please leave me here alone while you find dry wood and build a fire. Dry the extra manta and place it over me, I want to be warm. My baby is coming."

The first cries of the baby were heard by the two men, together again and working to keep a sputtering fire going using damp wood. Honmana bathed and dried her son, holding him close to her body with the manta providing a snug covering. A span of time later, only the little head with its crop of black hair was visible as the new mother walked toward the fire. Her companions had built the fire near a rocky overhang and between two trees in a comparatively dry place. They helped Honmana settle down on a bed of soft juniper branches and leaves where the warmth of the fire provided new strength.

The rain ceased. The baby cried.

"Well, this is a noisy little *kwaatsi*, boy or girl?" Yutanuu shyly posed the question as Quitoya poked a stick into the red hot embers.

"I have named him Aroyo. This is where he was born. His father is a Castillian."

"In a few days when mother and baby were stronger, the group continued on to Oraibi. A loving and heartwarming welcome greeted the somewhat ragged group when Honmana's grand-mother came forth to meet them on the path to the stone abode. Her great-grandson rapidly became the center of attraction in the home as the villagers came to hear about the flood and other exploits connected to Honmana's long absence.

Chapter Eleven

THE QUEST

Honmana was restless. Life at home in the Oraibi Pueblo for which she had longed for after existing in any way possible on the trail, had something missing. She was not happy even though little Aroyo kept her occupied and filled her days. The missing ingredient was Captain Tovar. No courier had come with his message stating a date or place where they could meet.

"It is impossible for me to find complete peace and be happy in this continual waiting to receive word from the captain. Grandmother, I am going to find the army and locate Don Pedro. Something may have happened to him. I must know and he must see his son."

"How will you travel? It would not be well for you to journey alone. Do not make that decision now. Give yourself another night to decide." Grandmother had plotted to act on her own. She would tell Honmana's companions, Quitoya and Yutanuu, of her granddaughter's plans and ask them if they would accompany her.

The two men strode leisurely into the patio the next morning, full of smiles and greetings. Honmana sat in the sun watching Aroyo crawling around from one reed and feather mat to another where a small basket or pottery piece had been placed. This was his mother's way of teaching him to be resourceful in his many quests to satisfy curiosity. She had resolved to locate the captain on her own if necessary and told the two men who were now sitting alongside on the ground, of her travel plans.

"Are you not needed here to take care of little Aroyo? Let me under take the journey. I will cover the ground at a fast pace and bring back the information you seek in a matter of days!" Yutanuu, younger of the two men by three years, stood, thumped his chest and pointed to the southeast.

Quitoya responded. "It is not necessary that you go alone, my friend. Others may try to prevent you from completing the task. Two heads will be better than one on such a trip to the headquarters of the conquistadors!" Honmana was secretly amused by the interplay of these two friends who had previously demonstrated their interest in her. She controlled her composure however, and gave no outward indication of her thoughts. Listening intently, she still refused to let the Hopi men go without her.

"I am afraid that no one would believe you and might even detain you for much questioning. In that event you might return empty handed from your mission. I will tend to my young son and care for him on the journey. We can go together which will be best for our mutual support and protection. Do you agree? Captain Tovar must see his son!"

* * * * * * * *

Lunch time brought a break in Siki's narrative but the discussion continued over the table. "It is not clear to me where the expedition finally camped. They looked for the legendary Seven Cities of Cibola. The first site in Tierra Nueva was near Hawikuh, a Zuni village. So many people must have been involved attending the horses, cattle and sheep, tradesmen, blacksmiths and others doing the miscellaneous chores in addition to the Spaniards, Mexican natives and Indians comprising Coronado's army and the expeditionary total force. Certainly a very large area would be required." Siki looked inquiringly at Cindy.

"In certain library references I recall, the historians say Coronado's encampment site was on the west bank of the Rio Grande near the present town of Bernalillo, New Mexico. The expedition occupied most of a pueblo and set up additional tents in the surrounding area. It might have been suspected as one of the legendary seven cities sought by the Spaniards but it was not rich in gold and precious stones. In fact, the ruins of Pueblo dwellings can still be seen there!" Cindy concluded.

"I appreciate this information. Some items of interest are undoubtedly lost in the many generations repeating Hopi history on which I depend. As a descendant of Bear Clan tribal members, my knowledge would relate to certain events in that clan that would be told differently in other clans, although it all comes together in the recollections of various people." Siki mulled over several points in the discussion. "From your description, Cindy, I believe the settlement near Bernalillo was called Tiguex by the Castillians. Let's see what the journals of Pedro de Castaneda have to say about it." The bound volume was handed to Cindy who began on dateline April 30, 1541.

Correspondence from Captain Hernando de Alvarado and Fray Juan de Padilla who wrote from Tiguex describing the bountiful crops, fine pastures and plentiful water, influenced General Coronado to move to that land. Captain Don Garcia Lopez de Cardenas, with a force of fourteen Spaniards and a number of Mexican soldiers, was ordered to Tiguex where he established a camp in the open, outside the pueblos. The Indians were hospitable but when they learned the Spanish planned to spend the winter an undercurrent of dissatisfaction became obvious to Cardenas who knew from the moment he arrived that they wanted to rebel and all the Spaniards felt the same. They were in the midst of many hostile pueblos hoping that larger forces of the army would soon arrive.

With the onset of snow and cold weather, Cardenas requested the natives to vacate one pueblo and move into the others, there being twelve in the group. Although resentful, the Indians complied without resistance.

After more than a week of severe weather and scarce water, Coronado reached the Rio Grande and Tiguex where quarters were ready at Alcanfor Pueblo. The Rio Grande was crossed and all segments of the army were assembled at Tiguex on April 23, 1541. The massive assemblage of over 1500 persons including Mexican allies and Indians was expanded by a thousand horses, thousands of sheep and cattle and three wives of Spanish soldiers with their children who had made the original trip with the expedition.

* * * * * * * *

"Over 400 years have passed and the weather has not changed much. The hardships endured by the army and people of the expedition have largely been overcome by modern transportation facilities and the spread of cities and small towns. Heating must have been a real problem in those stone and adobe structures of the sixteenth century." Cindy thumbed aimlessly through several pages. "This evening I am going to continue on the trail of my ancestors. My research indicates more involvement with affairs in the court of Spain and some links to the New World. It is very interesting so far!"

The trio of Hopis had covered many leagues following the Rio Colorado Pequeno which guaranteed water supplies. It was a different route than that traversed by Captain Tovar's contingent which crossed the desert to Antelope Mesa. The arrival at Hawikuh brought mixed reactions from Honmana and the two men. Expecting to see a large encampment of the military with many horses and soldados, only a fragment of Coronado's expedition was left. Cibola, land of the Zuni, had been vacated.

Honmana and her companions, along with small son Aroyo, were billeted in a section reserved for the native people who had remained when the army entourage had originally occupied the pueblo and much of the surrounding area. Several Indian guides who had accompanied Cardenas to the great river canyon welcomed the Hopis, renewing friendships.

Tiny Aroyo and his beautiful mother became the center of interest and activity for the Indian women who brought gifts, animal skins and blankets to make them more comfortable. At a time when one of the women was holding and playing with the young boy, Honmana managed to draw one of the Zuni guides to one side.

"Do you know if Captain Tovar is in this camp? He was very good to us when bivouacked at Oraibi and other Hopi mesas with his small force of soldados."

"You apparently are not aware that Captain Tovar, Cardenas and the main army left for Tiguex on the Rio Grande where

Kuaua Ruins Near Bernalillo on the Rio Grande. CORONADO'S army billeted here the winter of 1540. The area was known as TIGUEX.

(Bell-Photo)

headquarters are now established. Only a small attachment remains here under junior officers. Certain of the local inhabitants put up strong resistance at several pueblos against a takeover by the expeditionary force, but the advance cavalry units fought their way through. Many pueblos are situated along the Rio Grande."

Honmana tried not to look disheartened. The perceptive Zuni read the expression on her face. "Do not be dismayed. The Spanish captains have been dispatched in many directions. Specially formed groups go out to test the resistance and abilities of certain pueblos reported as being ready to oppose the Spaniards. Others follow up reports of inhabited or uninhabited regions said to contain fertile valleys and rivers. Undoubtedly the Castillians plan to expand the boundaries of the areas already occupied. We have heard that the explored regions are added to the maps in the General's headquarters. Many do not like this since it would mean Spanish domination over the Pueblo tribes and under the flag of New Spain."

"Do you talk openly of this?" Honmana was wide-eyed upon hearing this information. The Zuni guide, Kalisomi, was unperturbed by her reaction.

"No. No. I trust you from our past experiences with Captain Cardenas and know you will share these thoughts guardedly, as I have with you."

Wishing to speak immediately with Quitoya, Honmana stepped outside and started toward the adjacent building. She screamed as a blanket was thrown over her head prior to being picked up bodily and placed on a horse with another person already in the saddle.

Inside, Kalisomi heard her screams and cries for help as did Quitoya just coming to the door of his quarters. The horse raced away as the two men witnessed the abduction. On the mount was an army lieutenant who had been waiting for an opportunity to kidnap the Hopi woman for his own purposes. They headed north at a gallop along the river bank disappearing in a thick growth of trees. A short distance behind, the lieutenant's orderly followed.

"Woo-hee". Kalisomi's yell was heard throughout the building and outside where women were baking. "Honmana has been kidnapped!"

Bedlam reigned inside where the women scrambled to look for children, picking up the younger ones in an effort to reach the seclusion and safety of their rooms. Aroyo was held tightly in the arms of a young Indian girl as the men rushed outside to provide assistance-this most dreaded of crimes experienced among the Indians. Abduction of children and women when caught on a trail away from the village had been occurring with more frequency since the main army had moved on and the coming of renegades with no land or pueblos of their own and who made raids at unexpected times. Personal items, blankets and supplies were also common targets.

The Zuni guide met Quitoya, both running to a nearby corral where they appealed to the *caballista* for two horses. The excitement and story told by the men convinced the corral keeper, who recognized Kalisomi as a member of the native contingent connected to the army, and authorized use of the *caballos*. He also gave them knives which were the only weapons they had.

Fortunately, the dust lingered along the trail. As they passed the first trees, the absence of dust swirls was noticed. Turning back they came to the place where the riders ahead of them had veered off into the forest.

Honmana, meanwhile, was kicking, scratching and fighting off the soldier who had encountered more than he bargained for. They had stood toe-to-toe but she had caused the man to trip and fall into a clump of bushes when the orderly came from behind and clamped arms about her body. The officer regained his feet and stalked forward, an arm raised to strike her full in the face.

Thrashing sounds among the trees had caused the Zuni and Hopi guides to dismount their animals and silently reach the scene. As one, they leaped upon the Spaniards and all five, including Honmana, fell to the turf of grass and leaves. Twisting and flailing with her arms, Honmana twisted from under the orderly and rolled to one side. As the four men fought in the shadows of the forest, she heard the clicking sounds of knives whose blades shined in arcs as the filtered sun's rays caught the thrusts and wild parries.

Quitoya lay on his back endeavoring to push the heavier orderly, a large black bearded man, off of his body. To Honmana's dismay, she noted that his knife had been wrenched from his grasp and hit the ground before her. The orderly's hand was raised for a fatal plunge when Honmana recovered the weapon and flung herself on the back of the adversary. The knife entered his side in a mortal wound. He rolled over, sprawled in the grass as Quitoya came to his feet and turned to assist the Zuni. It was unnecessary since the lieutenant had been thrown against a tree, striking his head causing what appeared to be a momentary black out. It was more than that. He had fallen on his own knife. Blood flowed from the wound.

"Give me the final thrust. I cannot face my fellow officers or my regiment." The Castillian peered pleadingly into the eyes of Kalisomi.

"Rest in peace, soldado." The Indian used the officer's blade for the final dispatch.

Sanctity and protection of the home were of prime concern to the pueblo dwellers. The men, some of whom had met the Spanish head on as warriors before being subdued the year previous, dashed to the corral but were refused mounts when unable to produce an army permit. Brandishing spears and clubs a dozen yelling and shouting warriors took off at a run after the pursuers on horseback who had now disappeared on the trail ahead.

After running at an easy lope sustained for nearly a league, the band sighted mounted horses emerging from a growth of cottonwood trees. Coming closer they recognized Quitoya and Honmana riding double on one steed with Kalisomi following leading two horses. On their backs were tied the bodies of the orderly and lieutenant, hanging loosely as they swayed with the pace of the animals.

With his right hand raised high in a peace sign Quitoya spoke to the warriors as they gathered around."You are a welcome sight and your coming to rescue Honmana is very much appreciated. As you can see, with the help of the Great Spirit, we were able to overcome these culprits and they have met their deserved fate."

Kalisomi also spoke. "I am thankful that you came. It makes me feel proud to know that our people are bound together in in effort to aid or rescue those in distress. This is evident even though an alien army now occupies our homeland. We must proceed now to deliver the bodies."

At the corral the still forms of the lieutenant and orderly were removed from the backs of the horses and placed in custody of the caballista.

"A terrible struggle took place between these two soldados over the woman who had been abducted. When we arrived at the scene they had stabbed each other to death. Their knives are still red with blood as you can see." Kalisomi waited for his explanation to be accepted.

"It is best that you leave immediately. I will take care of the horses." The sounds of hoof beats preceded the appearance of two riders coming at a gallop. The corral attendant had closed the gate as the soldiers dismounted. Passing by Kalisomi and looking at the bodies, they questioned the caballista.

Honmana retrieved her son, thanking the local women for taking care of him. They listened to the story of her abduction, but later whispered among themselves, blaming the Hopi woman for the event because of her beauty. During the next day Honmana recovered and rested from her ordeal. Sharing a meal later that day with her companions and Zuni guides where stories of the excursion to the Firebrand River were re-told, Kalisomi advised that the officer now in charge at the camp planned to hold the visiting Hopis and charge them with the death of the soldados.

"This man is very suspicious and wants to blame someone, probably to avenge the deaths. Questioning will begin tomorrow. You had better leave tonight."

"Hope is in my heart that we will find Captain Tovar at the new headquarters at Tiguex. Can you help us?" Honmana sounded desperate.

"I will help you and so will the local Indians who work at the corral. Pack your belongings and what food is available and meet at the east end of the corral by the gate when the moon rises above the horizon. Three horses will be ready."

Honmana placed her left hand over her heart and the right hand over the heart of her Zuni friend. "My son and I and my companions will never forget your courage and what you are doing for us. Thank you."

Quitoya discussed weapons with several warriors who displayed lances, clubs and knives taken after an encounter with renegades, both white and Indian, who had banded together and were attempting raids on the smaller pueblos and outlying villages. Formed of disgruntled followers of the expedition and tribal outcasts, these groups also attacked isolated travelers, particularly displaced families comprised mostly of women and children who had lost their male members and were moving to another village for protection. Yutanuu appeared, loaded with light leather pouches of maize, pika bread and other food items provided by the local residents who had grown fond of the visitors during their short stay. The Zunis convinced the Hopi men of the necessity of using short, sharp bladed lances and knives when confronted by the roving bands. Several weapons were presented with the admonishment that all three be familiar with their use.

Prior to their departure that night Honmana gave Kalisomi a hand written message requesting that it be given only to Captain Tovar in the event he came to Hawikuh.

"The trail east is well traveled. Be wary of soldiers who may try to detain you at pueblos they have occupied. May the Great Spirit protect you on your journey." Kalisomi strode to each of the mounted trio, testing the halter buckles of the caballos and pressing an arm of each of his friends. Taking a step backward he waved them on. Little Aroyo was sound asleep, cradled on the back of his mother.

Long stretches of arid land confronted the group. However, spring days were cooler than summer heat and daily travel was not so wearisome. Honmana studied the bronzed Yutanuu sitting tall and straight on the Spanish saddle and looking strong and fit to meet any situation that might arise. From a knoll, she sighted a row of structures about a league distant.

"Look ahead to the right of the trail. Hopefully the people in this lonely place have not been raided and their homes and families are intact. Since our experience at Cibola, I am concerned about what has happened to the people as the army passed through."

"It is best to be optimistic. The army's actions probably had much to do with the reception and attitudes they receive from the natives." Yutanuu surveyed the small community.

The village's buildings were made of dried mud and reeds, compared to the stone structures of the Hopi. Children ran forward as the adults emerged from their houses to greet the riders.

"We welcome you and wish that you will pause in your journey to rest and visit with us." An elderly man beckoned them to dismount as he spoke.

Aroyo was looked over carefully by the children and women when Honmana displayed him in her arms. Mats and blankets were brought and placed on the ground for mother and child as it was feeding time. The women proceeded to obtain food and water for the visitors.

"We understand that the Spanish army passed through your area the past winter. Your people appear to be well and your homes do not bear the scars of pillaging." Quitoya's forthrightness pleased the local men.

A spokesman identified himself as head of the local clan. Our experience with the Spaniards has been peaceful. They did not attack or do damage here. On the contrary, the commander himself talked with the help of interpreters to our head men of the tribe. His name was Coronado and his objective was to impress us of his peaceful intentions and asked to allow time for his Friars to express their Christian teachings. This was done. The men still discuss much of what was said in our kiva ceremonies."

On the trail the following afternoon after an early start for the day's journeys, a dark green outline on the horizon indicated the presence of a river with its bordering foliage and trees. Excitement and some tension arose as the trio anticipated what might lay ahead. This changed as a feeling of dread came upon them and grew as they progressed, passing scenes of desolation and destruction amid the blackened ruins of pueblos.

"We have not yet reached the river that we seek but these outlying villages give evidence of disastrous confrontations between the native inhabitants and the Spanish." No one in the stunned group responded as Honmana halted her mount momentarily then moved on.

TIGUEX

They circled the environs of a large settlement containing tents for the soldados who had moved into them after a winter in the large pueblo. A few banners and regimental insignia waved in the breeze. An Indian stopped his chores, looked up and raised an arm in a friendly gesture as the Hopis passed then came to a halt. Upon questioning him, Yutanuu learned the encampment was at Arenal Pueblo. Asked about Zunis from Hawikuh, the man motioned to the north side of the area where the Indians were lodged.

Continuing, the party approached a row of single story, mud buildings where Indian women were tending outdoor ovens. The aroma of baking pita bread was a delight, beckoning the weary travelers. Dismounting, they tethered the horses to a rail fence separating the dwellings from the trail. The women and a few men, mostly Zunis, came to meet them with friendly greetings and an invitation to rest, eat and talk. Aroyo was taken inside a dwelling where Honmana was aided by several women in the bathing ritual of the small boy and a change of clothing was offered and accepted.

Accompanied by a Zuni who had been in the Cibola encampment and several guides and scouts attached to the army, the Hopi men entered an adjacent building. Pita bread was served as the group discussed news of events in the various pueblos to which was added the excursion of the Castillians into Hopi mesas and subsequently the great river and canyon.

Yutanuu had stepped outside and gone to unsaddle and care for the horses when two *soldado de caballeria* returning from a routine camp inspection stopped and dismounted. They inspected the saddles and bridles which bore insignia of their owners, Castillians in the expedition. On the spot, Yutannuu was accused of stealing the caballos and taken into custody, then forced to lead the animals to a corral about one hundred yards distant near the troop quarters. He was thrown into a small mud hut which served as a *carcel.* One of the soldiers left immediately for the commandant's office to make his report.

The other soldier stood guard outside the barred door, taunting the prisoner and calling to him in contemptuous terms and expressions. This kind of treatment infuriated Yutanuu who boiled with inner rage. He vowed to retaliate. His opportunity came when the guard was momentarily out of view. Yutanuu slipped a hand between the metal bars, deftly sliding the outer latch from its locking position.

The guard returned, stooping to retrieve something from the ground. At that moment Yutanuu pushed heavily on the door slamming it into the guard and knocking him off his feet. He leaped upon the man pounding his head into the earth until he appeared to be unconscious or dead. As the Hopi rose to his feet, the other soldier accompanied by four mounted men rounded the corner of the hut. Seeing the guard prone on the ground, the men rode straight into Yutanuu, forcing him to the ground where he was trampled by the horses hooves. Upon inspection of the bruised and crushed body, a knife appeared in the hand of the soldier who plunged it into Yutanuu as a lethal finish to the encounter.

An order was given to the horsemen who lost no time in locating Quitoya, Honmana and her child. They were made to walk to the commandant's compound and placed in a room with barred windows. Here they were told of Yutanuu's attempted escape, assault of the guard and subsequent death. The astonished captives were shocked by this news. Quitoya comforted Honmana in her grief as she rocked back and forth with Aroyo in her arms and tears streaming down her face.

While Quitoya was interrogated about the horses and how they were obtained, Honmana was taken to a large room in another section of the building. Aroyo was left in the care of an Indian woman in the anteroom.

The commandant, resplendent in the dark blue and red uniform of his rank, sat at a large table. A flag of New Spain hung in the background. A silver ornamented helmet with white feather plume lay before him. An Indian aid and interpreter, reviewing the circumstances leading to placing the prisoners in custody, turned as the door opened and Honmana entered.

"Honmana!" The exuberant aid rushed to her with both hands extended in traditional greeting. "It is such a surprise to see you!"

He addressed the commandant. "This wonderful woman and several Hopi men were guides on the expedition of Captain Cardenas to the big river and canyon, now called Rio Colorado and el Canon Grande."

Captain Zaldivar, who had been wounded at the battle of Arenal Pueblo and would soon proceed on the march east with the remaining army personnel, stood to welcome Honmana.

"This is indeed a pleasure. From first reports I would not have expected someone so striking and dressed in appropriate Indian costume. I am Captain Zaldivar."

" Your greetings are greatly appreciated but the harsh treatment and death of our companion was uncalled for. In truth, we might have expected something like that." The courageous woman paused, as the Captain was closely scrutinizing her. "I am Honmana of the Hopi Mesas."

The captain asked Honmana to be seated and dismissed the interpreter. "That was a most unfortunate circumstance with mistakes made on both sides. I am indeed sorry about the whole episode." He took note of the amulet Honmana wore, her only ornament.

"You wear an interesting amulet. Is it emblematic of the Hopi people?"

"This ancient medallion signifies the Bear Clan of the Hopis. It was given to me by my grandmother who is matriarch of the clan."

"We have much to learn about the native people in the northern provinces.

"You speak Spanish very well, Honmana. I am pleased to meet with you. I know a small number of Hopi words but I am more interested in your history and customs, much of which I learned from a close friend in this expedition, Pedro de Tovar. His foray into your region and the tales he told of your high mesas and various events are highlights of our excursion into these parts."

"Captain Tovar treated our people very well and in fact, he and some of his men helped settle a controversy which arose between clans and turned back an attempt of a band of renegades to rob and murder on Antelope Mesa. My closest friend Kyaqa was killed in the confrontation." Honmana studied the commandant for a few moments. "We have a reason for coming. Is Captain Tovar here in this camp?"

"No, he is not here. The main force continued the march eastward only a short time ago. When Coronado's headquarters were here at Tiguex Don Pedro was dispatched with a small contingent to Sonora, the northern province of New Spain."

"Will he return soon?"

"The Sonora area is a trouble spot with killings of couriers on the military road and an apparent uprising involving troops and the local natives. It is some distance from here and it may be months before he returns. Do you have a need to see him? Or a message perhaps?"

"Please excuse me." Going to the door, Honmana entered the anteroom and reappeared with Aroyo in her arms. He had been happily sitting on a floor mat playing with one of the guards, rolling dried, round gourds between them. His excited gurgles and squeals had been heard by his mother.

Expressions of amazement and understanding registered as Captain Zaldivar rose and came forward.

"So this is the reason for your long journey, to find Tovar?"

He took Aroyo into his arms, holding him for a closer inspection. The lightly tinted olive skin and other features caused the captain to exclaim. "He has the determined chin and challenging eyes of Tovar, yet the profile is a combination of his beautiful mother and handsome father. What a joy this little fellow must be"

"His name is Aroyo. He was born on the bank of a river where we had been saved from a flash flood raging down from nearby coulees. No one has been told of this. My deepest hope and desire is to have Captain Tovar hold his son and to see his face light up as you have. Is it possible for us to remain here until he returns?"

"My dear Honmana, many factors must be resolved." The captain returned the boy to his mother's arms. Going to his chair behind the table he motioned to Honmana to be seated. She propped the sleepy-eyed Aroyo so his head lay against her neck and shoulder. An aid soon came in with a padded headboard into which Honmana transferred the boy, now asleep.

Zaldivar continued."The vanguard of the army and support units are on the expedition's eastern route. Part of the region was traversed in advance for information about the terrain, Indian settlements, population, water and food supplies and all the items necessary when entering unknown territories. It is possible that the journey may be a long one, lasting over a year. The general means to explore a vast area containing what appears to be much diversification. You have hardly had time to notice that we are in the midst of making preparations to remove all remaining personnel, equipment and horses for our trek east to join the main force. The twelve pueblos here are practically abandoned as the Indians refused to move back after several encounters with our troops. A sad state of affairs, but the situation came about and now, when the Spaniards have departed, who knows what will happen? The people are widely scattered, living in other villages."

"You are saying that not much will remain for Captain Tovar and his soldados when they return?" Honmana was very dejected.

"The probability exists that Tovar will by-pass this area and head directly east to the Expedition. Our stay in Tiguex is terminated."

"It is best then that we return to our land of the high mesas. In my heart I shall forever hope that the Captain is safe from harm and that he will contact us when it is possible. Will you pass that message to Don Pedro when you see him?" Deep in Honmana's dark eyes were reflections of apprehension, but still, hope.

The captain recognized these indications which also contained a determination to surpass all obstacles. Her countenance glowed with the radiance of love and a resolve that her mission would be fulfilled.

"You may rest assured that the message will be delivered. Further, I will arrange for provisions to take care of the first week or two of your homeward journey." An orderly entered the room placing a paper in the commandant's hands. He was informed that the Hopis had stated the three horses had been loaned to them by corral attendants at Cibola and were army property. The animals had not been stolen.

"Your companion has been truthful in an interrogation just completed since it was decided that the horses were not stolen. He will be released, as will you, I might add, However, since all beasts of burden must be utilized in the army's movements, the animals have been impounded and returned to service. Undoubtedly this action will be to your benefit as the steeds would make your group targets for theft and even murder in the region through which you must pass."

"Captain Zaldivar, your kindness to us will never be forgotten and is deeply appreciated. We will be ready to leave in the morning." Honmana tugged at the leather thongs on Aroyo's headboard to make certain they were tightly fastened.

"May I look at your son once again?" The captain peered down at the sleeping child."This is an unmistakable sign that we will all be joined together in future generations, Indian and Spaniard. Surely the Holy Father accepts this union. I am sorry that Friar Padilla is not here to give the blessing." The captain crossed himself. He placed his hands on Honmana's shoulders. "We must have faith and look forward to a grand re-union. God speed on your journey." With that, he turned and left by a side door.

Honmana and Quitoya returned to the living quarters where they were greeted whole heartedly by their newly acquired friends. News of their release had already been received and the Indian women had prepared a special supper to honor their acquittal.

A newcomer had been added to the group. He was Yongo, a Hopi from Antelope Mesa released from a work force of Indians designated to clean up debris at Arenal Pueblo. He had been visiting at the pueblo when the Spaniards attacked, leaving the premises a smoldering ruins. With the departure of the army, many such crews had been disbanded, placing the restoration work in the hands of the former inhabitants.

A young man of sturdy build, Yongo was a warrior adept in the use of bow and arrow as well as outwitting an enemy. His jovial personality and optimistic outlook made it easy for him to be accepted by new friends, including Honmana and Quitoya who told him of their plans for leaving.

"One of our party, Yutanuu, met death when trampled by a group of mounted men who did not wait to hear his side of a controversy over three horses. Will you join with us on the return trip to our Hopi Mesas? Honmana and her small child will depend on us for aid and support as may be necessary on the journey."

"My stay in this region has been too long. I appreciate your confidence in me and welcome the opportunity to travel with you. What can I do to help prepare for the trip?"

"The commandant is providing supplies for us, thanks to the impression and mutual understanding between him and Honmana. Not much remains to be done. We will leave tomorrow."

Honmana spoke to the women. "Your thoughtfulness on our behalf is much appreciated. We plan to leave in the morning and so advised captain Zaldivar. He is arranging supplies for us. As you undoubtedly know, we will not have horses to ride."

"Talassi, the woman who had provided living space for the Hopis, responded. "I think we understand Honmana's situation. Since this camp is soon to be disbanded, it is probably a good time for us to think about leaving for our home pueblos. We have discussed this previously. Later today we must talk to our men." The Zuni women nodded in agreement.

At a meeting that evening the Hopi trio was advised by the Zunis that several additional days would be needed by them to obtain provisions and for packing and termination of their army attachment. Further, in order to establish a definite rendezvous, the Hopis were requested to plan to camp at a grove of cottonwood trees on a bend of the Rio Grande called Silver Bow, so named for the appearance of the river in full moonlight. It was approached coming from a *tsomo* on the west bank and was a traditional resting place for Indian travellers.

Nahdaq, a strong looking, handsome man of mixed Indian blood and much taller than the other men, cautioned the Hopis. "The trail north following the river has been unfortunate for many Indians, mostly small groups who are more vulnerable. They have been attacked by renegades and another motley lot who apparently live off such encounters, killing the travelers and taking all of their supplies and belongings. Be alert to the smoke of campfires, hearing loud voices or being caught in open country. We wish to assist you in your response to any such attacks by presenting these three new sets of *awtas* and *hoohus*. They are the finest we have."

The Hopis expressed their appreciation for the information and new weapons. "We will surely be on the lookout for anything unusual and will slow our progress so that you will overtake us in a short time." Honmana looked with gratitude over the group that would soon follow.

* * * * * * * *

Siki took a notebook from the stack on the table. "This contains historical information important to an understanding of the attitude of the Indians concerning the conquistadors. I will read it for you. Further, a report by Castaneda in April, 1541 indicates an assignment of Pedro de Tovar to correct trouble by the natives and unrest among the soldiers in Sonora Province."

Indians from the pueblo of Arenal, two leagues distant from the army encampment, had reported to Captain Cardenas that an unruly Spaniard had molested an Indian woman. After investigation of the matter the culprit could not be identified by the husband. This was the beginning of the distrust with which the Indians from then forward regarded the pledge of peaceful coexistence which had been given them. Unrest in Tiguex was heightened by harsh methods of collectors and soldiers in obtaining clothing and food for the army. At Alcanfor, a Mexican who had been guarding the horses ran into camp bleeding and wounded. He said the natives of Tiguex, after killing one of his companions, were driving the horses of the white men to their pueblos. Captain Cardenas with seven or eight mounted men went to the scene of the commotion and found the pueblo of Alameda abandoned. A short distance beyond were the carcasses of several horses killed by Indian arrows. Proceeding across the Rio Grande where the Indians had forded the stream with all the horses they could round up in the fields, he discovered twenty-five or more dead mounts and mules near the pueblos on both banks of the river. After a war council with his Captain and Fray Padilla in which agreement was unanimous, Coronado ordered war to quell the rebellion. Fortified and enclosed by palisades, Arenal Pueblo withstood several attacks with great loss of life on both sides until it finally burned out by setting fire to the timbers. Moho Pueblo met the same fate after a siege of about eighty days ending in March, 1541. Other settlements were leveled and burned, the natives fleeing to other locations. Zia Pueblo, located west of the Rio Grande, provided Coronado with much needed provisions through the winter. Then the march eastward to Quivira was mobilized.

Siki interposed. "Although these documents are credited to Castaneda, these events were undoubtedly reported by Captain Cardenas since he was in charge and involved in person while the chronicler was absent at the time. The following probably had its source in the general's staff and written by Castaneda in the period April 20-23,1541."

Distressed by reports from Sonora valley that Melchior Diaz, the local commander, had met death accidentally and soldiers were causing trouble in the southwestern Mexico province, Coronado sent his Chief Ensign of the expedition, Pedro de Tovar, to restore order. Further, couriers traveling the trail to New Spain had been attacked by hostile natives. With order restored and messengers able to travel the route, Tovar was to return the soldiers stationed at San Geronimo, Sonora and as soon as possible follow the main body east to Quivira. The general's dispatch stated that

Tovar would find letters under crosses set up on the way which would contain instructions for overtaking the army.

HOMEWARD BOUND

The quietly meandering Rio Grande seemed to keep pace with the Hopis, providing a feeling of support as they traveled leisurely on a course as straight as possible. The wide swings of the river brought them often to its banks. By late afternoon, after having covered about five leagues, the small but assiduous group came upon a large pile of white and gray, weathered logs which at some time in the past had crashed over the river's banks, pushed by the force of tremendous flood waters. It was a sight to behold causing Yongo to speculate on the distant mountains from where the wooden mass must have come.

"Surely a giant wave of water brought these logs to their final resting place. Look at that enclosure! Except for a roof overhead, it is similar to the log structures built by the Spaniards."

"Aroyo has been fussing and squirming. Let us stay here for the night. We have come far, our first day out." Honmana looked at her companions for confirmation.

Quitoya swung his pack off his back, making a visual survey of the area and surrounding country. "It is a good place and no signs of unwanted company are evident." They strode into a clearing within the piled timber.

Honmana unrolled a grass mat, placing her son on it and unfastening the thongs binding him to the headboard. She then went about the task of gathering round and flat stones with which to circle a fire. The hot rocks would provide heat for water contained in clay vessels she carried.

"Will it be safe to build a fire? The trail has been dusty today. Hot water is needed by Aroyo and plenty will be available for allof us." Honmana peered quizzically at Quitoya and Yongo.

"This place is like a small fort. If anyone wants to attack they must come in through the only opening- and we will be ready. We will place thin dry sticks at various locations to provide a warning if any one approaches. Come Yongo, let us prepare our warning system. Honmana, that hot water will be welcome." Once outside, the two men decided that a continuous watch through the night was essential, with one acting as sentry while the other slept. The positions would be reversed whenever the sentry needed sleep.

In early morning, just as the sun's rays reached the river bank, the cracking of a twig caused Quitoya to freeze where he stood at the entrance. He was instantly joined by Yongo then Honmana, both with bow and arrow ready. Another series of snaps and a small deer bounded across their line of vision. The moment of apprehension, then surprise, rapidly turned into uncontrollable laughter as all three joined in the merriment.

"Well, at least our warning system worked!"Quitoya looked at Aroyo." Even the little boy is gurgling with joy!"

The gurgling soon changed to coughing as Honmana went to his aid." His forehead is very warm. He seems to have fever." She applied a dampened cloth to cool and sooth the boy but the coughing and now crying continued." We must stay here until Aroyo is able to travel." He calmed into fitful sleep in his mother's arms.

A day of nursing, application of native condiments and long used natural ingredients in hot soup, brought Aroyo back to his usual happy ways and responses. They stayed another night in their compound and set out the next morning eager to be on the trail. Coming to the crest of a small hill strewn with boulders and brush Yongo pointed excitedly. The *mooha* grove is down there, the place we are to wait for our Zuni friends!"

The river flowed for many leagues north and south in a spectacular manner, winding between the low bluffs of earlier canyon walls. Honmana removed the headboard placing it on a grassy patch at the base of a large boulder. Aroyo was sound asleep. As she attempted to sit beside her son the swish of an arrow and the sound of its impact on the rock above caused the three to drop to the ground as other arrows struck the rocks.

Crawling to other positions behind boulders and with bows in hand, they sent a volley of arrows at moving figures advancing up the hill, darting between bushes and boulders. Honmana's arrows pierced the bodies of four attackers who screamed when hit then rolled on the ground until laying motionless. Knives flashed as hand-to-hand combat ensued with Yongo and Quitoya facing multiple antagonists.

Shielded by a ravine on the south side of the hill, a lone man crawled behind the large rock protecting Aroyo. He reached around the base, stealthily pulled the boy and the headboard out of sight of the combatants and scurried back into the ravine and downward to join a group of Indians in a sheltered cove a short distance downstream.

Honmana's deadly accuracy with the bow sent arrows into more of the opposition as attempts were made to rush her vantage point. She saw Yongo drop to the ground under the weight of an adversary who now stood above him with knife poised for the fatal thrust. Honmana's arrow went through his neck causing him to reel backwards and tumble down the slope. Quitoya, the larger of the two Hopis, stood struggling with two opponents.

One dropped of a knife thrust and the other stood at bay wielding a knife but holding back until three or four of his fellow assailants could join him in the contest.

To the dismay of Honmana, the wild yells of ten or more Indians filled the air as they came racing over the crest of the tsomo, brandishing spears and clubs. As they charged down the slope Honmana's fears changed to exultation when they attacked the renegades head-on. She recognized several of the men as Zunis from the army encampment. The bandits picked up anything worthwhile as they endeavored to escape the onslaught but several were killed in the pursuit.

"My son is gone! They have taken Aroyo!" Honmana screamed the news as she searched around the boulder. "Quitoya! Yongo! I believe he was taken through that gully!" She pointed down the hill to the right.

Chapter Twelve

THE ORDEAL

The lifeless bodies of a dozen or more men were strewn about the hillside. Pinpoint marksmanship of the three Hopis had taken a deadly toll of the attackers. At close quarters, the two men had fought with a fury Honmana had never before witnessed. When the arrival of the Zuni warriors momentarily distracted the Indian hovering over the downed Yongo, he thrust his legs upward pushing the man off balance. Simultaneously, he grabbed at the knife, turning it with a lunge which sent the weapon deep into the attacker's ribs. The man was dead when he hit the earth.

Quitoya quickly gathered five men and left on the run down the sloping hill, noting the imprint of footsteps on the bank of the ravine. The fresh trail, now showing deep impressions of a running man, turned south at the end of the gulch and pointed toward the river. Further downstream, a campsite clearly provided signs of a band of approximately forty to fifty people and their hasty abandonment and departure across the river.

"These individuals undoubtedly have taken the boy and plan to reunite with the others, those assailants who fled after our short, but furious battle." Quitoya squatted on the ground, beckoning his companions to do the same." We will rest, then join the others in our group."

One of the Zuni warriors spoke." We who arrived later have not been tested to our limit. May I suggest that four of us follow the trail of the culprits who removed the boy from his mother. See, here is a leather thong similar to those on the headboard of the

young boy we saw at Tiguex. I found it as we entered this place."
The piece of leather was held in the air for all to see.

Quitoya sprang to his feet." That is definite proof that they have
the boy. Go as you have suggested, Nahdaq, when you have
located the bandits one of you can return to notify us. We can then
form a larger war party. In the meantime, I will join with the other
warriors and take the women and children north along the river
trail. The Great Spirit be with you." He looked with compassion
over the four men as they picked up their bows, quivers and war
clubs. They were eager, competent men, able to accomplish their
objective.

Two days of dreary walking with no word of the whereabouts
of her little son, had placed Honmana at the edge of her patience.
"Another group must be dispatched to hunt down the kidnappers.
I want to be part of the search effort." She selected the finest arrows
from a large skin bag at her feet. Standing, she took up her favorite
bow and turned to face Quitoya." We must prepare to leave at
daybreak."

Meanwhile, Nahdaq's search party, after crossing the Rio
Grande, followed the trail in an easterly direction. At dusk they
found a junction indicating part of the band had turned north and
the remainder south.

"It appears that a large group went south from this point.
Possibly they have the boy. Do you have thoughts about which
direction we should pursue?" Nahdaq peered questioningly at his
companions.

"The greater number of small footprints in the dust indicate
more women and children are included in that part of the band
headed south. It is possible the boy is in their hands."

The man responding was noted for his tracking ability and detection of pertinent signs.

"All right, we will rest here and leave in that direction tonight when the moon appears."

Later, after following the well-defined trail several hours, their efforts bore fruit when they saw campfires ahead against a dark back drop of trees. As the first light of dawn came, figures could be seen moving about the fires. What appeared to be a hunting party departed at a trot following the tree line to the south.

Nahdaq and his comrades lay still behind bushes growing in a grassy meadow until the hunters were out of sight.

"We will enter the camp near the first fire at this end. It appears that only women are left, cooking meat in their pots." The smell of cooked food wafted over the meadow." They might not know who we are. Do you suppose that we will have a hot breakfast?"

Little attention was paid the men as they leisurely strode into the camp. Each man headed for a different group near the fires, observing infants and small children, but alert to a chance recognition. Nahdaq approached a woman and inquired if a young boy had recently been brought to the band, adding that he had lighter skin than some of the others.

"I heard of such a boy. He is not with us. Our once large group separated so the men could hunt in different areas. Our supply of meat is getting low."

Nahdaq noticed that the woman held her head down and did not meet his gaze." What is the name of the leader of the other group? I wish to talk to him."

The woman hesitated, then spoke in a low voice." I know that you are not of this band. They killed my husband as well as others and made the women come along as captives and to raise children for the tribe. The warrior who made himself chief is Iquana. He has the boy."

"I am very grateful for this information and sorry to learn of your plight. Do you wish to go with us when we leave? Three other men are here with me."

"It would be impossible now since my young daughter is also here and it would be a very great risk. Your concern is appreciated. I will tell you in confidence that plans are underway for our group to escape by continuing south to the land of our pueblos and friends. We will not rejoin the band that went north following the river under Iquana's forced authority." The young mother's upturned face registered a smile as she slipped two pouches of hot meat and vegetables under Nahdaq's loosely fitting blouse.

The Hopi squatted down, fastening the warm bundles to thin deerskin thongs hanging from his inside vest-garment. He returned the smile, clutching the young woman's hand for a moment." Thank you."

The woman nervously squeezed his hand." It is time for you and your companions to leave. The hunters may be returning at anytime."

Nodding his response, Nahdaq walked through the camp giving signs to the others to join him at the outskirts. They regained the trail, running half a league at an easy pace until stopping at a waterhole to rest and consume the food. After discussing the Indian woman's information, they departed following the course of the river, upstream.

During the night one of the hunters from Honmana's group returned to the camp requesting additional men to carry several deer which had been victims of a successful hunt. The hunting party returned at mid morning with the deer carcasses tied to long poles carried on the shoulders of a man at each end. Although the people were overjoyed to receive the welcome meat, Honmana was impatient and concerned over the delay of their departure in search of her son. She looked quizzically at Quitoya.

"We should leave now to find the bandits. The women are busy skinning the animals and preparing the meat. Plenty of men are available for the search, which may be more difficult as time passes and the band has separated."

"Please turn and look down the trail. We are going to have visitors." Quitoya picked up his bow and called softly to others to be ready with their weapons.

"That man leading is different from the others. See the garment and headband he wears." Honmana placed an arrow in her bow.

Armed with lances and bows, the group of six stopped about twenty paces from the waiting Hopis and Zunis. Four remained behind while one accompanied the apparent leader, a man of powerful build and medium height. His black hair reached to his shoulders, the bright red head band providing vivid accent to his brown face. He carried no visible weapon.

"I am Iquana. The boy is in my possession." He gestured toward Honmana." You are the mother of the boy. You come with me as wife. We raise the boy in my tribe." He stood with legs apart in a solid and formidable stance. His expression beckoned nothing but compliance with the request.

"What is your tribe?" Honmana was defiant.

"I am Apache chief. Many of my people and those of other tribes have joined me. Come with me and I will show you the boy."

"Why should we trust you? You are undoubtedly responsible for attacking us on our peaceful journey, as well as other bands on this trail. You and your bandits kill and pillage as a way of life. I will have nothing to do with you, but you will take us to my son and hand him over."

Iquana's scowl deepened." The words I speak are a command. Come with me now, alone, or you will never again see the boy."

Unobserved by those on the west bank of the Rio Grande, Nahdaq and his men had crossed the river downstream. Proceeding along its bank, they heard the chatter of persons engaged in a betting game or similar activity. Stealthily approaching, they observed several Indians squatting under a large cottonwood tree. One, standing aside of the others, held a bundle up to the chest, occasionally patting it and swaying from side to side.

Bending close to the ground with the others, Nahdaq whispered." It is a woman holding a small child. It must be Aroyo!"

The men crawled forward, keeping hidden until they were a few yards from the unsuspecting foe. As one they leaped upon the men with knives drawn. Matched four on four, the element of surprise enabled them to gain advantage and quickly dispatch their adversaries. However, a fifth warrior came into the fray plunging his knife into the back of one of Nahdaq's men in a fatal thrust. The assailant was swarmed over and dispatched by the others.

Nahdaq went to the Indian woman and removed a covering from the head and face of the child she held. "It is Aroyo, Honmana's boy!" The child peered into the warriors face and eyes momentarily then broke into a smile, raising his arms to be taken up. He was nestled in soft pieces of cloth with thongs holding him to the headboard.

The woman relinquished her grasp and passed Aroyo to Nahdaq.

"He is a good boy and gives much pleasure when allowed to play and crawl on a blanket." She produced a bracelet of bear teeth and small shells strung together on lengths of deer skin." This is his favorite plaything. He likes to hear the pieces rattle and feel each object with his little hands." The boy reached for the bracelet which the woman relinquished.

"How do you know the boy and his name?" The woman, who made no attempt to flee, gave Nahdaq the feeling of compassion and sincerity.

" I know that he was recently brought to our camp after a fight on a hill near the river. Who he is, I do not know. You see, I am also a captive of this tribe. My name is Pluma."

"It was our small band that was attacked on a hillside farther south where we rested before locating our camp site for the night. The boy is Aroyo, son of Honmana, a Hopi woman." Nahdaq paused. "Where are the others in your band? We must locate our people and warn them of their presence."

"The women and children are with the warriors north of here across the river. Your people are a short distance along the trail where Iquana, our leader, went to speak to them. I believe he wishes to bring the mother into the tribe and under his control."

"How many warriors are with this man who calls himself chief?"

"Five men accompanied Iquana. In his way, he feels invincible and can gain anything he demands."

"Then these men were here,ready and waiting, to go to his aid?" Nahdaq's voice was tense.

"Yes,one man was nearer the trail so that he could receive a signal. He ran back when he heard the commotion and has been slain by your warriors."

"We must prevent any such unwanted arrangement and re-unite the boy with his mother. Come with us while we observe what is happening."

Nahdaq spoke to his men." How is our companion who was wounded?"

"We have turned his face to the east, Nahdaq. He received a fatal wound."

"I am sorry about that, he was a fine warrior and friend. We will return for his body." The men came forward to see the boy. They expressed their satisfaction upon seeing he was healthy and active.

Nahdaq placed Aroyo in the arms of the native woman and turned to his companions." This woman is Pluma. She is not our enemy. Her chief is on the trail a short distance from here for a meeting with our people. He has five warriors with him. We will approach them peacefully, but be wary and ready to engage them if necessary."

Keeping out of sight among the trees between the trail and the river, the group pressed forward until they were within hearing of the chief, loudly proclaiming his demands. Bows were hastily strung with sharp pointed arrow heads which would penetrate the flesh of any man or beast. Continuing their approach, they observed the four warriors behind Iquana who stood with one man beside him.

The chief, Iquana, disturbed at the utterance of words which themselves were a command from a woman, seized his aid and forcing him in front as a shield, started toward Honmana. In the same movement, he reached under the aid's garment and grasped a hidden knife which he brandished above his head as a sign to his warriors. With a blood curdling cry he pushed forward.

A volley of arrows from Nahdaq and his men hurtled into the warriors disabling two men. From the cover of the trees the men ran forward. Before a barrage could be returned, they were engaged in hand to hand fighting.

An arrow from Quitoya's bow pierced the body of the unfortunate aid who fell to the ground at Iquana's feet. The chief lunged within a few feet of Honmana when Quitoya landed on him, the force of the downhill charge sending both rolling in the dust. The two men stood up with knives ready, circling like wolves at bay watching for an opening. It came with a fury that Honmana and her people had never before witnessed. A gash in Quitoya's upper arm spirted blood while a long red cut appeared on the chief's upper body as they stabbed and slashed with their weapons. Other wounds appeared but the men showed no signs of fatigue.

The chief reached into the soft dirt and threw a handful into Quitoya's face. The dust and particles seared his eyes. He saw the out line of his adversary coming at him. In a move dictated by an inner instinct for self preservation, he made a feint to one-side then bending to a half-crouch, lunged at the figure which had momentarily turned to the left. His knife found a soft spot in the belly which allowed it to be buried to the handle. Quitoya released his grasp on the knife. Iquana made one final effort to swing around and thrust his blade but the energy evaporated and his body fell into the dirt. The bodies of his warriors lay prone on the ground a short distance away. The encounter was over.

An exhausted Quitoya staggered out of the dust swirl and was met immediately by Honmana and other women bearing water jugs and lengths of cloth. He was forced to lie on the ground and was stripped of his clothing where blood had oozed through, revealing wounds which were thoroughly cleaned and bound. Honmana washed his face and applied a cloth pad soaked in cool water to his brow and back of his neck. His half-closed eyelids opened wide as he looked deeply into her eyes and expressed his gratitude.

Excited jabbering filled the air. Honmana stood up to see an Indian woman with Nahdaq and his three companions approaching in the forefront of the men and women of the band. In the woman's arms was a small form cradled in a headboard.

Honmana ran with arms outstretched." Aroyo my son, you have brought my son!" She looked at Nahdaq and the woman who placed the boy in his mother's arms. The excitement of the boy's return brought joy to all as they pressed to see his happy face and arms flailing in the air. An atmosphere of peace and contentment pervaded the people as they realized that their adversaries had been soundly defeated.

HAPPIER DAYS

A month at their camp on the Rio Grande enabled the wounded men to recuperate and heal. Hunters brought in many animals including deer, bear and rabbits to provide the skins and meat necessary for the excursion ahead. Yongo kept busy spearing and netting fish which provided several fine feasts for the entourage of Hopis, Zunis and a blending of others having Pueblo and Southern

Indian backgrounds. The two cultures had been slowly integrating over the years. The woman, Pluma, as an example had been taken as a servant for one of the Conquistadors when the Expedition passed through New Spain's northern province of Sonora. Many such men and women worked as cooks, seamstresses and attendants for the animals which were a large part of Coronado's huge force.

After a week of meeting people and getting acquainted with new friends, Pluma went to the river one morning to observe Yongo's fishing prowess. Kneeling at the river's bank, she searched the inner recesses of a large size deerskin pouch she carried, finally producing two metal objects and a roll of *cuerda* which she showed to Yongo.

"These are used by the Spaniards to catch fish. The metal objects with sharp points are hooks. The string forms a line to be tied to a hook through this small opening."

"What you have will be ignored by the fish. They must be pierced by a lance or caught in a net." Yongo stepped into the water, a backwater area bordering the meandering stream.

"No, no, you must try this. First you cut off a piece of flesh from a fish you have speared and place the hook through it. Next, toss it out in the water, holding on to the line. The fish will bite on the *carnada*, swallowing the hook and all. You will see!"

Yongo obliged since he liked this woman, Pluma. Almost immediately he felt a tug in the line.

"Give the string a quick jerk, then pull in and see what you have!"

Pluma stared at Yongo who stood several yards out in the water. The fish broke the surface as the hook pierced the flesh along the jawbone.

"Hold the line *tirante* and come to the shore. I will help you land your fish." Pluma ran to an extended point of the river bank.

Yongo slipped and stumbled into the water as he headed towards the shore line but held firmly to the line. He came up soaked and shouting at Pluma who had ventured out into the water.

"Here, take the line. I will throw a net over the fish when it is near enough to see." He threw the net, snaring his catch. With the fish squirming and thrashing within the folds of the net, he carried it to shore.

In his excitement Yongo placed the large specimen on the grassy bank, still in the net.

"Your method is a fine one. I think we will catch plenty of fish." He took Pluma by both hands and together they danced around the prize to the delight of many children who had come to participate in the obvious merriment and soon were dancing themselves.

"I am happy for you Yongo but you will find netting and wading into deep water unnecessary most of the time, if you use this *pertiga*." Pluma produced a long, slim sapling from a willow. She had removed all branches. Tying one end of the line to the pole, she handed it to the eager fisherman.

"With the baited hook free at the end, form loops in the line. Hold the willow in your right hand and cast the line over the water with a sudden motion of your other hand, coupled with a sweep of the pole. At the right moment, release the coiled string and the bait will carry it out into the water." Yongo looked puzzled as he pondered the instructions. Pluma demonstrated the casting action.

A few throws and practice found Yongo ready to outsmart the fish. The line swirled through the air and settled on the water with the hook and bait disappearing beneath the surface.

"Something is biting the bait. See the line tighten and go deeper!" Yongo pulled in many fish with his new method. He became an overnight hero to the band for his expertise as a fisherman. Pluma received many compliments when Yongo explained how she had taught him to fish with line and pole.

The journey continued. At the confluence of Rio Chama and Rio Grande the party split into two groups with some heading northeast to the Taos region. Now numbering eighteen, Honmana's group followed the Chama for many days. The Zuni, Nahdaq, identified a pointed spiral of red rock which he said marked a trail westward toward the mountains. The Hopis admired the broad savannah whose grassy plain made travel easier and provided a great variety of birds, their feathers to be woven into skins and fiber for sleeping mats and robes.

In the distance smoke signals rose from pueblos located along the Rio Chama indicating religious ceremonies were underway or some other communication usually understood by prearranged instructions. Hunters on the west side of the plain returned to report the finding of a settlement now in ruins, constructed centuries prior by the Anasazi, ancestors of the Pueblo people. The entire band moved on to the area, viewing crumbled structures of several stories and large kiva circles where wooden roofs had long ago deteriorated and plunged below. Mud and sandstone bricks and stones were strewn about the plaza areas which were surrounded by sides of buildings and walls of about five feet in height still standing. Several outdoor baking ovens stood beckoning, having weathered the years in still usable condition. Old grinding *metates* showing years of use, lay near the ovens.

Food was plentiful offering an expanded diet of maize and beans growing in ancient agricultural plots. Wild turkeys nesting in small stands of trees were available along with deer and rabbits.

"We shall have plenty of pika, beans and berries. Why not establish our camp here and prepare quantities of food for the future?" The men agreed with Honmana and began the task of removing stones and debris from the sheltered plaza. While several women and children went to the fields to pick corn and beans, others prepared to grind the maize into corn flour and set out lines to dry various kinds of meat which would be hung in strips.

Pluma and Yongo searched for wild rice, chili peppers and other herbs." I will make soft flour tortillas stuffed with many *ingrediente* which are savored by my people and a favorite food in New Spain."

"What is a tortilla, my *panadero* friend?" Yongo's Spanish vocabulary, slowly expanding,was being tested on Pluma! Her native language was liberally sprinkled with useful Spanish words learned during her association with the soldados.

"It is somewhat similar to pika except it is rolled flat and formed into round sections eaten held in the hand, after the filling is inserted. They can be baked crisp if desired." Seeing the smile on Yongo's face, she poked him in the ribs." You are making fun of me. I will not prepare any tortillas for you. The others will eat them and tell you how good they are."

Yongo took the exasperated woman in an embrace." I am only fooling. Really, I am glad to know what a tortilla is. Also, what you are doing will be appreciated by everyone in our little band, including me." Pluma responded by placing her hands on his face and rubbing noses.

* * * * * * * *

Exploring the ancient pueblo settlement became a daily event as the accomplishments of their industrious inhabitants became more apparent. Partial walls, foundations and piles of stones and adobe bricks indicated imposing structures once stood at the site housing hundreds of people. In the outlying area weathered canal systems had brought water from the foot hills where excavations had been made for basins designed to capture and hold run-off from rainstorms and the melting snows of winter. The canals led to fields under cultivation in those early years. A fresh water spring in a nearby plaza furnished bubbling cool water for daily consumption.

Sitting on a mat watching Aroyo play with another youngster, Honmana spoke to Quitoya. "A question keeps running through my mind. Will that little boy ever see his father? With such a large company of soldiers and multitude of people in the assemblage, Captain Tovar may never learn that we were at Cibola and Tiguex inquiring about him."

"It is most likely that your message will be delivered. Captain Zaldivar will surely exert every effort to contact Tovar. I believe the movements of the army and casualties in battle would assert the greatest hindrance to a meeting." Quitoya sat with his eyes toward the sky, obviously in serious contemplation. "Since all wounds are healed and the supplies of food are adequate, it might be best if we break camp and continue our journey to Oraibi. A message from Tovar might have already arrived."

"Your words and strong helping hand are a great aid to me. I am thankful that you are here to protect my son and me. I agree that we should move on." Honmana laid a hand on his arm as an expression of friendship.

Four days later found them at a mountain trail which passed through and over the great Continental Divide, discovered and correctly named by Coronado and certain Conquistadors knowledgeable in such matters. The Zunis enroute with Honmana also realized that the rivers on the east slope drained into the Rio Grande and on to "a great bay where the land meets the sea." Water on the west side of the mountains flowed in a northwesterly course meeting a large river which, many leagues distant, terminated in another sea of great expanse.

At a campsite two weeks later, Nahdaq spoke before the group." We have come a long way together but now is time to part. From this point our trail leads south to Hawikuh in Zuni land. The route of the Hopis lays ahead to the west. You will have no trouble in following it and as far as we know, no soldados or bandits have come this way since arrival of the Spaniards. Game is plentiful here, let us have a feast before nightfall!" All were in agreement. One of the Zunis produced a shallow drum fashioned from the lower half of a basket found in the ruins, to which he had secured a tightly spread skin. The pulsating beat added to the celebration as all joined in the dancing in the light of a huge fire.

Farewells were difficult the next day. The deadly encounters, travail and the good times had combined to form strong bonds within the small band. The final parting and diversion of trails south and west soon found them out of sight. Large boulders and ancient lava flows confronted Honmana, her companions Quitoya and Yongo, and Pluma who walked beside him. Pluma was always cheerful and helpful in carrying the young boy, Aroyo, to relieve his mother on the daily trek. They camped at a great pueblo, now deserted, in the ancient culture known as Chaco. The Hopis had heard about it in tribal lore but no one of the group had visited the marvel of construction and beauty nestled in a huge open cavern inside a massive cliff formation.

Three days travel placed the group in Hopi *tutskwa* and eager to see their mesa-top villages. Kawaiokuh, Antelope Mesa's largest village, provided accommodations and a resounding welcome by residents who gave freely of food and garments, now needed by the travelers. Since it was Yongo's birthplace, they stayed an extra day during which old friends found a suitable residence and convinced Yongo he should settle down after his experiences and travels. Moreover, it was obvious to all that he and Pluma were deeply interested in each other!

The next stop was Oraibi and home! Honmana's grandmother met the travelers with open arms and a welcome of love and affection. Later, while she was occupied feeding and playing with Aroyo, her great grandson, Honmana went outside to speak to Quitoya. Her expression was downcast.

"No message from Cibola. I do not know if Captain Tovar ever arrived there or if something happened to him. My thoughts are so mixed it is impossible for me to think out what to do next."

"Perhaps more time is necessary. The exact course for an army cannot be predetermined definitely. The location or present duty of the captain may be difficult to learn. Certainly, someone at Hawikuh will advise our people when they pass through there and load salt from the mines. We have a fine rapport with the Zunis."

"What you say is true. I will wait and tell Aroyo about his father in the hope that someday they will meet as father and son."

Quitoya longed to take Honmana in his arms but he knew the time was not right." I can not help but think of Yongo and Pluma settling in Kawaiokuh. They are so happy. It will not be long until those two will have a wedding ceremony!"

* * * * * * * *

"What happened to Captain Tovar? It seems that he could have attempted to send a message to Honmana somewhere along the way in his army travel." Sam Michaelson was bothered by this apparent lack of fulfilling his commitment to the Hopi woman.

Siki responded, based on her knowledge of accounts of the Expedition and clan history.

Having restored order in Sonora, Captain Tovar headed a mixed contingent from San Geronimo utilizing a trail traveled originally by the army in reaching Hawikuh. At this Zuni pueblo Don Pedro's soldados rested several days, gathering supplies and attending the horses after an exhausting journey. Tovar prepared a message for Honmana placing it a courier jarron and leaving it in the care of an army scout who had been in army service. The vessel became lost in a collection of army cast offs, broken stirrups, armor and a few Spanish coins. Not until several years later was the inscription, names and address interpreted by an Indian resident who knew enough Spanish to understand the lettering. Much later, when Hopis visited the Zuni settlement, the jarron was given to them for delivery to Honmana.

Following orders, Captain Tovar went on to join the main army, oblivious to the knowledge that Honmana and her companions had inquired for him on their visit to the area. Possibly Captain Zaldivar's wounds, received at the battle of Arenal Pueblo, were disabling as he made no contact with Tovar concerning the Hopis. By this time the expedition had returned from its eastern trek. Another winter was spent at Tiguex. Since no gold or other precious metals had been discovered, plans for further excursions to the East were abandoned. This decision was reached in part due to Coronado being thrown from his horse and trampled under the hooves of another. After a long recuperation period his mind did not seem to gain its former alertness and clear thinking. On the trip south to New Spain he became unable to mount a horse and was carried in a leather litter rigged between a pair of mules.

At Mexico City Coronado gained a measure of health and was appointed by his longtime friend Viceroy Mendoza to the government council and other duties. He served well in these capacities until his resignation due to ill health in June, 1554. Francisco Vazquez de Coronado passed on September 22, 1554.

* * * * * * * *

"All was not well among the troops or the friars where dissension had risen following the general's decision to depart for the Mexican capital. These events can best be understood through the writings of Castaneda who apparently followed the situation closely. Mark, you have been very attentive during these sessions. Will you please read these transcripts?" Siki once again produced the historical documents.

"I would like to do that. This is an interesting part." Mark took the journal and read with the energy and finesse of an accomplished youth!

As the physician and surgeon who attended him was a gossip, he told the General about dissent among the soldiers. He then planned secretly, seeking out caballeros who thought the same way, of methods to bring about a return to New Spain. They had meetings, had petitions signed by all soldados and presented them to General Coronado. The General announced he would not allow the petitions to be considered unless the captains and caballeros approved them by signing a statement. They expressed their opinion that they ought to return to New Spain, since they had not found any wealth or any settled area where distribution could be provided for the whole army. As soon as the General had the signatures the return to New Spain was announced. The return march began in April, 1542.

At Cibola the General ordered the release of all Indians who had been acquired as servants for army personnel. This was in keeping with Viceroy Mendoza's instructions concerning treatment of the natives. Among the women servants some were living with soldiers. In spite of the order, one soldier of exceptional valor, Juan de Troyano, took his companion to Mexico as partners in matrimony. In this writer's view it would have been better if all had been taken to civilization where they could be taught among Christians.

Fray Juan Padilla informed the General that several friars wished to remain in Tierra Nueva and work as missionaries to convert the Indians. This was accompanied by a request for soldiers to stay with them. Although the request to retain soldiers was rejected, the general approved Padilla's plan for the friars and furnished them with equipment and escorts to their respective locations.

Fray Luis de Escalona choose Circuique on the Pecos River in the Pueblo country saying that with the chisel and adze which he still possessed, he would erect crosses in those towns and baptize the children he might find on the verge of death, thus sending them to heaven. Since he was old, he would employ the short time that might remain to him in saving the souls of these people. Fray Juan de la Cruz remained alone at the Tiguex Pueblo. He was very much respected by everybody including Coronado who ordered the soldiers to bare their heads whenever they might hear the name of Fray de la Cruz.

Mark stated." This page of the journal is signed by both Pedro de Castaneda and The Franciscans.

"You did really well on that reading, Mark. We appreciate your taking part." Sam sat at the table turning the jarron between his hands.

"It strikes me that something more may be discovered from this urn than the names, craft sign and date that we recognize."

"How about the date June, 1540?" Mark looked up, his face solemn." That was the time the army was on the move and a courier might have been easily attacked and subdued by hostile Indians. If that happened, the urn could have been missing for a long time, then found and delivered later."

"That is a good thought, son. In fact, it may tie into the account of Sergeant Juan Herrera who was dispatched at San Geronimo, Sonora province to accompany two couriers carrying messages from Viceroy Mendoza to the general of the army. The men were waylayed not far from the army post. Sam reached for a notebook." Here is the record. The sergeant's report read as follows."

We were attacked by several natives about two leagues on the trail to Tierra Nueva. They surprised us by leaping down from an outcropping of boulders standing on both sides through which the trail passed. We gave a good account of ourselves but were thoroughly pummeled and finally left for dead and kicked into the dirt alongside the trail. When nightfall came the cool air revived me. I found one messenger dead and the other barely breathing, both were Indians from southern Mexico. Our weapons and dispatch bags were gone. In an effort to save who I thought was a dying man, I struggled to carry him to the fort where we arrived at daybreak. The man was attended but died while receiving medical aid. Because of my ordeal, the maestro de campo transferred me to army headquarters at Mexico City where I was confined in a hospital. Postscript: This report was prepared at the request of hospital authorities. I wish to add that my nurse Isabel de Pucha provided wonderful care which enabled me to recover and take an assignment in army headquarters. Isabel and I Joined in marriage and now reside on the post.

"We are on to something here, " Cindy exclaimed excitedly! "It really pays off to stay up half the night reading these notebooks and references as we have been doing. My transcript contains a memorandum of correspondence received by Isabel, the sergeant's wife, from Elizabeth Burrington at Madrid, Spain. It describes social events at the King's court and conveys the message that she plans to leave for the New World when transportation can be arranged!"

"Here is another piece of information." Cindy turned and read from notes." Our mutual friend, Christina Blake, who entered the nurse's training program at Madrid Hospital de Primera Saugre, the same facility that you attended to learn about procedures in a military field hospital, has graduated and is now stationed at Seville with the expectation of going to the New World when her commission is arranged. You may recall that her brother Tom, a lieutenant, went to Mexico a few years ago. Have you had an occasion to see him?"

Siki smiled happily at those across the table who were so engrossed in their search. "Those notes were obtained from records in the National Archives at Mexico City. Copies were made available to me at a meeting attended by a large group of teachers, professors and historians all interested in various stages of New Spain's early history. Of course, I was compelled to capitalize on spare time in the investigation of sixteenth century material. Senora Isabel Herrera was a prolific letter writer as you shall see further on."

"Please forgive us, Siki, we do not wish to derail the continuity of your fascinating narrative. Why do people pursue research with such a relentless fervor?" Sam, with journal on his lap, peered quizzically at Siki.

Siki responded." It is much like climbing a mountain. The urge to reach the top creates an inner tension in the mind and body which will not be relieved until the objective is attained. The unfolding pages of a notebook or journal also contain an aura of mystery which constantly beckons."

PART TWO

Chapter Thirteen

PATH TO MANHOOD

During what had been a long narrative by Siki, Mark had gone to join a group of young people in the visitor center. His father and mother noted that the elderly lady seemed to drift off into space, deep in though as she sat quietly. Cindy broke the silence.

"From what I have read, the Hopis and some other Pueblo tribes are descendants of the Anazazi who were ancient cliff dwellers. When did your people first come to settle in this mesa region?"

Siki roused herself and smiled, apparently amused at the question.

"I have pondered over that question myself. In my younger days I studied archaeology and the origins of this land in classes at Northern Arizona University. Many disturbances occurred that shaped the land, affecting the climate and its ability to support habitation. In ancient times the volcanoes, torrents of water and wind carved the terrain. In the adjoining painted desert old funnels and formations of volcanoes can be seen still standing in the ancient desert and rock promontories, extensively weathered over the years.

"In comparatively modern times, the years 1066-67, a volcanic eruption in the San Francisco Peaks area sent tons of ash into the atmosphere. The heavy ash fall in this region created ecological zones where animal and plant life thrived among ponds of fresh water and marshes. The mixture of sand, ash and water provided a richer soil able to support abundant green foliage, trees and grass. These changed ecological conditions attracted several groups of people who inhabited growing settlements for many years.

"In the meantime, the continuous flow of desert winds and erosion of the soil due to years of constant farming and breakup of the ash mulch blew the loosened cover into sand dunes, against mesa walls and into dry river beds. The inhabitants began to seek other areas resulting in abandonment of arid regions. The Hopi mesas absorbed several immigrations as did the more distant Rio Grande valley. This great change also affected the people, who you describe as cliff dwellers. The arid conditions caused them to leave their settlements among the canyons and life in the steep slopes of the cliffs."

The following morning Siki was bright and eager to continue her story. Sam and family had returned from a trip the previous evening to Flagstaff where extra batteries for the recorder and a supply of tapes had been purchased at "Greco's", a local drug and variety store. Upon being questioned casually by the proprietor, Sam had said he was interested in Hopi history including the early years of the Spaniards and conquistadors. Mr. Greco's response stressed the "great and ancient history of this area" and suggested a visit to Northern Arizona University library for information and access concerning reference volumes on the subjects.

When the equipment was ready Siki looked earnestly at her audience. "It is not my wish to become involved in the many sources that make up scores of oral histories and the written accounts. Each clan has its storehouse of information concerning its people and events. Our history is not all legends, myths or memories of mystic happenings in the ancient days. I want to tell you more about the people of the Bear Clan and others, and their impact on historical events. In other words, I wish to continue with the persons who were involved, I am sure, in the incidents leading up to Mark's discovery of the Coronado jarron. Please feel free to interrupt anytime that you wish."

In his boyhood years, Aroyo learned the rudiments of desert farming by helping in the fields. It was a frustrating process to raise meager crops which would provide the Hopis with food through months of winter. Supplies always seemed to be adequate derived by sharing the output of hundreds of small plots. He participated in the ceremonial rain dances which brought the water necessary for basic needs of the people as well as agriculture. An active part in Kiva meetings demonstrated to others that he was deeply immersed in the Hopi concept of the Great Spirit and their wish for a peaceful life within the bounds of historic tribal culture.

Paqhua, son of Yongo and Pluma, became Aroyo's closest friend by extended visits to each other's homes on different mesas. Exploratory hikes around the base of the mesas provided information on the location of fresh water springs which they noted flowed out along the southern edge of the towering cliffs. The outpouring of cool water came from stone reservoirs located deep within the rock masses and continued flowing through long dry periods when no rain fell. The two boys became proficient in scooping out basins, lining them with mud and red clay, then allowing them to dry and bake in the sun. Where possible and abundant water was present, shallow, clay-lined ditches conducted the precious fluid to basins located at intervals near the numerous patches and fields of maize and cotton which could be readily nurtured by the large, hand-carried water jugs.

Good physical condition was a priority of the men, many of whom became warriors. Youths participated in regular training from an early age. After rising early, a daily event was a bath at the foot of the mesa in cool spring water. Muscles were hardened by running up and down the mesa trails. Supervised by their fathers, the youngsters utilized a ledge below the village to practice shooting with bow and arrow. Sand or rock piles about four feet high were erected, spaced thirty to forty and up to seventy yards apart. The mounds supported arrows placed vertically with the feathers exposed as targets. Both fathers and sons shot arrows, testing bows and judging their strength and range. Hardened leather shields were placed in the hands of the boys who were taught their use as a defensive weapon. Hopi warriors carried diversified weapons including bow and arrow with quiver, throwing stick, stone axe or club, and lance and shield, though not necessarily at the same time. Training of the youth included hand crafting of these items. Bows were rubbed with a sticky gum obtained from the horn of mountain sheep. The treatment included application of strips of animal tissue along the length of the bow which was then left to dry. Bowstrings were made from animal hide. Arrows were tipped at the end of the slender shaft with feathers used to stabilize the missile in flight. Both were obtained from the San Francisco Peaks area by tribal hunters, along with specified types of wood.

Aroyo and Paqhua demonstrated their prowess with bow and arrow with deadly accuracy. Small animals on the run and birds in flight fell victim to the slim arrows, providing ceremonial feathers, lining for bed mats and capes, and fur skins for varied

Pueblo ruins-Mesa Verde.　(Bell-Photo)

uses.

Although the Hopis centuries before had located the Mesas and constructed villages high above the desert plains as a defense measure, war was always felt to be imminent. In the years 1540-41, two new adversaries threatened these pueblos, clinging to the six hundred feet high escarpments of four flat-topped hills. The new challenges came not only from the Castillians but also from new peoples of Athabascan origin in northern areas, the Apaches, Navajos and Athabascan Indians.

Hopis, the Peaceful People, had always accepted strangers and impoverished Indians of other pueblo tribes into their midst where many assimilated into Hopi life. In the kivas, talk of outrageous deeds and pressure by the Spaniards forcing the people to adopt a new religion caused much concern. The Peaceful People responded in their way, intensifying traditional activities. The young generation of girls and boys was taken into the kivas for intensive learning and participation in tribal religion and ceremonies. Oral histories and legends were repeated and retold by the elders who were determined to preserve their ancient sense of being and life style in harmony with the earth, its basic influence on daily, monthly and yearly life of its inhabitants and coexistence of all living things.

As with many young boys, Aroyo had his favorites among the many myths and legends about insect, bird and animal life. One reflected the child's concern that ants are so thin. The legend explained.

Black Mesa was a place where ants liked to live on its eastern slopes. Their underground homes contained great colonies of many residents with some having large ant hills on the surface. The ants wondered why so many of their kind had been overlooked by the leaders of the Kachina societies. After awhile Chakmongwi, the village crier chief, received word and announced that in a few days an initiative into a Kachina society was planned. Much preparation was necessary. On the fourth day several of the Ant children who were to be initiated had to dress as Kachinas as is done by children of human parents when they are to be initiated into a Kachina society. The ceremony was to be held in the kiva where upon arrival certain Ants made a sand picture on the floor after which the Ants brought in their children who were ready to be initiated in the kiva. After all the children had arrived in the kiva, the ant Kachina priest told the story of the society in the same way as it is now told by the priest during the ceremony. At this time four children dressed as Koyamsi, clown kachina, completed their performance, Their antics made the children very happy. Unknown to those inside, an Ant had been told to sit on a boulder outside the kiva entrance. When the ceremony inside was finished, the Ant made a signal by swinging one of his front feet intensely to attract the attention of some waiting kachinas. They came at once, running in a group circling the kiva several times. Entering the kiva, they took places near the sand picture then set upon the Ant children, flogging them so violently that they were almost severed through the middle part of their bodies. When all the children had been beaten the kachinas ran away leaving them in the kiva. Since at that time they were nearly cut in two, that is the reason why ants now have bodies so thin in the middle.

WORLDS OF EMERGENCE

In the span of years between childhood and manhood, the middle period shaping the future sense of being for a young boy, Aroyo felt the need to know more than he had learned in the kiva ceremonies. He turned to Quitoya for help.

"The lessons learned by children are many and need to be understood and accepted, but certain things bother me. Where did we come from? Why am I here? Are Hopis different from the people in other tribes?"

"The questions you ask are provided answers in later sessions in the kiva. These usually occur when you are older but I recognize your need to know now, since you are older in many ways. Let us go to a cave a short distance from here to talk. We will take pika along to go with water for refreshment.

"I will obtain lots of pika for us." Aroyo soon returned with two food pouches hanging from a strap across his shoulder.

A circuitous climb was required to reach the cave. Aroyo's eyes widened at its expanse with walls etched and painted with human and animal-like figures. "My friend and I have seen this opening from below but did not climb up to investigate."

"This is an ancient habitat of our people before they built mud and stone structures and kivas partially immersed in the ground. Later, the present dwellings were constructed atop the mesas. Do you remember the opening in the floor of our kiva, surrounded by a few stones?"

"Yes. It is a place for spirits to come from, called Sipaapuni, the symbolic opening for emergence from another world."

"That is correct." Quitoya motioned for Aroyo to sit near him.

"Several events happened before our people appeared in this place many years ago. At first no land, mountains, mesas or valleys were here, only space, where nothing existed. No sun, wind or rain existed here. Then *Taiowa*, creator of all earthly things, looked about in the void of space where he lived, and thought that life was needed as well as a habitat to sustain life. Taiowa was known as the Great Sun Spirit, who had such great power and force that he formed the ingredients for what we call earth and placed the first living creatures in the form of insects in deep under ground caverns. This was the First World."

Aroyo was attentive and grasped the concept of creation. "We are people, so the insects must have been alone with no birds to eat them. Besides, that dark cave was a good place for them. They could not do much down there."

"You are on the right track, Aroyo. Over a long period of time, Taiowa saw that nothing was progressing and the beings he had created were not of much consequence. They needed to be aware of their creation and they did not comprehend the meaning of their existence."

Quitoya pondered his next words for a few moments then explained how Taiowa called upon his nephew, Sotuknang, giving him the power to take the substance of earthly matter and form its shape, adding air and water gathered from endless space. This was part of the diety's universal plan which included the creation of life in the First World.

Needing a helper who would remain on the earth, Sotuknang created Kokyangwuti, Spider Woman. Legends of other clans identified her as Spider Grandmother. Using molds of earth and moisture, she brought forth plants, trees, bearers of nuts and seeds and many varieties of birds and animals.

Spider Grandmother was instructed to go into the underworld cave, talk to the creatures and tell them to stop fighting among themselves. The insect beings listened when told that Taiowa wanted to rearrange their fate, place them in a better environment and correct deficiencies in living things. They agreed to depart from the cavern and join with Spider Grandmother.

"It was a long journey and during that time the Sun Spirit transformed the creatures into animals. Spider Woman relocated them in a different cave of large dimension above the original. The inhabitants changed from an inferior condition to a better life in their Second World. They somewhat resembled bears and dogs with fur covering their bodies and skin between their fingers similar to animals adapted to water.

"Could these animals find food and raise their young pups?" Aroyo chewed on pika bread as he assimilated the information. "Was the Sun Spirit satisfied with the Second World?"

Quitoya also munched on pika, reflecting on his recollection of the mystic and ancient oral histories of the Hopis concerning origin of life and its emergence from the Lower World into a higher level.

"Taiowa tried to keep his promise of bringing all living things to perfection and undoubtedly providing food and substance for the creatures living in caverns. These beings seemed to be happy at first but they soon began quarreling and even eating their own kind."

"Did he kill them to keep them from eating each other?"

"Other plans were evolving for these animal-creatures when Taiowa saw what they were doing and that they did not grasp the meaning of life. Living in the underworld in caves was a burden to any progress. The Sun Spirit was pleased with Spider Woman's results on Earth. He told her to bring human life into being since she had been given the wisdom, love and knowledge that would help all life brought into existence. Four earth colors, red, yellow, white, and black, were gathered by Spider Woman who created four forms in the image of Sotuknang. Then she made female partners for them patterned after her own likeness."

Quitoya peered closely at Aroyo. "This may sound complicated and it is true that much was involved and it transpired over many years. At this point in time it was called the Third World, bringing more light and warmth to the atmosphere and providing water for the fields. The creatures emerged into this new world led by Spider Grandmother who, by the way, was able to change her appearance to that of an animal or human. The beings became aware that their bodies were changing, losing their fur, tails and webbed fingers. Spider Grandmother explained that they were now people and no longer mere creatures. She exhorted them to live in harmony, to do away with evil and not to destroy or injure each other. They must not forget that Taiowa, the Sun Spirit, had created them originally out of the void of space and now provided a way for them to understand the world about them and the meaning of life."

Aroyo fidgeted as he looked around the cave. "Some of the drawings depict people at work and making things. Also, the shapes of animals and birds are similar to those living in the vicinity of our mesa. Did the people occupy this cave as a place to live?"

"As we have discussed, our legends and myths tell of three stages of creation in which the environment for living was in the Lower World. Centuries passed and Taiowa decided that it was time for the people to inhabit this new Upper World he had created. Spider Woman showed them the way and they emerged through the sipaapuni into the Fourth World which is our world today. Caves like this one were probably the first places available but the people soon started looking for different regions where they could grow corn and erect their homes. Spider Grandmother kelped them again and created the sun and the moon. In the Upper World, powerful light and heat were available from the sun by day and reflected at night in regular intervals from the moon. This occurred about twelve times each year and provided a method of counting the passage of time between intervals of the full moon, helping to determine the right time to plant corn and schedule ceremonies.

Aroyo looked earnestly at Quitoya. "Were the people now satisfied and happy with their lives?"

"Before the people settled on the present land in this region, they made many migrations. They went in all directions as instructed by Masauwu, a deity appointed by Taiowa, the creator, as Guardian of the Fourth World. He is the lord of fire and death. Various groups banded together, developing their own languages and later becoming clans. The clans then constructed houses, kivas and worked in the fields. Ruins of their villages dot the countryside many miles apart. The people had felt after many years that something was missing from their lives and were drawn to Tuumanasavi, the Center of the Universe. Masauwu had instructed that this region near Black Mesa was where the people would come after completing many migration cycles. Living on these mesas, the clans became unified as Hopis, the Peaceful People. Some bands never returned." Quitoya stood to stretch his legs then again sat beside his young friend.

"Aroyo, I hope some of your questions have been answered. It is very probable that your quest for understanding and knowledge will continue throughout your life. Ceremonies of the clans depict certain phases in the Road of Life which includes all four worlds. From each world preceding, the place of emergence is represented by the small opening in the floor of a kiva, the sipaapuni, always placed at a prescribed location. In the quest to find the great sipaapuni, legends depict the people paddling reed boats and rafts across large bodies of water to reach a dry place since the Third World had been destroyed by sinking beneath the sea. Only the tops of mountains were left, forming small islands from which the fugitives sought the shore of dry land with space for all to live. Under the guidance of Spider Woman, the people continually traveled east sometimes having to cross an island on foot to the opposite shore where they again built and launched their primitive craft for navigating the water.

"Spider Woman admonished them to let their inner wisdom and the spirits guide them in locating their own place of Emergence. This occurred in a land where the boats were propelled to shore by a smooth, persistent current.

"It was a narrow, sandy beach at the mouth of a large river flowing from a gorge extending as far east as was possible to see. Very high rock walls and cliffs always seemed to block their way as the people pushed against the current in the Lower World. After more days of paddling, a point was reached where the craft could be landed. A breach in the sheer walls allowed the fugitives to leave the canyon and proceed toward the mountains. Their place of Emergence occurred near the San Francisco Peaks area, bordering what is now our land. Masauwu, who owned the lands in the Upper World met the travelers, telling them to leave the mountains and giving permission to settle on the land in the new environment.

"So you see, Aroyo, in answer to your question 'where did we come great from?', it could be from across the great sea to the west of this place."

The boy sat quietly, turning all that he had learned around in his mind. The faint sound of a twig breaking or snapping alerted Quitoya. He had noted the feathers, sticks and other debris strewn about the dirt floor and assumed that animals and birds had inhabited the cave over the years. Hearing another snap, he moved closer to Aroyo and said in a whisper, "Go behind that large boulder. I heard a movement or something. Take a good size rock with you and place it where you can use it as a weapon, if necessary, then be ready to go to the village for help. I will investigate further back."

Before Quitoya could fully stand erect, three figures appeared from the deep darkness of the cavern, rushing at him with such force that all four rolled on the ground as they met in a frantic tumble. One scrambled to his feet just below the boulder shielding Aroyo who saw three men dressed in rags and skins. The boy raised a rock in both hands, slamming it down on the head of the attacker, knocking him to the floor where he lay without movement. The other two renegades, brandishing clubs, pummeled Quitoya who fought fiercely with arms and legs flailing.

Although reticent to leave, Aroyo did as he had been instructed, making his way down the steep, rocky incline of the mesa, then running all the way to the village. Bursting through a gate into the first plaza he came upon in a cluster of buildings, he beckoned wildly to a group of warriors who immediately came to his side. He spoke between gasps of breath.

"Three bad men attacked us at a cave on the east side of the mesa. My friend Quitoya is struggling with two of them. I smashed one on the head with a rock. Quitoya told me to come for help. I will show you where the cave is located and the trail leading to it."

In a matter of minutes the Hopi men had gathered weapons and started down the mesa path at a run. A large warrior, seeing Aroyo had not had time to regain his breath and strength, swooped the lad up onto his shoulders.

"Lead us to these men who would attack a lone man and a boy. We will deal with them." The big man smiled at Aroyo.

Aroyo recognized him as a member of the Bear Clan and hung on as they jogged toward the cave site. Tapping his friends head, he pointed to the boulders marking the route up the bluff.

"Thank you Big Bear". Aroyo named his new friend as he was placed on the ground. "I wish to stay with you and go to the cave to find Quitoya."

"I see no prints or evidence of anyone being here recently other than the small prints of the lad here." Big Bear spoke to the other men as he scanned the ground closely, then looked up the side of the mesa. "Let us all take this path to the cave, but be on the lookout for any movement on either side."

Entering the mouth of the cave, the rescuers were greeted with a grisly sight. One man, identified by Aroyo as one of the assailants, lay prone at the base of a large boulder, his head smashed and dried blood permeating the soil. Another's neck and upper torso were red with blood from many knife wounds and his face badly mutilated, indicating that a ferocious struggle had taken place. Identification in death would be impossible. Further into the cave's recesses Quitoya was found on the dirt floor where he had been dragged and stripped of his clothing. Beaten with bloody clubs which lay nearby, he had apparently been left for dead. Blood oozed from the wounds and one arm appeared to be broken.

The big man quickly made an examination. "This man has taken a vicious beating, but he is still alive. He must be taken to the village where the women can provide treatment."

"He is Quitoya. His house is next to Honmana's grandmother, the Bear Clan matriarch." Aroyo explained that he and his friend had climbed to the cave earlier and indicated he wished to accompany him to Oraibi.

"Your friend is a tough taaqua. We will find and punish his assailants." Big Bear waved an arm. Two men stepped forward.

"All right, take him to where this boy instructs you. We will search the cavern and look around for any evidence of the renegades." Big Bear motioned to the others to spread out, then ventured into the dark depths and tunnels requiring torches to be carried.

A large cache of weapons including clubs, spears, arrows and coils of cordage was found in a chamber adjacent to the entrance area. Extending further was a natural passageway leading to another cavern where sleeping mats were stacked. A short tunnel led to an outside opening located on a promontory projecting from the bluff. This provided an observation point revealing two well-traveled trails leading to the village of Oraibi on top. Further, a complete scan of the eastern side and edge of the mesa and a view of the original cave entrance could be made. A path shielded by large boulders, led down to the base of the rocky cliff.

Returning to the stockpile of weapons, Big Bear and the three men accompanying him sorted out some of the items. "These arrows have markings of several different tribes. Do you suppose that a raid on Oraibi is in the making? The stockpiles represent a lot of work for some group. Quantities like these indicate that many would be involved in an attack launched from these caves. The attackers could arrive by ones and twos to avoid a large band being detected. Then a surprise attack could be launched."

"This amount of cordage, cut into proper lengths, could be used by many men to scale the cliff above to the mesa surface." Honshoki, a stocky Hopi warrior, picked up a length of the coiled rope, tied several knots at intervals then attached a wooden club to its end, swinging the section back and forth.

"We have not used these in our tribe but the people living in ancient cliff settlements utilized this method of going up or down in an emergency. The individual ropes supplemented rigid ladders and those made of cordage and wood steps. With a whirling motion and well-placed throw, the wood piece at the end carries the cord up and lodges between the rock crevices, holding the cord line firmly for climbing. Many warriors could reach the top in this manner."

Big Bear broke out in booming laughter. "I am not laughing at what you have said, my friend. Can you imagine the heads of these renegades coming up to the rim and we are there waiting to bash their heads in and watch the bodies fall from the cliff?"

The big man finally controlled his mirth which contained a

strain of contempt for anyone attempting to reach the village in that way.

"We will tell the others of what we have found and establish continual surveillance under cover from the top. Who ever plans this attack will be greeted by an unpleasant surprise!"

* * * * * * * *

Under constant care of the matriarch, Honyanqua, her daughter Honmana and several others, Quitoya seemed to respond at times then fall into a coma. Signs of torture and multiple knife wounds covered his body. Deep cuts nearly severed one arm above the elbow. On the third day he succumbed to his wounds and loss of blood.

Quitoya's sister on First Mesa arrived with relatives and Naso, a beautiful Hopi girl introduced as the dead man's daughter. Aroyo, who had been kept busy running errands and carrying water, was immediately impressed by the young maiden who asked if she could help him with the chores. Many friends, including Yongo and Pluma came to impart their condolences and place prayer feathers in the household and about the plaza. It was a busy time for Honmana, the young people and other helpers who baked pika bread and prepared corn meal for distribution to all who came. The active life and exploits of Quitoya and his ready willingness to aid his fellow man were discussed over and over again.

Honmana was deeply distressed at the loss of her true friend who had saved her life during a terrible storm and flood which resulted in the birth of her son. He was her protector in events at the great northern river and canyon. She recalled the journey to the Zuni pueblos, the army posts of Coronado and the hazardous trek via the mountains in a remarkable region she probably would never see again. She related these events to Naso who listened attentively and became aware of the unexpressed love that had been shared by her father and this woman. Honmana had asked her to stay with her for an unstated period of time. Permission was given by her aunt who returned to her home at First Mesa.

Chapter Fourteen

WAR CLOUDS

War fever ran high as the villagers prepared to repel an attack which they perceived to be imminent. Rock piles, shaped to appear natural, were stacked at intervals along the eastern tumpavi. Set back several feet from the rim, the accumulations of rocks were doubled above the cave area. Warriors and townspeople were assigned stations along the mesa rim. Big Bear and Honshoki had been appointed by the elders to oversee the activities. Weeks went by without any additional evidence of intruders. Tension eased in Oraibi but scouts were sent each morning in the adjacent area.

Aroyo, Naso and friend Paqhua, who had remained when his parents returned to First Mesa, became a trio doing daily chores together and developing skills with the lance and bow as well as participating in games played by girls and boys. Naso won many foot races in competition with girls of the pueblo and proved to be fleet footed and skilled in a game using stout sticks to move a leather ball back and forth across a field. The objective was hitting the ball over a line scratched on the ground at the ends of the playing field.

The two boys and Naso had been fascinated by the concept of grappling ropes and their adaption to scaling cliffs. They sought out Honshoki who was found sitting in the plaza. Aroyo was the spokesman.

"We wish to learn how to climb cliffs using a wood block and cordage. The materials were left in the cave. Can you teach us?"

Honshoki studied the trio for a moment with a trace of amusement then leaped to his feet. "To what use would you put this feat? I have thought about teaching the men, but our warriors indicate they do not have the need to climb cliffs in that manner. You may lack the strength to pull your bodies up toward the sky!"

"We run each day and are taking the training to develop our strength for throwing spears, wield a battle axe and engage in wrestling." Paqhua flexed his arm muscles. "We are past sixteen."

Aroyo was excited. "We wish to explore the mesa walls for hidden caves. This would reveal any further activities of our enemies. Also, we can reach out croppings where eagles and other birds nest. The feathers are necessary for ceremonies and prayer sticks."

"I can help too. The boys have said we do things as a team. and support each other." Naso stood erect to show that she was an inch or two taller than her companions.

"Well, I believe your powers of persuasion will match your abilities to perform the tasks. Let us go to the cave and obtain the cordage. You had better wear sandals that strap to your feet. Get ready and do not forget selected your bows and quivers. We will leave here shortly." Honshoki selected a favorite lance and before returning to the plaza instructed four men to follow the edge of the mesa to a marked place above the cave which contained the cache of weapons. They were to wait there until receiving a signal from below.

At the cave the stored arrows were tied in bundles and carried to the entrance. Most of the other weapons were tied and dragged to the opening. Honshoki judged the distance to the top of the ridge, measuring an appropriate length of cordage and securely tying a club to one end.

"This length of rope will be used to climb to the edge above. We will tie knots at intervals the length of an arrow. These provide something to grasp with your hands and to push with your feet." The young trio pitched in, helping Honshoki prepare the rope.

Swinging the rope in a circle, Honshoki pointed to a rocky ledge halfway to the top. "I will try to snag this club between the rocks." The second effort was successful. He jerked on the cordage, testing to assure that it was securely held, then pulled himself up, using hands and feet. After looking down at the trio watching, he let himself down.

"As you see, one can go up or down on this single rope ladder. Who wants to try it?"

Naso stepped forward, grasped the rope and with apparently little effort pulled herself to the ledge then came down. The others applauded her, taking turns to accomplish the exercise.

Honshoki was pleased with his proteges. "You have done well. Now we will try for the top." With a twisting motion he sent coils upward which dislodged the wood letting the rope fall at his feet. He then gathered the knotted cordage, swinging it in a wide circle before releasing the free end. The heavy wood club landed just short of the top. The others tried the maneuver several times before the wood finally lodged securely in the rocks.

Honshoki tied a bundle of arrows to the rope, then looked upward shouting, "the load is ready!" Men appeared appeared above and pulled the arrows upward to the rim then sent the rope back down. In this way all of the weapons were cleared from the cave and confiscated for local use. With bow and quiver fastened about their backs, the young trio individually ascended the rope followed by Honshoki. They were greeted by the waiting men who were visibly excited about this method of coping with the mesa cliffs.

Batches of arrows were sorted by the elder warriors who studied the colored rings, markings and feathers. The craftmanship and assorted signs produced characteristics associated with several area Indian tribes; namely, Utes, Supais, Navajos and Pauites. Certain battle axes bore marks and figures depicting animals and humans, many without heads!

One old warrior summed up the investigations. "The variations in arrows led us to believe that several tribes or bands might be involved. However, a close scrutiny of several battle axes indicated primative figures and signs associated with people called barbarians. The mutilated bodies in the cave indicated terrible beatings, probably with an axe, according to Big Bear who looked them over. The third person evidently ran away when when he heard our rescuers coming. Aroyo said the three men were very shabbily clothed in animal skins, their black hair was long and unkempt and they attacked with clubs."

Another elderly man continued. "It is possible that the weapons had been obtained by raids on several tribes and hidden in the cave which the barbarians had chosen as a temporary habitat."

A few days later, the Yavaconeni (Far Away People) tribe visited Oraibi bringing items to trade for corn. Their handsomely tanned deer skins and dippers made from the horns of Big Horn sheep were highly prized by Hopi women. The Conenas, as they were known through the Indian grapevine, were welcomed and treated as guests. Two of their elders were invited to a meeting in a Kiva where they were told about the events in the cave and questioned about the possibilities of barbarians located in the region.

An elder Conena responded. "Our warriors captured two men of that description who wandered into a camp asking for help for their destitute women and children. These people are called Head Pounders who kill an enemy by beating his head with a rock or stone axe."

"Then we must destroy any of them who enter our boundaries. Is that not the answer?" One of the Hopi men posed the question.

"The captured men stated that several in their band had been convinced by a stranger that killing and destruction were necessary for their existence. The man departed with a few warriors to lead a life in that manner, but one by one had themselves been killed. The people in the band who would talk seemed to have no recollection of their tribe's past and were wanderers."

When Big Bear heard of this he bristled, confiding in the warriors. "Do not listen to those old men. One of our finest warriors had been killed. Who is in our midst committing such crimes we do not know. They certainly must be strangers with enough knowledge of the terrain to work themselves into our realm. We must continue scouting activities and increase our efforts to find anything unusual near our mesa. A band of desperate men may be out there!" He asked Honshoki to assign the southeastern end of the mesa, where Oraibi was located, to the young people, two boys and a girl who had scaled the cliff.

"They can slip in and out of the rocky ridges and discover if something is taking place unknown to us." The others agreed.

During daylight hours the trio climbed the bluffs from bottom to top, eagerly searching for signs of intruders. Another cave and a small area on a shelf-like projection of rock were found with indications of war preparations. Human footprints, debris, a few weapons and markings etched on boulders pointing in the direction of paths between areas, gave evidence of advance planning. The landfall on the slopes of the mesa provided access to the top without the obstruction of sheer walls. Concealed behind one group of boulders were earthen water jugs filled for human consumption.

Hidden from observation below, Aroyo, Naso and Paqhua prepared crude maps on sections of white rabbit skin indicating outcroppings and promentories accessible from the top surface of the mesa. Hopi marksmen could be lowered at these points to overlook activities of the enemy. An assault could be ripped to pieces by bowman stationed at strategic locations. Paths, large crevices, cave entrances and staging areas at the base of the mesa were also pinpointed. Presented to Big Bear and others, the maps and personal narratives were readily accepted.

* * * * * * * *

Siki paused in her narrative allowing a young man, the director of the vistor center, to speak to the group. "Please accept our invitation to visit the section of our center containing an art gallery which may be of special interest to you at this time. In it are drawings and paintings depicting conflict between the Pueblo tribes embracing the period 1542 - 1556.

"Hopi villages were the object of raiding parties. The isolation and life of the Peaceful People stimulated curiosity in other tribes who tested the high mesa pueblos looking for anything they could plunder and take away. But the Hopis became noted for their corn and sheep which were the objects desired by the Navajos, recent arrivals from northern regions. Sheep corrals and corn fields, many located in the perimeter of the mesas, were easy prey for raiders who took what they wanted sometimes without opposition in certain unguarded open spaces.

"Other forays were made into the settlements where villagers were confronted in fierce fighting. Their plunder included women and children who were taken into families and brought into Navajo culture and environment."

Sam and Cindy rose to thank the young man declaring that the gallery would surely be visited.

Siki resumed her narrative.

* * * * * * * *

The attack came about noon four days later. Coming from Black Mesa which bordered the Hopis to the north, Indian warriors made their way through Oraibi wash, moving close to the side of the mesa where they possibly could not be observed. Others, having positioned themselves during the night, were preparing to scale the cliff.

The young trio had arrived early and were perched on a promontory part way down the bluff. A movement in the distance caused Aroyo to exclaim. "Look northward in the dry wash under the shadow of the mesa wall. Something is moving."

Naso, peering through cupped hands to shield the brightness of the sun, responded. "It is formed of many people. One stepped into the sunligm momentarily and his silver medallions reflected bright light."

A few minutes passed and Naso spoke again. "I can see many colors and men carrying things. It is a war party! Bodies glisten with red, yellow and white paint. Small banners of colored cloth are attached to their battle axes, bows and spears. We must warn our people!"

Paqhua, who had been peering in the opposite direction, held up a hand. "See down there along the escarpment, men are gathering at the white vein of rock! They are swinging ropes in circles. Some are climbing upward!"

Aroyo shot an arrow up and over the mesa top. It bore a ribbon of white cloth signalling an approaching war party from the north and a red ribbon indicating an assault via the cliffs. The arrow may have also served as a signal to the opponents as the attack began at several points along the bluff.

Within minutes of sighting Aroyo's arrow, Hopi warriors took designated positions a few feet back from the rim while others descended to out- croppings and promentories of the ancient, weathered mesa cliff. Villagers from Bahavi, a small village a league distant from Oraibi, appeared at the mesa rim, plunging rocks down, scattering the main force below. Warriors hurtled rocks on climbers endeavoring to scale the bluff and using battle axes, smashed heads appearing at the edge. Arrows from the young trio and other marksmen hidden on ridges and boulders along the precipice, found their mark as bodies fell to the rocks below.

Fierce hand-to-hand fighting confronted the few who success-fully scaled the rim. Most were killed and captives were thrown over the cliff. After many attempts at ascending the precipice were repelled, the remaining warriors abandoned the project, retreating to the base of the mesa.

The main force stopped at the trail leading up to Oraibi. Big Bear looked them over.

"Our enemies are Utes, Navajos and renegades among them with no colors of their own. The stout logs we have piled at the plaza wall and gate will slow them, giving our bowmen excellent targets."

Honshoki observed. "Maybe they will follow a battle plan from the past, according to the old warriors."

"What is that plan?"

"A small force will advance part way to look us over and check the barricades. After a few minutes of discussion they will turn back and rejoin the others."

"Then what can we expect?" Big Bear clasped both hands around the handle of a stone battle axe.

"The second time will be an attack in force on our bulwarks. That is the time for our bowmen to shoot straight and often."

Big Bear peered thoughtfully at Honshoki then passed an order to the defending warriors to stay their bows until the second approach of the assailants.

A wildly shouting crowd stormed up the trail in three columns, attempting to breach the stone and mud wall of the plaza, reenforced and backed by piles of logs. They were repulsed by a resolute body of warriors and villagers all equipped with a weapon with which to face the enemy. Volleys of arrows struck the foe with deadly accuracy, thinning their ranks and littering the trail with bodies of dead and wounded.

The mass of attackers, darting back and forth as they advanced up the trail, included bowmen who inflicted many casulaties on the Hopis, shooting their arrows from behind boulders on the mesa slope. In desperate charges, warriors struggled upward with some going over the wall. The defenders were ready, slashing and smashing with lances, knives and battle axes.

The defense was overpowering, led by Honshoki and Big Bear who in the thick of the battle continuosly exhorted his compatriots; shouting, "Stand your ground! Stand your ground! We will rout these intruders who wish to capture our women and children and make us slaves!"

Retreating down the trail, the attackers were in full flight, scurrying for cover among the large boulders below which years prior had fallen from the rocky walls of the mesa. Attempts at regrouping and fleeing north in the dry gorge were prevented by the relentless barrage of arrows from the cliffs on that route. Finally, smaller groups made their way south where the band came together fleeing to the Little Colorado River. It would then be possible for them to follow the river north and thereon to their villages.

The Hopis had other plans. Big Bear quickly organized a large unit of warriors who pursued the enemy relentlessly, forcing a crossing of the river valley where they took refuge in the ancient ruins of Wupatki which once dominated the area. Occupying a campsite on a hillside where they could observe movements in the deserted pueblo, the Hopis rested from a pursuit lasting the previous day and all night, aided by a full moon.

Before sun up the next morning a young runner arrived with news from Oraibi. The warriors gathered around as he spoke to

Big Bear.

"Big Bear, the news is not good. Naso and Aroyo were captured as they reached the base of the mesa. Enemy warriors took them north toward the Navajo village. Paqhua, who saw what happened, climbed a rope to the top of the mesa and ran to Oraibi with the information."

"Did a rescue party go after them?"

"Yes. Honshoki and our warriors have followed them, His message to you stressed the fact that they total only two dozen men since many had to stay to protect the women and children at Oraibi and the balance of our fighting men are with you. He said if it is possible, you must hasten north up the river to Tokanave (Navajo) Mountain. From that point your forces couLd join. We must free our two young people now in enemy hands!"

Big Bear addressed his men. "This is a serious affair which we mean to end. We will launch an attack immediately. Divide into three parties and probe through the old pueblo to determine in which part they are lurking."

While two groups stealthily searched the ends of the ruins, Big Bear and his party approached the center, crouching so as not to present an upright target. Several arrows whizzed by revealing the location of their opponents since two bowmen were momentarily observed. Shouting his personal battle cry, the big man broke into a run towards a deteriorated stone wall, brandishing a battle axe. The warriors followed at his side. The wall was easily surmounted providing a short leap into the enemy ranks which were small in number. The fray lasted only a few minutes as the Hopis mercilessly speared, axed and bludgened their opponents.

With his back to a wall and a knife at his throat, the Navajo chief raised both arms in a signal of surrender. He and twenty-two men were bound with hands behind their backs and made to sit along the wall while the dead and wounded were dragged to the opposite side of the narrow enclosure. Except for two Hopis who had been treated for deep body wounds, only superficial injuries had been received.

Soon the other two parties returned having located no one. A warrior reported what they had discovered. "A tunnel was found leading from the rear of the old pueblo to a spring of water. It is apparent that the others escaped that way."

The Navajo chief spoke. "They were stragglers and *kwitamuh* from other tribes that no one wanted. We did not think they would run away in the face of a battle, but that is surely what happened."

Big Bear retorted. "If they return, our warriors will kill them. That will be their reward for attacking Oraibi."

He turned to his warriors. "Keep a close check on the bindings of these prisoners. It is time that we cross the river and start north."

Accompanied by several warriors, Big Bear crossed the plaza out of ear shot of the captives. The men knew of the situation at Oraibi and the abduction of Aroyo and Naso, and agreed with the decision to join another Hopi group at Tokanove mountain. The runner was so advised.

"Moreover," the big man ordered, "when you return to Oraibi see that arrangements are made to have food supplies, extra weapons and cordage needed by our warriors delivered at a bend in the Little Colorado River where it turns west to meet the great river. We will camp there."

At the time of his departure, the young runner was accompanied by a warrior and the two wounded men whose cuts were tightly bound for the journey.

* * * * * * * *

PURSUIT AND RESCUE

Four days passed. The Hopi band, reinforced not only with supplies and weapons but about thirty additional warriors, had left the plateau of the river and were traveling northeast for a rendevous with their compatriots coming from another direction. Guards were assigned daily to watch over the motley group of captives trudging along with hands bound.

Setting a comparatively fast pace, the other contingent of Hopis had advanced within a league of the Navajo village. Honmana and two warriors familiar with the region approached Honshoki and Loloma, son of Bear Clan kikmongwi, who was his representative since the older man was unable to travel. Honmana scratched descriptive lines in the sand as she outlined a plan.

"Many small buttes and gullies surround the Navajo settlement which is not on a high mesa. A gorge of some depth extends from the village toward the mountains and Tokenova. Instead of meeting with Big Bear's band and attacking in one large body, I wish to suggest that they make the approach through the gorge and we station ourselves among the boulders and outcroppings which provide excellent cover. We would be in a much better position to force the release of our two young people as our bowmen could decimate the opposing warriors from the cliffs."

Loloma disagreed. "We should not plan to attack with our forces split in two groups. The enemy might out number us two to one with disastrous results."

"In my opinion we can defeat them as only remnants of their battle forces remain. Their regular fighting men fled south after being routed at the battle for Oraibi." Honshoki peered directly into the eyes of the chief's son.

"At any rate, Big Bear and his warriors must be contacted and notified of our plans. You who know the terrain would make the greatest speed." Loloma stepped toward Honmana. "Are you able to undertake the journey with your companions?"

"We are ready. However, one man should remain to lead the way to the canyon which could be easily mistaken in these barrancas. Remember, these eager warriors must be kept out of sight of the enemy until everything is ready. We will need more than a day to reach the mountains. Probably two days will be required to return and enter the gorge which is normally a dry wash. Big Bear's band, moving between the cliffs toward the village, will undoubtedly be sighted by scouts. Soon after, the Navajos will gather in force to meet them. This would probably occur at a place in the canyon where a landslide has blocked half of the trail."

Loloma directed his question at Honshoki. "Is this plan complete? Can you think of anything that has been omitted?"

Honshoki patiently replied to the young man. "In order to rescue the captives, we must be in a position to intercede the Navajos as they retreat to their village. We will deploy our warriors and bowmen in such a manner that this can be accomplished. Our positions will be carefully planned and made ready for the encounter. It will keep us busy until we are notified that Big Bear and his warriors have arrived!"

Satisfied with the explanation, Loloma turned and placed a Bear Clan amulet on Honmana together with prayer feathers on her garment and that of Wupataqa, the warrior guide. "May the Great Spirit be with you."

As the courageous woman and man started off at a loping pace which would be maintained for many leagues, all of the band watched until the two diminishing figures disappeared from view.

Big Bear was dismayed when the two Hopis arrived at his camp.

"Have Honshoki and the warriors been wiped out?" He ran forward to embrace a tired Honmana and extend a hand to Wupataqa. Others brought water, pika bread and cuts of venison shared from the evening meal.

"Do not worry about Honshoki. They have not engaged the enemy and will deploy themselves to create the greatest disaster ever known to that tribe. Of course, you will meet the main force head on in the dry wash. It is not far from their village."

"The dry wash, where is that, pray tell?" A scowl appeared on Big Bear's face.

All listened as Honmana described the gorge and explained the plan of attack in detail. Her warrior companion added his knowledge about the route and approach to the gorge.

"This is not what we have had in mind. Another route across a plateau leading into the enemy's village will serve much better. We will be able to see his forces and judge his strength and numbers. Should we be locked in a canyon like stranded sheep?" Comments and a nodding of agreement backed up the big man's statement.

"Loloma and Honshoki must be questioned about their plan."
Honmana spoke with authority. "So little time remains. Our warriors could be detected by the Navajos, as they are positioned right under their noses, so to speak. Furthermore, how would those men be utilized on an open field?"

"Let me think about this and talk to my able brethren, warriors who have gone through much already but are ready for the next confrontation." Big Bear started to walk away, then turned to Honmana.

"Do you have word of your son Aroyo and the girl Naso?"

"As far as we can tell, they are still being held captive." Distress registered on the woman's beautiful countenence. She looked up and beyond the big man, seeing the bound captives lying and standing among a grove of short cedar trees.

"What have you here? Did you chase them from somewhere south of Third Mesa?"

"We engaged them at Wupatki, the old ruins near the Little Colorado River. Some renegades among them fled through the ruins and escaped through a tunnel at the rear. In this group is a Navajo chief who surrendered in the heat of battle, prodded by a knife to the throat!" Big Bear laughed as he recalled the episode. "The captives have caused delays in our long march but I believe they and the chief will be usefull for a trade when we encounter their warriors and demand release of Naso and Aroyo."

Early the following morning the war party moved eastward leaving the mountains behind. Before the sun had risen fully over the horizon, Big Bear strode to Honmana's side.

"Much thought must have been given to the assault plan developed by Loloma and Honshoki. You were sent many leagues into the wilderness to convey their message. We will participate as planned and hope that the arrangement is the right one. We will know soon, won't we? "

"Thank you, Big Bear. Whatever is effective in obtaining the return of our loved ones - that is the important element in this whole maneuver. Further, the Navajos need to be taught a lesson!" Honmana's bright smile gave the big man the lift he needed and cleared his mind of any negative thoughts concerning the forthcoming encounter.

By mid-morning the next day the band had traversed a system of barrancas which, but for Honmana and Wupataqa, might have found them disoriented or at worst, lost. In the sandy, well-packed river bottom on which they now travelled, the war party was joined by two Hopi scouts from Honshoki's group, who led them into a canyon which twisted and meandered beneath high rocky walls.

One of the scouts spoke to Big Bear and Honmana. "We must depart now. The others are to be advised that you are in the gorge. By our estimate, you will arrive where the old landslide is located by midday. At that point in the canyon you will undoubtedly be under observation of scouts from the village.

Honmana prepared to leave with them, shifting her pouch, bow and quiver to a better position for running and climbing. "I can inflict more punishment on our adversaries with bow and arrow from the cliff, than trying to wield a heavy battle axe here on the ground. We will join you for the victory march into the village!" She placed a hand on Big Bear's arm for a moment, looking into his eyes, then was gone on the run trailing the scouts who turned onto a path leading upward to the rim of the canyon.

After continuing through the wash a distance of about one league, the warriors were assembled into full battle array. Big Bear and four of his ablest men made up the first line. Their lances were held vertical with feathers and small, colored cloth banners flying in the slight breeze. Other weapons hung, ready for immediate use, from their garments.

Next came a row of eleven captives, the Chief in the center and all with hands bound behind and tied waist to waist with heavy cordage. Two lines of Hopi warriors carrying bows, lances and axes with a second line of bound prisoners followed. Four lines of warriors, ready to meet any form of combat, formed the last rows.

The formidable group stopped at the landslide, waiting. Within minutes a small party of Navajo warriors appeared around a turn of the gorge, advancing within hearing distance.

Big Bear stepped forward two paces. "We demand return of our Hopi son and daughter taken from Oraibi." His voice boomed through the canyon.

An opposing warrior, dressed in the finery of a chief and brandishing a spear in the air, took two steps forward then stopped. He thrust the spear into the sandy earth. "Your demands are hollow. The young spies are our captives. They are for ransom. We demand two hundred sheep and six thousand sheafs of maize. We will accept no less."

"Let us see the boy and the girl." Big Bear thrust his own lance into the sand and stood firm, arms folded across his chest.

Naso and Aroyo were brought into view. Each was tightly held by a warrior as they stood alongside the Chief.

Big Bear nodded to the men behind him who parted ranks, revealing the line of captured warriors. "You had better change your offer. Do you recognize the Chief of one of your bands? With him are twenty helpless warriors who are our prisoners. Turn over our young people and we will give these men to you in exchange."

Having checked the strength and deployment of the opposition as was their custom, the Navajos withdrew, disappearing around a protruding wall of the Canyon. Unknown to the Hopis, stray horses and those captured in battles with the Spaniards along the Rio Grande had been obtained by the Navajos, mainly through trading with displaced Pueblo tribes.

An unfamiliar sound, somewhat similar to subdued thunder, echoed down the canyon. To the amazement of the Hopis, mounted horses came into view, their riders whooping and yelling when they saw their opponents scurrying to sides of the gorge and upon the landslide. From above and behind the mounted men arrows flew from the rocky cliffs. The markmanship of the bowmen resulted in many riders and steeds downed, bodies bristling like quills of a porcupine with arrows protruding in bunches. Many horses faltered and fell to the ground, others came on, galloping into and over the captive warriors, still tied in a line. The Chief was trampled under the hooves.

Big Bear and his men speared and leaped on the riders as they milled around a narrow section of sand and boulders along the landslide. The bunched animals and men were unable to maneuver as the Hopis came at them with battle axes.

A second assault followed. Arrows from the cliffs again took their toll and riderless horse galloped into the melee. Mingling with the first group, the added horses and men surged in a circle, as if caught in a backwater against the landslide which covered two-thirds of the canyon floor. Many mounted warriors were targets for deadly lances and arrows. The Hopis gained the advantage and surrounded the hapless attackers whose ranks were now badly depleted. Some of the wounded hung onto their horses, going round and round in desperation.

From her viewpoint high on the canyon wall, Honmana made careful use of her strong bow, making each arrow count. As the last of the horemen passed, she noticed the original party had taken refuge in a small recess and over hang at the base of the gorge where the two young Hopis were held hostage. In the opposite direction she observed a war party forming outside the village with one segment already started toward the canyon. Rapidly covering the short distance down a crevice to a ridge where Loloma, Honshoki and several warriors were grouped together in animated conversation, Honmana arrived, excitedly telling about her observations.

"We have been given the opportunity to rescue Aroyo and Naso if we act quickly. Only four of the enemy are holding them."

Honshoki spoke to the group. "Honmana is right. The trail down to the bottom of the canyon will place us in a position to cross over and approach along the wall in a surprise assault. When we have gained release of the captives, we will return to the trail."

Loloma agreed. "In the meantime several of our bowmen will be advised to work their way down the cliff and position themselves to re-inforce you if necessary. Others will delay the approach of the main force with their arrows."

Against the wishes of Honshoki, Honmana followed his men, running to the opposite side of the gorge with them. Creeping along the wall she held her bow with arrow in place, ready for a movement or sighting of the adversaries. Within yards of the opening a warrior stepped out and peered in her direction. He fell forward with an arrow piercing his neck.

In an instant the Hopi team ran forward, meeting the opposition in hand-to-hand combat at the cave entrance, then out on the sandy terrain. Naso and Aroyo seeing Honmana at the opening, dashed to her side.

"Go across to the trail!" The shout came from one of the warriors.

But by then the approaching war party was in sight, deluged with arrows, some of which bounced off the sheer canyon wall. From the cliff trail, warriors led by Loloma swarmed out onto the canyon floor, meeting the rescued Hopis about half-way across. At that moment Honmana fell to the ground, an arrow protruding from her back. Two men urged the two young people on, lifting Honmana from the sand and carrying her to the trail. They continued upward several yards to a small clearing where the two captives had stopped, hidden behind a large boulder. Naso ripped off a section of her manta and applied the cloth to Honmana's wound which bled profusely. Aroyo pondered on whether the arrow should be pulled free.

The warriors returned to the scene of the battle, joining their fellow Hopis who had met the oncoming Navajos head on. Battle axes and clubs were swinging wildly on both sides as the conflict continued. Bowmen ran from the cliffs into the gorge attacking the rear of the enemy warriors and momentarily halting their advance.

A loud shouting rang through the canyon! Having subdued the remaining horsemen, the Hopi warriors led by Big Bear sounded out their battle cries as they came at a run, rounding the bend in the gorge. Charging ahead they met the foe, their weapons smashing and cutting with such force that many of the opposition endeavored to retreat. Bodies of dead and wounded lay in the sand.

Big Bear fought his way to Honshoki's side. "Come, my brother, we must cut through and part the enemy's ranks. This battle has gone long enough. We will finish it although our forces are outnumbered six to one!"

Now joined in their enormous task, the two men fought as if charged by a mythical spirit. Were these gallant fighters the reincarnation of the warrior brothers Pokanghoya and Polongahoya, the grandchildren of Spider Grandmother? They had appeared on numerous occasions over a vast period of time to defend and protect the people under many circumstances. These warrior dieties also had human qualities, teasing their grandmother and engaging in mischievous humor to identify with the people.

With the canyon walls on two sides confining the space to maneuver and their forces split in two, the Navajos fought fiercely. But the renewed ferocity of the Hopis following the example of their two leaders coupled with heavy losses, caused the Navajo warriors to give up the battle in defeat.

Loss of life also occurred among the Hopis who tied the dead warriors on the backs of horses and set out for Black Mesa where the bodies would be buried. This required leaving the gorge and passing the Navajo village which they ignored except to allow the inhabitants to claim their dead at the battle scene and treat their wounded.

Another group of Hopi warriors entered a nearby grove of trees, cutting poles from which litters would be made to carry the wounded who could not walk on their own. Water was obtained for use of Hopi men experienced in herbal medicine and applications to treat various wounds. Honshoki, who had received several slash wounds and abrasions, was among those treated.

Honmana was placed on a litter and carried to the treatment area where the arrow was removed from muscle cords of her back. Aroyo and Naso comforted her, applying bandages as required for the bleeding and healing.

Big Bear and Loloma stopped to check her condition and express words of consolation. The two men then visited Honshoki sitting in the sand with the canyon wall at his back for support. They sat cross-legged on the ground near him as he spoke.

"Some surprise! I did not know the Navajos had horses. Rumors had been received about animals left behind by the Spaniards. In the years since the conquistadores left the region, the horses have multiplied!"

"Our people have shown little interest in the animals. Some of the eastern tribes, Apaches and others, are gaining reputations as excellent horsemen!" Loloma considered his next statement. "We are taking a few for pack animals and several of our warriors are interested in them. The future will tell if horses fit into our life style on the high mesas."

Big Bear thought about his previous discussion with Honmana. "We would have been trampled under their hooves if our warriors had been caught in the open plain as originally planned. That handsome woman, Honmana, did a fine job of convincing me and the others that your scheme of meeting the enemy in the gorge was workable. The foresight of placing our bowmen on the cliffs was the advantage we had to match their superiority in numbers. I will never forget how out of control the mounted warriors became when coming up against the rock slide." He laughed loudly in retrospect. "They are still going round and round in my mind!"

Loloma interrupted. "I cannot be given credit for devising the battle plan. Honmana contrived the scheme in detail. She drew illustrations indicating such knowledge of the terrain and ingenuity in placement and deployment of forces that it was undoubtedly the wisdom of the gods coming through her."

Big Bear responded. "What a gift Honmana has. We can all be thankfull it was imparted to us. We must see that everything is done to bring her back to health and to protect the young ones Naso and Aroyo."

The three men, each a leader, quietly sat thinking about the past, present and future. The battle was over. The mission was accomplished. The memories would linger for years to come.

* * * * * * * *

With each step of the two warriors carrying the litter, Honmana felt searing pain in the area of her back where compresses of herbs and leaves had been bound tightly against her body. Herbal medicinal mixtures applied to the wound in the form of powder, provided an elixir which flowed through her body bringing on a deep sleep and absence of pain. In this quintessential state she envisioned a palatial ballroom. At her side was Pedro de Tovar.

He was attired in full dress uniform with braided gold epaulettes on the shoulders and insignia of his regiment and the national army of New Spain. They were surrounded by beautifully gowned ladies, distinctive government officials and military men.

Don Pedro, who was holding her tightly by the hand with their arms touching in parallel, turned and met Honmana's adoring gaze. "You are breath-taking, my love. Never has such beauty as yours adorned this place with all of its grandeur, gilted walls of red and blue and chandeliers of a thousand candles easily out-shone by your presence. Your gown, blending Spanish and native color and quality, easily commands the center of attraction and attention."

Honmana, moving closer, was radiant. "You are elegant and look very handsome yourself. I am the envy of all the ladies, with such an escort."

"Shall we venture out on the terrace for a breath of fresh air?"

Don Pedro nodded toward a splendid archway flanked by pink marble columns.

Sitting in an ornamental settee built for two, they were encompassd by flowers and shrubs of a terraced garden. The warm night air was soothing. Honmana felt the arms of the man she loved embrace her.

The dream ceased. A jolt, upsetting the smooth sway of the stretcher, brought back reality.

* * * * * * * *

Chapter Fifteen

ROAD OF LIFE

A measure of serenity had entered Aroyo's life. His friend Naso had returned to her aunt's domicile and Paqhua to his parents on First Mesa. As an aftermath to the tribulations encountered in his time spent as a captive and eventually rescued, he began thinking deeply about the Hopi way of life.

Honmana was still bedridden much of the time. Whenever possible her afternoons were spent in the warm, shaded area of the plaza where she rested on several thick mats, padded and raised at one end to provide a partial sitting position. With the passing of her grandmother, she had become matriarch of the Bear Clan. Her aunt Manawya had come to live in the abode and provided needed care.

One pleasant day she observed Aroyo carrying bundles of firewood for the baking oven and called to him. "Our system of clans and matriarchal lineage is sometimes confusing. I want you to know more about your forebears. You, of course were well acquainted with your great grandmother, the matriarch, since we lived here together. Your grandfather, my father, was Nuvamsa a Havasupai. Our home was here until my mother, your grandmother, passed on. Due to circumstances at the time, Nuvamsa returned to the Havasupais who lived in the canyon of the Great River." She then related events that occurred during the occupation of the mesas by the Castillians and her journey as guide to the canyon with the resultant death of her father. She told how her companions had rescued her during the flood and that her son had been born at the time.

Aroyo listened attentively but at the conclusion appeared unusually solemn. "Mother, I would not want you to go through a flood again and I am glad that your companions Quitoya and Yutanuu were there to save you and then bring us both safely to Oraibi. Something I have wished to talk to you about is a subject that Quitoya said is important to all Hopis, the Road of Life. His unfortunate death prevented him from continuing beyond our discussions of our Emergence into the Fourth World." The young man sat alongside his mother who always looked forward to these occasions.

"My son, the journey into successive lower worlds and then into the Fourth World are part of a spiritual path which the Great Sun Spirit created. It is represented by a symbol known as *Tapuat*, mother and child, in which the child emerges from the womb of Mother Earth. The lines in the Creation Symbol form a maze. Mankind must follow the lines and passages within the maze as it represents the Road of Life."

Aroyo seemed mystified but groping for understanding. "How do I know that I am on the Road of Life?"

"You are traveling on one segment now, my son. Our forefathers made it possible as the Creation Symbol reflects the path of evolution leading to the present world in which we live. Purity of mind and being in tune with the Creator are essential in the individual fulfillment of His universal plan. You will feel it inwardly as an initiate in the WuWu Chim ceremony and others when the elders circle the village four times as an indication that it, and we, are part of the earth and the universal plan. The Creation

Symbol carved on a stick of wood is placed on the altar at Walpi in the kiva during the ceremony."

* * * * * * * *

Siki paused in her discourse, as if she, herself, was deeply caught up in the religious significance of her statements. "Much is to be learned before understanding of the whole is forthcoming."

" I have some thought provoking information to add about this. While in Flagstaff, the Northern Arizona University library let me look over their reference books. I made copious notes from these sources." An animated Cindy Michaelson imparted her knowledge, supported by the basic research contained in her notebook.

The Creation or Earth Symbol is known by the Cuna Indians in Panama who describe the cross in the maze as the Tree of Life, shaped by the cord and skin of the embryo when Earth Mother bore her children. To certain other tribes in the Americas much the same meaning is associated with the symbol. Coins of Knossos, Crete dated 200 B.C., have a Minoan Labyrinth identical to the carved image on the wall of Casa Grande Pueblo in Arizona. Other Cretan coins displayed the labyrinth of Daedalies. An Egyptian medallion carries the Osirecon of Menes which predates the Crete coins. This depicts labyrinths of water, entered by boat for the afterlife. Similar religious interpretations have been associated with the symbol and its Tree of Life since its spread all over the world.

Cindy was excited about her inquiry. She looked around the table. "I dwell on this question: are the Hopis related to these far-off people who lived in such diversified environments but share nearly identical religious beliefs pertaining to their creation?

"Here in America, archaeological discoveries dated by carbon-14 tests prove that man has existed here twenty to thirty thousand years. Hopi myths and traditions assert that they came much earlier, not via the Bering Strait, the generally accepted route for all American Indians."

"Cindy, you are really into this. More exists than has yet been uncovered I agree; but what establishes a basis, for example, of previous routes taken by ancient people to this continent? You understand, I am not doubting you." Sam eagerly awaited his wife's answer.

"Oh, that's easy. !" Cindy turned over several pages of her notes, then began to read. "Some of this is in my stale shorthand, so please bear with me. Probably the earliest crossing of the vast ocean separating Asia and America is the description of a voyage to a land beyond the Great Eastern Sea set forth in Shan Hai King written in China and dated 2250 B. C. In it a two thousand mile journey is depicted in various regions of the newly discovered land. It contains accurate geographic presentations of several landmarks now well-known in America; for example, the Grand Canyon, then designated as the Great Luminous Canyon. As with other ancient writings and oral histories, this Chinese classic was looked upon for many years as a mythical narrative. Now it has been declared to be a positive portrayal of the areas visited.

"Kuen 327, completed in the fifth Century A. D. , is another prominent Chinese book relating the experiences of a Buddhist priest, Hwui, and his voyage across the sea to a distant land, Fu-Sang. The land to which he traveled has been identified as Mexico and Yucatan.

"Another question: did people follow to colonize?Were they on the ship? Did their migration bring them here? Did they bring the message of Creation and its symbol, the maze?"

Siki thoroughly enjoyed the discourse. It had been a welcome break in her own narrative. "Obviously only the surface has been scratched in the search for knowledge and information on these subjects. This is very refreshing to me. Cindy, you have made a fine start and should pursue additional sources to find answers to your questions".

She rose and left the room returning in a few minutes accompanied by an Indian girl who carried a tray of assorted cinnamon and other sweet rolls just removed from an oven. Coffee was included.

"It is time to relax and get up and walk around if you wish. You will enjoy this pastry which our young women bake once or twice a week."

"These rolls are delicious. Thank you very much." Cindy sipped at her mug of coffee. "May I say one more thing about the fascinating origins of the Hopis as well as other Indian nationalities in this region extending south through Central America?"

" The oral transmissions of beliefs, myths and customs find common ground among Aztecs and Hopis. A postulation published at London in 1827 tells of the arrival of Mongolians in great numbers on the west coast of America in what is now called Mexico. They came from Tollan, a kingdom in Mongolia which appears frequently in Aztec legends and for which they named the city of Tollan in the new continent. Other sites took names from the the native country as did Anahuac, designating an area embracing a large lake and the present location of Mexico City."

Siki commented. "Worldwide research and translations are now available. In fact, only recently have written languages been developed from the varied native tongues. It might be possible to tie different groups of people together, one to another, in some future time. Our origins do seem to parallel others."

* * * * * * * *

Siki resumed her narrative.

Aroyo and Paqhua exchanged visits to their mesas as often as could be arranged. In their teens, the two boys began to take notice of the maidens who went about their chores barefoot, barelegged and with barearms extending from their woolen mantas. An attractive girl augmented her appearance with powdered corn meal to whiten her face and fashioned her hair with butterfly whorls.

The young people in those days met at formal *ovekniokwi* (picnics), play periods and corn grinding parties. Dances were a regular event for after which groups of boys and girls left together for a leisurely walk along the mesa. Food packets of *somiviki* were provided by the girls and shared with a boy escort when they stopped for a picnic supper. Grinding parties extended later into the evening, brought serious couples together, the young woman being escorted to her home where he stayed with her. In this manner, wedding proceedings were announced.

Aroyo thought only of Naso and sought her out at the various events. After about two years they were ready to be married. Honmana had her hands full at her household. White corn meal, as well as blue corn meal ground by the bride, were placed on trays carried to the bridegroom's residence. The following day, the trays were returned laden with choice ears of corn, as was the custom. After three days at the laborious task, friends of the bride brought in their own gifts of ground maize. The wedding could now go forward.

On the fourth day at dawn, the two families and relatives assembled. Roots of the yucca plant with water added were pounded in separate bowls by the two mothers, resulting in soapy suds. Kneeling before their future mothers-in-law, Naso and Aroyo's heads were washed thoroughly with relatives participating by pouring handfuls of suds over the couple's bowed heads. With much laughter and gaiety, friends rinsed the hair with small vessels of water each had brought for the occasion.

Taking a small quantity of corn meal, the groom and bride went to the edge of the mesa looking east from Oraibi. After touching the corn meal to their lips, they threw the meal toward the rising sun.

Aroyo embraced his bride. "You are now my wife. My love for you soars into the sky. My prayer asks for health and long life."

Naso responded. "You are my husband who I request the Great Spirit to keep safe through our journey of life together. I will love you always."

A wedding breakfast was prepared the next morning. For several days relatives and friends throughout the village removed new cotton from seeds and turned it over to Aroyo who gave it to the men doing spinning and weaving on looms in a kiva. The cotton cloth was woven into a complete trousseau for the bride, consisting of two blankets, one large and one small; a fringed white sash and a pair of moccasins and white leggings made from deer skin. A reed mat was woven in which the blankets would be rolled.

At a feast prepared for the villagers, Naso appeared wearing her bridal finery, then returned to her husband's house. Normally she would have gone to live with her husband in her mother's household. Since both her mother and father were deceased, the lone surviving aunt gave permission for the couple to remain in Aroyo's domicile.

*   *   *   *   *   *   *   *

Four years had passed. Breathing was an effort for Honmana who was now unable to rise from the bed. She welcomed the midday visits, Aroyo and Naso, kneeling at either side. Her old friend Yongo had come from First Mesa with piki bread and other food items prepared for his son Paqhua's forthcoming wedding.

"I am glad we are together this day. The many wonderful experiences we have had in past years keep running through my mind. Living side by side in these dwellings, Quitoya was like a father to you, Aroyo. He has been missed. Yongo, your visits and those of Paqhua have always been welcomed."

"I have something to show you, brought to me early this morning by a woman and man of the village. They had just returned from a visit with Zuni friends at Hawikuh." Honmana reached beneath the bed cover.

"This small courier vessel bears my name. It was found in a collection of miscellaneous items left at Coronado's encampment. Both the general and Captain Tovar's names appear on it.

Yongo took the object, turning it over and closely examining the inscriptions. " It also bears the date Junio - 1540." He twisted the upper and lower sections in an effort to open the jarron, with no success.

"These many years have passed and the long expected message has finally arrived. Captain Tovar was your father, my son, and I am giving this to you. Some day you may find a way to open it. Do not be confused about this knowledge. Find your roots in your own way. Consult the elders and learn all you can." Honmana looked lovingly at her son, daughter-in law and long time friend for several minutes then her eyes closed, peaceably, into eternal sleep.

A few days after the burial and their return from Black Mesa, Aroyo questioned Yongo. "Did you know about this? I mean, that Captain Tovar was my father?"

"While you were still carried in your cradle board, your mother, Quitoya and Yutanuu traveled to Cibola where Coronado's army had headquarters at Hawikuh. Honmana told them that she wished to locate Captain Tovar as you were his son."

"We all know about the conquistadors and that Tovar and his men came to our mesas. I do not understand how my mother knew him."

"You see, Aroyo, Tovar was in charge of the small force of Castillas, some mounted and a few foot soldiers, who appeared at Antelope Mesa one morning. Your mother first met him later at a meeting in Oraibi when the chiefs from all Hopi villages convened to formally meet the Spaniards. Your mother represented the council of elders and chiefs. She presented gifts to the captain on behalf of all Hopis in accordance with specified ceremonials. Within a few days after that event, the Castillas moved their forces to Third Mesa, locating near Oraibi. Captain Tovar was a decent man who did not oppress our people. He and your mother became friends and he was accepted by your grandmother, matriarch of the Bear Clan.

"Was the mission to Cibola successful? Were they able to talk to him? "

"The captain had been dispatched at the head of an army contingent into Sonora in northern New Spain where uprisings of the Indians were underway. The main army had gone on to Tiguex on the Rio Grande, then east to explore a vast country some of which was previously penetrated by a small advance unit. Only a small contingent of soldados remained to close down the encampment. No word was available as to when Tovar would return, although it was apparent that he had been ordered to rejoin the expedition." Yongo could see that Aroyo was endeavoring to sort things out.

"Your mother and her companions went on to Tiguex, still hoping to obtain word of the Captain. It is evident that upon his return to Cibola, your father arranged to send a message enclosed in the jarron. Circumstances at the time caused the courier vessel to be misplaced until it was finally discovered and brought to your mother.

" During their stay at Tiguex, Yutanuu was killed by mounted soldiers who trampled him purposely after accusing him of breaking out of confinement. When it came time to leave Tiguex, I joined your mother and Quitoya. The Spaniards had held me captive for a time after a raid on a pueblo. They released me when convinced I was Hopi and a visitor to the area."

"Thank you for telling me about what was an unsuccessful

search for my father, Captain Tovar. It must have been very tiring for Honmana as I was a small child requiring daily attention and it was a long journey for all."

After Yongo had departed for First Mesa, Aroyo found himself wondering how life would have been with his conquistador father. What were the villages and the people like in his environment in New Spain? Were they happy, successful at farming, or warriors always away at a distant place to fight other people? He rubbed an arm. His skin was a lighter brown than most of his friends, but others on the mesa were darker or lighter and nothing was made of it.

At a cold water spring in the desert or among the large boulders on the mesa rim, Aroyo sat quietly, pondering over the information he had learned about his father, mother and the civilization that existed far to the south. Stories about Spanish friars with their bodyguards of former soldados spread throughout the Pueblo tribes. These were remnants of the great expedition still in existence across the mountains and among the people of the Rio Grande Region. He ultimately reached the conclusion that the Hopi way of life was best.

Thereafter, he felt free to raise a family, two sons and a daughter, and enjoy a happy life with his wife Naso. Ceremonial events were very much a part of their lives. Continuing over the years in the kivas, the elders discussed the Castillians and pondered over the future of the Hopis and what may be in store for them.

Chapter Sixteen

FORAYS FOR GOLD

After a break during which Mark obtained cold drinks for everyone from a vending machine, Siki placed the situation on Tierra Nueva in perspective.

Forty years had passed since the Castillians visited the Moqui (Hopi) towns. Coronado's expedition had faded in importance. However, the frontier of New Spain had pushed northward where rich mines furnished the mother country with revenue and wealth in large quantities of silver, exceeding that previously obtained from regions conquered by Cortes and Pizarro combined. Enterprising entrepreneurs of the frontier led farmers, miners and friars north where they saw new opportunities. A cycle of renewed activity was underway to find and exploit new mines and the region's inhabitants in the search for souls to save and riches to be found.

Frequent expeditions to the north were made after colonization reached the head of the Conchos River in 1580. An expedition by friar Agustin Rodriguez into northern territory was launched from Santa Barbara on the Rio Conchos in 1581. Traveling north, they encountered strong resistance by the Indians and a rescue party led by Antonio d'Espejo arrived too late to save them from annihilation.

The battle was a surprise to Espejo who had previously passed peacefully through many Indian villages on the Rio del Norte. Ascending the river they had discovered a tribe of natives who displayed ornaments and figures decorated with feathers of diversified colors. Their cotton garments were striped blue and white in close similarity to cloth brought from China. Using signs, the Indians indicated that precious metals could be found about five days journey west. This and a persistent story of a lake of gold, influenced Espejo to continue as directed. Proceeding along the Rio del Norte, known in the northern province as Rio Pecos, they journeyed north receiving a welcome among numerous villages.

Having progressed over one hundred-twenty leagues, much of the route through vast groves of Poplar and walnut trees, the expedition reached the province of Tiguex containing sixteen pueblos. Many of the inhabitants fled, since in one of the villages Friars Lopez and Ruyz had been killed. This event had been noted by Espejo as the whereabouts of missing priests was an item on his agenda to investigate.

Taking exploratory trips out of Tiguex, the explorers found indications of mines containing rich ore deposits. In a province called Los Quires on the Rio del Norte, they found several villages containing thousands of occupants. These people worshiped idols and exhibited strange things including a pig in a cage and canopies identical to such structures found in China. The sun, moon and stars were painted on them. Judging from the position and height of the polar star, the captain reckoned their position at 37°, 30', north latitude.

Siki paused. "It is important that you know about the journey of Captain Espejo. It affected the Hopis greatly and indicated what might occur later in the Pueblo country.

"Coronado's expedition traveled the Pacific Coast route through Mexico entering Arizona and the Tierra Nueva region. Espejo journeyed through the mountainous section and rivers of Central

Mexico, entering the province of New Mexico at its south eastern border. Different lands and native Indian settlements were discovered and explored on each course. It is apparent that names of villages and spelling changed in different translations that may be encountered."

"Let me read about Espejo's travels. His discovery of the mountain people who had the earmarks of a Chinese ancestry intrigues me." Cindy rose from her chair, walking around the table to receive the proffered journal Siki held in her hand. "For my part, I am thankful that these documents have been previously translated from Spanish, it would really be a chore to wade through the process of translating. Well, anyway, we can thank Siki for these notes and for the opportunity to share the writings of Antonio de'Espejo."

Ascending the Rio del Norte we arrived at a province called Los Quires, finding five towns and fourteen thousand inhabitants who were idol worshipers. Curious things were seen at this place, such as a pig in a cage and ornamental roof-like forms shaped as those brought from China and painted with displays of the sun, moon and stars.

A succession of villages was found on the northerly course including Ciazia with twenty thousand people and houses painted in divers colors; Ameres Province with seven great towns and thirty thousand souls; Acerna, a great town containing about six thousand persons situated on a high rock having no entrance but by stairs hewn into the rock. The water of this town was kept in cisterns. Mountains in the vicinity showed signs of metals.

At Zuni, which was called Cibola by earlier Spanish explorers, were three Christian Indians left by Coronado in 1540. Our journey continued westward and north which the Zuni people said would lead to a mighty lake on whose banks were many towns and whose inhabitants wore golden earrings and bracelets. On the route a multitude of persons at Zaquato met us presenting many provisions and mantles of cotton.

Forty-five leagues due west in the mountains, mines were located which produced rich metals taken out with our own hands. Two rivers of reasonable size were found and numerous Indian pueblos were in the vicinity.

"Espejo's report of what he saw and the many thousands of people in the region surely indicate a diversity among the various tribes. I am particularly delighted with his China connection to those mountain people. What is merging here is the possibility of ancient colonists from Asia mainland, probably via boat. All I have heard of heretofore is the Bering Strait route then down through the continent from what is now Alaska. Plainly, major differences exist between the North American Indians and those of early heritage in Mexico who moved into the Southwest." Cindy sat with the journal held to her chest.

Siki's narrative continued.

Historical accounts written over the years differ in some details. Hopi legends set forth the problems and trouble forecast by the elders as a result of the Spanish conquest. The greed-inspired search for gold and silver in 1583 brought the Espejo Expedition to Tusayan, the Hopi province remotely located in Tierra Nueva territory. Castillas were again welcomed. The Hopis fed and bivouacked the men and in time honored custom spread cornmeal on the earth for their mounts to walk on. Four Hopi guides were assigned to accompany the contingent on the trip west. A large quantity of supplies was furnished including, cotton mantles in the size of one vara (thirty-three inches), blankets and food items. As anticipated, the Spaniards demanded more than was needed for their own use.

It is said that the expedition found mines containing silver in an area of mountains beyond the Hopi country. On the return trip Espejo bypassed the Hopi mesas going directly to Cibola. Later, they tried to gain admittance to Taos Pueblo but were refused, thereupon heading south on the trail to New Spain.

When Aroyo learned that the Espejo Expedition was quartered at Awatovi collecting supplies, he left immediately to consult with his friend Paqhua.

"This force, although small, can bring nothing but sorrow and misfortune to the Hopis. You have told me of the provisions and material demanded, must we sit back and speculate on their next claim for something they believe is due them? We should get rid of them!"

Paqhua considered his reply. "If it is a peaceful mission as they have implied, to force a war on them would be unwise. The material things they have taken will be replaced by villages on other mesas before winter sets in. Awatovi, being larger, functions as a supply center for smaller communities which may have had bad luck with their harvest. Behind your eyes are unspoken words. Why do you distrust the Castillians?"

"For many years I have listened to the elders in the kivas who have correctly forecast the actions of the Castillas. The list includes destruction of property, taking supplies needed by the people, killing those who disobey soldiers or friars and taking away our religion. All of these things have happened in pueblos at many locations. Now, after many years of isolation, we are in peril." A young man known by Paqhua came into the plaza and joined the two men sitting in a corner of the walled area. Aroyo acknowledged the introduction by Paqhua who stated that the newcomer had been tutored in Spanish language by a Zuni Indian who had served in Coronado's army as an aid to a captain.

The earnest young man, Cinotiva, spoke in low tones. "My companions and I have attended many horses in the corral which was enlarged by extending the fences. Two soldados, one an officer, looked over the caballos and commented that their animals had received excellent care and would be able to carry large packs on their backs when the mines were located and bags of gold and silver were loaded on them. When asked if the Indians at the mine area would give them any trouble, the officer replied, "Any provocative natives will be eliminated."

"Did they say where the mines were located and when they would leave here?" Paqhua was now concerned.

"Nothing was said about leaving, although instructions at the corral about watering and feeding indicate that it will be very soon. The officer said the mines were far off to the west."

Aroyo commented, "The old story of gold and silver mines and natives wearing gold bracelets and other finery is still spurring the Spaniards on. This Espejo group is motivated by greed and dreams of great wealth, which will have nothing but bad results for the people." He thanked the young man for the information.

"I must go now, we have unfinished work to complete." The young man hurried away.

Paqhua peered at Aroyo. "Are you thinking the same as I am?"

"Could it be that your devious mind is forming a plan to spy on the Castillas?" Aroyo could not suppress a wide smile.

Paqhua broke into laughter." Should we start by packing the necessities for an extended trip? We should also be ready to leave on short notice."

The Espejo Expedition was a mixed group of approximately one hundred twenty-five mounted men, foot soldiers, natives and mine workers knowledgeable in metals, ores and their extraction. Traveling west of the Hopi mesas, the assemblage crossed the Rio Colorado Chiquita, upstream before it entered a deep gorge. At this point a camp was established and used for several days.

Aroyo and Paqhua kept at a distance, following the expedition on a dusty trail through the lower Painted Desert. The uneven terrain was laced with cutbanks, coulees, mounds and cliffs cut into acres of red earth. In past ages, winds had teamed with occasional torrents of rain to carve out packets of gray-black earth producing strange shapes. Funnels of ancient volcanoes, lava and eroded table-top mountains stood above rock piles, the discarded side walls of weathered cliffs.

"Without their Hopi guides, Expejo and his gold seekers would be lost. Much of this is like a maze with one barranca leading into a gorge which circles back to another canyon ending in the first one." Paqhua silently recalled the days of their youth when excursions into the region with older men were part of growing up and training in recognizing geological outcroppings used as landmarks. The red soil supported vegetation for animals and birds.

"During our learning years, I do not recall ever encountering people from other tribes in this area west of Third Mesa. It seems to me that if mines do exist, they must be very old and the inhabitants who lived nearby left long ago. Possibly we will be present at a new discovery?" Paqhua, always optimistic, looked at Aroyo to share his enthusiasm.

"I agree with you. My thoughts have been running in the same vein." Aroyo pointed to a flat rock outcropping a few feet up the canyon wall. "Look, the soldados have scratched a large arrow and other markings on the rock. I recognize some Spanish words." Both men stopped to observe the signs.

"The arrow points to the left." Moving out into the center of the gorge, Aroyo called out. "From this point I can see a junction ahead. Some one placed the arrow to mark the route traveled as well as the direction to take. Well, we will also go that way!" Foot and hoof prints bore out the deduction.

As they rounded the corner of the gorge, Aroyo and Paqhua were set upon by two soldados, apparently the rear guard for the main force, who leaped from a ledge on the canyon wall. With bow and quivers filled with arrows strapped across their backs, the two Hopis fell under the weight of their assailants but immediately rolled from under the initial impact. Gaining the upper hand, they pummeled their adversaries, rolling in the sandy earth until able to stand upright. Vicious hand-to-hand combat was underway when the Hopis were hit from behind with clubs wielded by two additional soldiers who, with the help of the others, beat and wrestled Aroyo and Paqhua to the ground.

With hands tied behind and loose leg ropes binding their legs to allow walking, the two were pushed ahead on the trail. The barranca was far behind when the motley group entered a wooded area at the foot of a mountain where the expedition had established camp. Men were all about erecting tents in two rows with space in between as a roadway.

The soldados, striding behind their captives, came close and pulled arrows from the quivers. Each one was broken in two, the arrow head thrown to the earth, the other half replaced in the quiver. Soldados lined the path, laughing at the broken shafts and the two Hopis in pathetic array. They were marched past the tents and on around the base of the mountain about a hundred yards where stood the ruins of a once great pueblo. Part of the auxiliary support men of the expedition were established in tents in this area. High up the slope of the mountain could be seen the dark, open mouths of tunnels, deeply rutted paths and outcroppings of ore and waste from mines. Aroyo and Paqhua observed all of this as they were led to a still standing section of the pueblo next to a walled plaza. They were roughly pushed through the yard and into a cell-like room with two narrow window openings on either side of the door. The heavy wooden door, a makeshift slab, was constructed of half-round planks hewed from dead trees which littered the area. The Spaniards had nailed the pieces together with lateral sections. The whole was placed inside the rock lined doorway and braced with tree limbs.

The captives, peering through the slit-like window openings, could observe sweating soldados stripping off their dirt stained uniforms and washing in water filled basins scooped out years prior from the wide adobe wall. Orderlies brought earthen jugs of water into the plaza from an adjacent spring.

At sunrise the following morning, a tall, stern-faced officer flanked by two soldados and several orderlies entered the court-yard. The officer, a lieutenant in Espejo's small army contingent of ninety plus twenty-four mounted men, ordered the door removed and the two Hopis brought outside. Orderlies pushed them to the wash basins, directing through hand signs that they remove their tunics and clean themselves. Paqhua understood some of the words since his mother, a native of an the Indian tribe in the northern Mexican province of Sonora had spent nearly two years in a food service group attached to the Coronado Expedition. After cleaning themselves, the captives stood at attention.

Amid shouted commands, the Lieutenant called his group to attention as Captain Espejo entered the plaza accompanied by six officers and men. Walking stiffly past the Hopis then returning for a second time, the captain peered intently at the captives.

"They appear to be farmers, not warriors. Where are the soldados who captured them?"

The lieutenant gestured to the four men who stepped forward and stood facing the captain. Espejo spoke.

"Tell me how you captured these forlorn creatures." Paqhua and Aroyo stood proudly, displaying bruised faces, legs and arms, their garments torn and smudged from the encounter and long distance walked under duress.

A spokesman for the group explained in detail how the captives had been sighted far behind the main force, how they were jumped upon and captured after vigorous fighting.

Next, the Lieutenant called for one of the Hopi guides to come forward. The Hopi, showing no flash of recognition, indicated that he was unable to identify the captives.

"Enough of this. We will put these men to work clearing tunnel entrances and digging in the mines. Lieutenant, see that they are provided food and water and that they are under surveillance at all times." Espejo walked from the courtyard. He took two officers to one side. "We can never discern if two men like that are really scouts for a band of Indians. Sentries must be posted and small scouting parties maintained in the perimeter of our encampment at all times."

Later in the day, Aroyo and Paqhua were taken up the mountain where they were ordered to clear rubble and rocks from a mine tunnel. They were watched closely by two guards armed with clubs and sharply honed steel swords. Three days later when men came to wash in the plaza after a day of digging in the old mine tailings and inside the tunnels, the conversation overheard by the Hopis dwelled on ore findings. Veins of silver and gold had been found but the discovery that caused most excitement was that of men digging close to an ancient cistern for holding rainwater. Near its banks gold and silver bracelets, rings, trinkets and ear pieces had been unearthed. Espejo was jubilant, exclaiming that the old persistent stories of people wearing such finery were true. The truth being that inhabitants of the village had worn such ornaments in ancient times, not in the settlements now occupied in the region. The mining experts bagged ore samples from several tunnels and other points in a wide area of the mountain. These would be taken to New Spain where assayers could determine the value of the contents.

The first opportunity for a meeting with the captives came when one of the Hopi guides offered to take food and water to the cell, from which the door was removed for a time each evening. The guide Talowima a resident of Awatovi, had recognized Paqhua.

"Are you and your friend all right? We have learned little of your treatment as the Spaniards are a close-mouthed lot. Of course we have trouble understanding their language as they have the same with ours!" He managed a wide smile which was shared by the captives.

"Our treatment has been adequate and not harmful as might be expected. Water and food are meager but sufficient for our needs. Can you provide a knife to cut our bonds? Occasionally, one of us can slip a hand free With a knife we could sever the leg ropes and make our escape!" Paqhua's countenance formed questions for the guide to answer.

"We too wish to leave these people who are very demanding and always giving orders. They have found which they desire the most and we do not wish to stay with the expedition. We have heard that they plan to go south many leagues from here to the Rio Gila and then to the Zunis. That is more than we bargained for."

Aroyo. "Can you find weapons? We will need them, including bows and quivers of arrows for the journey home after we leave this place."

"A cache of weapons is hidden in the ruins. We have a plan for our escape. A word of warning is necessary. The past few days we have placed branches and matted grass across the wide, gaping hole of a kiva in the *kisonvi*. It is a trap for those who will undoubtedly strive to engage or pursue us." The guide produced a poyo. The hands of the captives had previously been untied for the evening meal. "Take this poyo and cut your leg bindings to be ready for our signal. The plan will proceed when my three companions arrive."

Soldados loitering in the plaza sauntered out to join a food line near the encampment tents. As the guide Talowima emerged from the cell carrying empty food plates, two guards came forward, peered inside to observe the captives, then began to lift the heavy door into position to be secured. On signal, the three Hopi guides emerged from a dooway into the courtyard. With clubs swinging, they knocked the guards to the ground where they remained senseless. The unwieldly wooden door fell over them. Talowima ran into the room where the prisoners had just completed cutting their ropes.

"Go over the wall and run along its length to the first opening around the corner. Go inside and follow a narrow corridor to its end."

Aroyo and Paqhua raced to the end of the plaza and disappeared into the ruins. Waiting in a room at the end of the passageway were the four Hopi guides and a store of weapons. Carrying what was required, the group proceeded as fast as possible through the many halls and rooms of the old pueblo. Obstructing their progress were a litter of stones and mortar from collapsed walls, old wooden beams and roof material fallen in during the many years since the structure had been abandoned. Arriving at small apartment bordering the plaza, they proceeded to the far side and into a space having a window opening from which they could view the yard area. A doorway was located below the viewpoint.

Most of the walls and roofs on the opposite side of the plaza had crumbled providing a direct approach over the rubble to the center courtyard. In a short period, many soldados had gathered below forming columns and awaiting orders.

"This is a critical point in our plan." Talowima leaned forward to talk earnestly with his compatriots. "The Spaniards probably believe only the two captives have escaped. We need to draw them to the plaza. Since only one doorway is available on this side, they would advance directly across to gain entrance."

"The arrows of six men will meet them instead of two!" Aroyo pulled an arrow from his quiver. "Every pull of the bow must send this little fellow to its mark."

"Exactly. We will station ourselves at other windows but remain out of sight. You, Aroyo, and Paqhua go to the doorway and let them see you."

"We will hold a lance high in the air and shout their battle cry, Santiago! "Paqhua grinned, "that will get their attention."

The ploy was successful. Amid shouted orders and cries of "Santiago", the soldados charged over the rubble covered slope. Paqhua and Aroyo picked off the advancing troops one by one as their arrows hit with deadly accuracy. Led by the tall lieutenant, the charge of the soldiers slowed at the remnants of the plaza wall, re-gathering for an assault. Over the top came the lieutenant flanked by his men. Those in the lead were pushed on by the large force behind. In groups of threes and fours the unwary soldados and the lieutenant dropped into the pit of the old kiva. As they rushed toward the doorway, those to either side were now prime targets for the entrenched Hopis shooting arrows from four positions. The arrows struck vital parts causing bodies to pile in front of the opening. Unable to observe the havoc being inflicted on the other side of the wall, men continued to appear and jump into the yard until officers in the melee called for a retreat.

Now came the opportunity for the defending Hopis to carry out the remainder of their escape plan! Checked out in advance by the guides, a veritable obstacle course faced the six men as they scrambled over the debris of centuries making their way to the northwest corner of the ruins. The outside wall contained a window opening allowing one man at a time to crawl through and drop about ten feet to the ground. No sentries could be seen. First out was a guide who first dropped his club and lance to the ground below then backed out through the opening. A second guide was emerging from the window when a sentry appeared shouting *cesacion!* With sword in hand he charged the Hopi who was picking up his lance but was able to thwart the initial thrust of the sword. He wheeled around and plunged the lance into the chest of the soldado. The loud shout of the sentry had been heard by two others who ran to the scene.

A thrown lance grazed the right thigh of Aroyo as he was hanging by his hands just prior to dropping to the surface. Landing in the midst of the fray he joined in, wildly swinging his club. One of the Hopi guides fell from a vicious blow to the neck by the flat side of a sword. Fighting one on one, Aroyo struck the right sword arm of the sentry causing the weapon to drop. Followed by a blow to the head, the man fell, blood spurting from his mouth. Rushing at Aroyo from the side, another soldado from the sentry group lost his balance, falling against the wall where he was impaled on a protruding splinter of wood beam. The remaining sentry was overwhelmed by a guide who jumped upon his back and in the fall to the ground plunged a knife into his stomach.

Meantime, Paqhua, Talowina and the remaining guide dropped from the opening to the outside surface. Seeing blood on the right leg, Paqhua tightly wound a length of cloth over Aroyo's wound. The Hopi guide was revived and given water. Talowima summed up the situation.

"We originally planned to travel through the woods then venture across a ravine to the tree covered mountain beyond which we would not be found. Now it would be most practical to take horses for our escape. The corral is down the slope at a small meadow bordering the trees. Do we agree on this next move?"

Paqhua looked at each of the men. "Considering our options, it is our best chance. The noise emanating from the other end of the ruins indicates most of the contingent is still there. We had better go now ahead of the Spaniards."

"We will approach the building. When you hear the sound of a screech owl, come running!" Talowima left with one of the guides.

Separated into three groups, the Hopis approached the corral from three points keeping hidden among the trees and underbrush. A rough structure of native trees cut into planks formed a lean-to completely walled at one end where saddles, bridles and other gear were stored. Horses moved restlessly in the corral.

At the makeshift building an Indian wrangler came out to greet the Hopis. A Zuni, he had been friendly to the men.

"It is our desire to leave this expedition. We wish to have mounts. Can that be arranged?" Talowima heard movement in the shed.

Looking furtively back at the building the Zuni kept his voice low. "Five soldiers are in the storage area marking their names on saddles, one is a *teniente*. Do you have an order to release the caballos? Why do you wish to leave?"

"No, we do not have such orders, but Captain Espejo has found the gold and silver. We have done our job and do not wish to travel the great distance ahead which is far beyond our mesas." Talowima's explanation was understood by the Zuni.

"I will try to comply with your request, but with one condition. It is also my desire to leave. You must take me along."

"That we will do." Talowima responded.

The wrangler nodded and smiled. "I appreciate this opportunity to return to my home. We will need five mounts. Is that not right? The four of you and myself."

"Actually two additional caballos will be needed. They are for the two Hopis who were captured and are now hiding in the woods with the guides awaiting your answer."

"This is a large request-seven horses. Now I am forced to accompany you since the Spaniards would take their anger out on me. Go over to the gate. I will bring saddles out one at a time." The wrangler entered the shed, soon re-appearing with a saddle and halter which he carried to the gate.

The guides entered the corral and returned with two horses previously fitted with halters. Talowima told the wrangler that bridles were unnecessary.

The Zuni brought two more saddles out to the corral gate area. However, on his return one of the soldados questioned why bridles were not taken.

"That is the request received. All I am doing is complying with it." He removed two more saddles from the racks.

At the door the lieutenant blocked his way. "I overheard your conversation. Only Indians ride without bridles. They rely on the halter, believing that the bit hurts the caballos' mouth. What are you up to?" He turned to his men and ordered one to guard the wrangler. The others accompanied him outside. In the corral he met Talowima and the guide as they returned with two more horses.

"I see these caballos are equipped with halters, saddles are here on the grass, but no bridles."

The teniente drew his sword and with the others advanced toward the two guides. Talowima let out the high pitched call of the screech owl. An answering call from nearby momentarily confused the soldiers giving Talowima and his companion the opportunity to hastily retrieve their weapons which were laying against the corral fence.

Simultaneously, the fugitives among the trees raced into view, lances held high. Inside the shed the Zuni plunged a knife into the guard upon hearing the screech of the owl. Saddles in hand, he brought them on the run to the gate.

A huge, black cloud had gathered overhead, casting a deep shadow over the corral area. The Spaniards re-grouped and started toward the Hopis when a loud crack of thunder rumbled across the sky. Seconds later a bright blue light bathed the area as a bolt of lightning smashed into the ground where the soldados stood. When the cloud cleared and normal light returned, nothing but dark, burned smudges could be seen on the earth. A period of time elapsed before the Hopis realized what had happened. Neither the animals or any persons other than the Spaniards were touched by the dazzling display which had left its mark.

Hearing shrieks and shouts coming from the camp and pueblo areas, the fugitives lifted fence rails to allow the remaining horses to run in a wild stampede toward the oncoming soldados. The expedition forces scattered into the woods. Some were trampled, unsuccessful in their scramble to safety.

Later that evening, many leagues distant, the six Hopis and lone Zuni stopped to rest at a cool, fresh water spring with sufficient grass nearby to graze the horses.

"Masauwu, the Great Spirit of Fire and Death, was with us today." Aroyo spoke quietly, "These mountains are the home of many Kachinas and dieties whose spirits know what Hopis are doing and come to aid them in time of need. Our legends speak of Masauwu who even now appears among us at times. We will tell the elders in the kivas so they will know that the Great Spirit is still our guardian." Each man lowered his head, immersed in his own thoughts. The Zuni understood, as he too bowed his head.

PART THREE

Chapter Seventeen

INSIDIOUS INTRUSION

Siki summarized. The families had grown; Aroyo with two boys and a daughter, Paqhua having a daughter and a son. In many ways they were as one large family, sharing exploits of the young people, participating in kiva initiation and ceremonies. It was a relatively peaceful time in their lives. An occasional religious visitor from New Spain was reported in other sections of Tierra Nueva but the Hopis were stubborn and independent in their religion. To the Spaniards they maintained a passive resistance. Chumuscado, who had followed Antonio d'Espejo with a small party, made no inroads. The Hopis secluded themselves within ancient boundaries on the mesas with Mountain Utes to the north some distance, the Navajos closer to the north and northeast, Apaches pillaging and ravaging in the south and Comanches of the Great Plains menacing traditional borders among the pueblos to the east.

* * * * * * * *

Far to the south at Mexico City in 1595, Juan de Onate exerted the influence of himself and others in obtaining a contract giving him the right of conquest and settlement of New Mexico province. Three years later in 1598 he had gathered a sizable expedition equipped for colonization of the pueblo country. Included were a group of Franciscan Friars, one hundred thirty soldiers, many accompanied by their families for purposes of settling the country, and seven thousand head of cattle sheep and horses. Onate was successful in obtaining the submission of several pueblos by performing extravagant ceremonies honoring the chiefs and other principals in the Indian communities. This program continued through much of the Rio Grande region resulting in the declaration of Spanish sovereignty over the whole territory extending from the Rio Colorado to the Great Plains and regions yet unexplored to the north.

The Hopis were not excluded. Onate, with his large military force and company, arrived in November, 1598. He met chiefs and elders at the larger villages on the mesas and in parting left gifts of sheep in large numbers and a few head of cattle. Formal submission in the name of the king of Spain was received. None of the friars stayed behind to begin missionary work but left with the captain's entourage. Such was the Hopi's determination to retain their ceremonial ancient myths and deeply rooted religion controlling all aspects of their way of life.

As in past planning, legends of vast riches in the northern regions persisted, placing gold and silver discoveries as prime objectives in any expedition. Onate was no exception. He dispatched Captain Marcos de Farfan to locate mines in the mountains west of the Hopis which Espejo had discovered years earlier. As a result of finding veins of many different colors, a variety of minerals was suspected. Captain Farfan obtained many ore samples which were deposited in bags and taken to New Spain for assaying. Through other sources, probably the Zunis, the Hopis learned that a good showing of silver had been reported.

Elders felt that the worst possible disasters would be forthcoming as a result of the continued intrusion by the Spaniards, the development of mines in ancient sacred mountains and the influx of friars in other sections of pueblo country.

"Through manipulation as well as a positive performance in dealing with native tribes, Don Juan Onate accomplished a great deal in laying the groundwork for colonization and government." Siki produced a bound volume.

"This contains examples of information and testimonial records maintained by Onate during 1598. His exploits included involvement in the Hopi region. Sam would you please read the pages marked?"

"Of course I will, Siki. We appreciate your giving us a full meaaure of Hopi legends, myths and the more recent history written by those who participated. This part was evidently written by Captain Farfan."

Marcos Farfan de los Godos, captain of the guard and cavalry, appeared before the governor (Onate) on December 11, 1598. He stated that he and eight companions had journeyed from the province of Mohoqui (Hopi) by order of his lordship in November of this year. Traveling six leagues west over a sandy and woodless region they stopped overnight at a place having a small spring. Water was plentiful for the men but not enough for the horses. After proceeding about three leagues the next day, they reached a river flowing northward (Little Colorado). Sparse pasture was available but water was plentiful with cottonwoods lining the river banks. A westward direction was maintained for three days with certain camp sites providing scant water and one containing a large, deep pool among pine trees on the slopes of a sierra. Snow was encountered as they progressed along the mountains where they were forced to stay over night without water.

With horses unsaddled and guards posted, two of the Indian guides indicated they knew of a spring nearby and wished to fill gourds and return with the water. Officer Farfan, thinking that they might run away, refused permission unless a trustworthy person accompanied them. Thus Captain Alonzo de Quesada went along requiring the guides to walk ahead of him. After a short distance they were surrounded by natives armed with spears and bows, identified as Jamanas Indians. They then walked into a settlement of several rancherias. The Captain reassured the group and two Chiefs that they were friendly and would do them no harm. He gave them beads and other presents, advising them that they sought the location of ore deposits or mines and wished their help. The journey was renewed with directions given by tribal representatives.

ATTESTATION - The mines were discovered. Captain Marcos Farlan de la Godos reported the events of his journey at the pueblo of Cibola, called Zuni by the natives, December 11, 1598. Testimony was taken from the Governor, Captain of the Guard and his eight companions who declared under oath what they had discovered. Ordered and signed by: Don Juan Onate, Governor and Juan Velarde, secretary.

Cindy Michaelson questioned Siki. "How did the submission of the Hopis to the Spanish regime affect the children of Aroyo and Paqhua? It must have been a time of stress for them with the input of conflicting ideology."

"The isolation of our mesas and villages kept the Spaniards from forcing their governing methods upon us as occurred at Santa

Fe and some pueblos in that section. Thus no changes were visible
to our young people and the affect of rumors and hearsay probably
had little impact.

"Captain Onate, however, gained success in establishing early
stages of colonial administration in the Province of New Mexico.
Authority over military and civil concerns was rigidly adhered to
by a captain general and provincial governor located at Santa Fe,
then a small outpost on the overland trail. In large independent
pueblos the office of governor and *cacique* were elected by the
inhabitants. A long list of lesser Spanish officials was appointed
by the provincial governor. In smaller pueblos and villages an
alcalde mayor supervised political as well as judicial matters. Friars
were installed initially in large pueblos to rule on religious
concerns and spread the faith. Missionary activity was eventually
carried to most pueblo communities."

* * * * * * * *

Our young people now had new chores tied into the tending
of stock animals. The list spread as tribal members became herders
of sheep and interested in raising chickens, hogs and cows. The
men, at the time, became expert at weaving wool blankets and
cotton cloth. The girls and women enjoyed the warm woolen
garments in the cold season and colorful apparel year-round. In
addition to animals, the Spanish introduced food plants. Acreage
adjacent to pueblos was utilized for new crops and the live stock
where possible but the requirement for additional land brought on
the development of new fields around the mesas and sometimes
several leagues distant where soil and water were adequate.

Aroyo gathered his family together to help in making a decision. "As you have observed, the mainstays of our diet, maize and cornmeal, are being supplemented by various melons, squash, root plants and other things. We can have this food in necessary quantities if we work hard to prepare the soil, plant the seeds and tend the growing sprouts through harvest time."

The oldest son spoke. "Since we must continue to grow our maize and corn, the extra work would not be excessive and the new food to eat would surely be worth the effort!"

"Paqhua, Pluma and your mother and I have discussed this matter and we believe that our two families, growing and sharing different crops, can accomplish fine results. Do you wish to say more about this project? We want to have everyone satisfied and happy about it before deciding. A section of land suitable for our needs is located south of here about two or three leagues distant."

One by one the family agreed that the plan was workable and since all enjoyed the friendship with Paqhua's family, they looked forward to getting started.

"I have another subject which I wish to share with you." Looking from one to another, Aroyo related the story of his journey through the land of Cibola as a small child strapped to a cradleboard carried on his mother's back. The participation by Honmana's two friends of many years who accompanied her on the quest to locate Captain Tovar of the Coronado Expedition was described in detail.

"These of course, are not ancient legends but family events so that you will know more about your roots. Captain Tovar was your grandfather. He was my father who I never knew."

Aroyo reached into his garment and produced the jarron. "Many years passed before this courier vessel was located in Cibola and delivered by friends to Honmana. She died before it could be opened." The children inspected the jarron intently as it was passed around. He placed it in the hands of his maana.

"Nainoma, I want you to have this. One day in the future you will discover the secret of opening it and read whatever message it contains. It is right that the urn be yours as the day will come, undoubtedly, when you will become matriarch of the Bear Clan and will cherish the meaning of its contents."

"Thank you father. I will keep it safe for our family. The knowledge we have gained today is a great comfort to me, and my brother as well."

"Moreover, my maana, you are the image of Honmana, with her grace and beauty. May the spirits give you a happy, full life and the love of your family now and in the future."

Nainoma went to her room and removed Honmana's favorite Kachina figure from its niche. The setting sun was a fiery ball dropping into the distant mountains as she stood at the wall of the household plaza situated on the outer rim of the mesa. She clutched the jarron and doll tightly, praying to the Great Sun Spirit for a long life and revelation of the contents of the vessel.

Wearing a blue manta and white deerskin leggings, her lightly tanned skin and long black hair bathed in the orange and red rays, Nainoma noted the flight of two large birds. They were silhouetted across the fading portrait of the Great Sun Spirit.

ODYSSEY OF THE EAGLE

Restless, Nainoma went to her room, attaching prayer feathers to the jarron and *kwaahu* kachina figure. Lying in bed, her mind was in a turmoil, with sleep finally bringing calm. However, sleep also brought dreams as she became *Nuvakwaahu* soaring in the sky and racing the sun to avoid the darkness of night. The eagle turned southwest and soon spotted white cliffs below, which, against the dark terrain, beckoned as a resting place. Early morning revealed a clear, placid pool of azure water at the base of the white rock fall. Green foliage and flowering plants encircled the basin providing a pristine locale for a refreshing dip and pruning of feathers.

Above the sheer, rock cliffs boxing the miniature canyon, bright shafts from the sun lighted the glowing rim in contrast to the shadowy gloom below. Desiring to bask in the warm sun and appraise the surroundings, Nuvakwaahu soared skyward circling high above the crags of a volcanic ridge jutting upward in a rugged line as far as the eye could see. It was the ancient Mogollon Rim, extending southward for hundreds of miles to form the boundary of a forested plateau.

As the flight continued, a panorama of deep ravines colored red, white, brown and gray, stretched out below. Many contained sparkling lakes of crystal and emerald cradled in their bosoms. In several large canyons flat-topped mesas, covered with deep canopies of green, loomed in vivid contrast to the singed cliffs which seemed to encircle them.

The powerful wings of the snow eagle, flying high in the sky, stretched out into a glide providing an overview of a large pueblo of ancient times. Villages settled in more recent years dotted the land scape. Somehow, Nainoma knew the old ruins were that of Casa Grande, inhabited centuries prior by a band of Aztecs who had migrated north from the City of the Lake, center of Aztec culture.

Questions arose in Nainoma's sleepless mind. "Were these people actually Hopis returning from their ancient migrations encompassing the continent? Ancestral buildings and villages atop the mesas of the Hopis had structural similarities. The measurements of housing units were identical in the height, width and design of windows and door openings!"

Imprinted on her mind were emblems, artistic pottery designs and ceremonies all of which had much in common. The flight abruptly came to an end at a small pool of fresh water inside a plaza surrounded by crumbling walls. Somehow the area looked familiar.

A picture of human sacrifice flashed across her mind. "Was that the reason for breaking away from the central authority of the Aztecs? Blood coursing through my veins could be rooted in these people. I wonder. But my immediate forebears provided the blood, a life stream necessary to all humans and animals. What mystery holds the secret of transmission of look alikes and familiar characteristics from generation to generation? I must not dwell on such things. My quest is pointed in one direction-to locate Captain Tovar, my grandfather."

A long flight revealed the Rio Gila then the Rio Colorado Chiquita and trail traveled by Honmana and Aroyo to Hawikuh, the Zuni village first encountered by the original Spanish expedition into Pueblo land. Flags flew from masts rising from a white structure, apparently headquarters for a Spanish governmental unit. The eagle swooped down passing over a courtyard where men in the robes of friars could be seen conversing with Indians and Spaniards, then flew to a high tree to perch, casting a wary eye over the nearby terrain.

A second eagle, Kwaahu, appeared coming from high in the sky and settling in the tree close to Nuvakwaahu. "So many thoughts from different sources are filling your mind. They are causing mix-ups in the route you must follow to reach your objective. Let me guide you."

"It would be a great help, but how can you do that?" The snow eagle was tired but appreciative of the offer.

"Your destination is south and somewhat to the west where the great ocean can be seen. When night falls, the constellation *Kwidi* will appear. Its group of three little eyes and a bright star forming a point directed at Mother Earth comprise a complex tool for navigation. We will remember the position of the bright star and go in that direction by day."

In her bed, Nainoma knew that a kachina spirit had come to guide her in the right direction. She sub-consciously grasped the kachina doll and held it tightly.

Rio Sonora was a welcome sight after a long flight over desolate terrain. It was the Despoblado, cut with deep barrancas and inhabited by the still unruly Indians of northern Mexico who had harassed and killed couriers and soldados moving north and south on the old route of Coronado. At Corozones, near the river, the two magnificent eagles came down in a wooded area from which Nainoma emerged dressed in the attire of the local maidens.

Her garment was in two pieces, the upper a white blouse with bright floral patterns and puffed at the shoulder with wide sleeves to the elbow. A full skirt of dark blue and white designs reached below the knee. Short white stockings and black moccasin-type shoes completed the clothing. Entering a white, well-kept building flying the flag of New Spain, Nainoma approached a male receptionist in the outer office of the Acalde Mayor. The young man expressed some surprise at this beautiful woman, standing straight and tall with an undisputable air of authority.

"Please tell me where I can locate Captain Tovar. He was located here many years ago."

"We have no Captain Tovar in our current lists, however, one of the military men may be able to help you." Nainoma was escorted through a hallway to the room of an officer where the clerk explained the purpose of the young woman's visit and departed.

The white haired, distinguished looking man peered quizzically at Nainoma. "Please be seated. Many years have passed since we have had an inquiry about Captain Tovar. In earlier days, long before this building was constructed or many people lived in Corazones, I served with a Captain Pedro de Tovar who was Ensign in a large military expedition. We explored the pueblo country many leagues to the north."

"Was Captain Tovar with you when the expedition returned? Where is he now?"

"Now slow down young lady. Let's take one question at a time." The officer readjusted his position in the chair. "We were separated several times during the two years on duty. He was dispatched, as were several others, on special assignments throughout the vast area. When the main force came together for the march back to New Spain we enjoyed exchanging stories about the journey. After the army disbanded Captain Tovar took the post of Alcalde Mayor in Culiacan." The officer rose from his chair. When he turned to approach Nainoma she had vanished. He went to the door way and peered into the hall. No one was in sight. With a sigh and expression of bewilderment, he returned to his desk.

THE FLIGHT TO CULIACAN

From Corazones high in the mountains to the continent's shoreline, the eagles encountered strong wind currents. "Are these the Santa Anna winds-one of the Pacific Ocean's special events? What are all those ships doing on the west shore of Mexico? Had they sailed on the demon winds all the way from China? Is Mongol blood dictating my thoughts? No, it must be my imagination, those are probably regular trade ships plying the waters to Spanish ports!" Through the eyes of the snow eagle, Nainoma's mind was in a turmoil.

The upward sweep of the winds caused the eagles to soar to new heights above the rugged coastal mountains to the east of the city below. Maneuvering down into deep canyons, they skimmed the tops of towering conifers rising in groves along the coastward ridge. The appearance of many wood and stone structures at the outskirts of the community influenced them to rise high in the sky for a better view.

"What are those puffs of smoke coming from groups of people down below?" Zip, zip, the airborne sounds of fired muskets and iron balls shooting by, too close for comfort, were new to the eagles, Nainoma and the kachina. They had heard about the arquebus, a small portable firearm supported for firing by a hook. These hand-held fire pieces were a new discovery.

After a few maneuvers, they were out of range of the sharpshooters. Kachina Kwaahu indicated that here was the destination they sought.

Nainoma looked upon the ocean as a sparkling jewel, with water enough to satisfy the whole pueblo country. As far as she could see along the coast line, trees and shrubbery provided a green mantle to the extent never seen in the desert areas. Yet explorers came from this country looking for riches and a place to establish colonies in her native mesa lands For a time in their migrations, her ancient forebears had lived and farmed in a lush green land blessed with rich soil and water. "Was this that land?" This was a puzzle she knew might never be solved.

Culiacan, founded in 1531 by Nuno de Guzman a conquistador formerly with Cortez, was a busy city with many large buildings and wide streets. The eagles flew to a central plaza near a multi-storied structure bearing a large bronze emblem over the entrance - the great seal of the government of Mexico.

Nainoma appeared in Hopi dress, a manta type garment of white cotton bare on the right shoulder; a beautifully marked light blue sash at her midsection. White leggings and moccasins of bleached deer skin completed her attire. Two long braids of shining black hair fell over the shoulders and front of her manta. Kwaahu, in traditional garb, stood beside her.

The spacious quarters of the municipality and military were of old Spanish design. High archways separated large rooms whose ceilings were decorated in bright red, yellow, blue and green combinations with bands of gold running from corners to mid-points of the domed overhead. Gold and silver candelabras provided the light of two hundred candles.

In the center of the *vestibulo* was a duplicate of the governmental seal brilliantly colored by inlaid tiles placed on the floor. An ethereal presence seemed to permeate the atmosphere of the adjoining room. It's domed ceiling contained panels of stained glass allowing shafts of light of various colors to beam down on the walls. Next to the entrance archway a large copper hued placque was mounted on a wall. Kwaahu and Nainoma looked up at the names listed under the heading:

HONOR ROLL — CITY OF CULIACAN
Nuno de Guzman founder - 1531

Hernandez Cortez	Tristan de Luna Arellano
Melchoir Diaz	Pedro de Tovar
Pedro de Castaneda	Francisco Vasquez de Coronado
Hernando de Alvarado	Garcia Lopez de Cardenas

"Captain Tovar had a prominent position as Alcalde Mayor. We will not see him as he must be deceased. Step over to the next panel. It will reveal something to you." Kwaahu moved a few steps and peered upward at a portrait of a young male castillian dressed in the metal armor and helmet of a conquistador. Nainoma followed.

Silent for what seemed to be several minutes, she spoke softly. "The name on the brass plate is Pedro de Tovar, my grandfather." Tears streamed down her cheeks. Kwaahu tried to console her. She regained her composure.

"Much of his countenance and bearing are in Aroyo, my father.

It is unfortunate that fate chose to separate Captain Tovar and Honmana. He tried several times, as did my grandmother, to communicate but it was not to be. He would be in his late seventies if he were still living."

Several other portraits were scrutinized closely as if every detail must be memorized. It was improbable that this journey would ever be repeated and Nainoma would want to relate certain descriptions to her family.

They returned to the portrait of Captain Tovar. A young man came forward. "The captain earned much recognition as a conquistador, our Alcalde Mayor and other important positions. Do you wish to see someone in this building?" He addressed Nainoma, the Kachina spirit Kwaahu was invisible to him.

"I do not wish to see anyone in particular but more information about the captain would be interesting to me."

"It is my good fortune to have recently reviewed our archives and investigated his records. Would you please come to my work place where we can discuss the material available?"

At the archive work room Nainoma made known her request. "Did Captain Tovar leave a diary or any manuscripts he had written? I am interested in his life and career."

"We do not know of manuscripts. He did, however, have a record of events and exploits in the expedition of 1540. He gave those papers to Pedro de Castaneda who produced a history of the expedition. Castaneda based much of his writings in his journals on Captain Tovar's material and others as well."

"Did the captain share in the credit for the chronicles?"

"No, I am afraid not. You see, much of the work done by Castaneda occurred some thirty to forty years after the expedition."

"Are any of Captain Tovar's original papers available?"

"It is unlikely that the papers will turn up. As researchers, we of course, hope that they will, sometime."

"Why was such a delay allowed? The exploration of the region north of New Spain would have been helpful to map makers and others who would be in a position to conduct additional excursions into the area."

"Undoubtedly the information was kept secret due to politics. You see, other nations were planning to send expeditions to the new world, including France, Portugal and Great Britain. According to reports, parts of the most northern region of the Pacific coast had already been colonized by the Russians.

"May I introduce myself, Diego de Alarcon. Culiacan is my home. I was born here." As he gallantly bowed, Nainoma took note of his excellent manners, demeanor and finely formed features. His skin color, bigote and apparel indicated a Castillian background much like that of Captain Tovar.

"It is my pleasure to meet you." Nainoma smiled discreetly.

"Where do you come from. I do not believe that I have ever met such a beautiful native girl and one so handsomely dressed." A slight stammer entered the young man's speech and a ruddy color blushed his cheeks.

"Hopinunu are my people." Nainoma smiled at his confusion as she responded." Our villages are located atop high mesas in the Painted Desert region of Tierra Nueva. We are called Hopi."

"Do you have Spanish settlers in your area? One of Coronado's objectives was the discovery of suitable land to colonize."

"Our mesas were visited by the conquistadors but no one stayed. Others, such as Espejo and Onate with their followers, came later looking for gold and silver. Their visions of riches took them west to the mountains fully stocked with food and supplies that we gave them. No word has since been received from the Spaniards nor have we seen them since."

Diego produced a map of Tierra Nueva drawn and dated 1558 which he spread on a large table. Nainoma, who had been sitting at the opposite side, responded to his request that she stand alongside and help him hold down corners while they perused the parchment. Her parents, along with friend Pluma, had tutored her in Spanish, a vocabulary limited to words transmitted from the time of Tovar and Honmana and subsequent additions. As in their legends and ceremonials, no written words were available since such communication had not existed.

"This is your homeland?" Diego pointed to the sketched mesas on which names of Hopi villages had been printed.

"My village is Oraibi on Third Mesa. Captain Tovar and his small group of soldados and horsemen discovered us at Awatovi on Antelope Mesa. Together they traced the explorers routes to the Great Canyon, Rio Firebrand and San Francisco Mountains.

Alarcon walked to stacks of wooden shelves containing manuscripts, notes, diaries and memoranda credited to various individual sources or chronicles. "This space contains just about everything available pertaining to the Coronado Expedition. Other sections in this building have material and histories of other events which occurred during the period the King of Spain dispatched his conquistadors, troops and explorers to the new continent separating the Atlantic and Pacific oceans."

Nainoma was impressed. "So much is available to learn about the people, terrain and differences of the various regions whose boundaries are shown on the map. As Hopis, we are an insignificant dot or two on this vast area." She laughed. Until this map had provided somewhat of a picture of Tierra Nueva and Mexico, she had not really comprehended the relationships and problems facing any move or attempt to bring different cultures together.

"I do not agree with your statement that Hopis are insignificant. Your nation has played a large and fascinating role in the seemingly slow but illuminating discoveries made by the explorers! For example, after receiving Captain Tovar's reports of a mighty river to the north, the general dispatched Don Garcia Lopez de Cardenas who saw the large river and the Great Canyon which made the channel appear as a shining thread a thousand feet below. The chronicler for that journey was Geronimo Merado de Sotomayer who had been appointed official historian for the Coronado Expedition and was one of the discoverers of the canyon. His report of that event has not been found but was certainly included in the details assembled by Castaneda. Some information contained in the various historical writings were undoubtedly based on reports of soldados, Friars and native interpreters. The appointed chroniclers could not have been at all locations reached by the main expedition and smaller excursions undertaken.

"This might particularly be true of an auxiliary expedition exploring the Pacific coast in an effort to find a waterway inland. Supplies were on board the ships for use of Coronado and his large entourage. I must back up somewhat to tell you that Cortes, the conqueror of New Spain, dispatched a fleet of three ships loaded with immense cargoes at Aculpulco to explore the northern waters of Mexico's coast line. In the year 1539, one year prior to the launching of the Coronado Expedition which left Culiacan in 1540, a relative of Cortes, Francisco de Ulloa, sailed past the peninsula of California to the head of the bay which he named Gulf of Cortes. There he found the tide plains and channel of a large river. Later reports indicate that Cortes wanted this knowledge so that he could send an expedition on that route to find the Seven Cities of Gold. He was at odds with Viceroy Mendoza who had placed his support with Coronado. Without penetrating the river further, Ulloa returned through the gulf, rounded the peninsula and sailed north for exploration in that direction.

Her interest heightened, Nainoma offered her thoughts. "The Seven Cities of Gold were either the Hopis or that of Cibola in Zuni country which also was comprised of seven cities. The Castillians found both groups but not the riches as expected in the overland routes."

"Yes, that is true. However, the supply and support contingent needed by Coronado were sent into the Bay of Cortes, led by Hernando de Alarcon, in an effort to find a water passage inland. Whether Ulloa's discovery of the river had been divulged or kept secret was unheeded. The land party of the expedition was on the march northward from Culiacan and Viceroy Mendoza gave the order for the fleet to sail as agreed to previously with General Coronado."

Nainoma traced a finger over the map." Designated here on the map as Rio Colorado, that river was known by the Indians as the River of the Firebrands, or simply Firebrand River. The Great Canyon and river discovery by Cardenas is part of my family's history record. My grandmother was one of four Hopi guides who accompanied the Cardenas expedition. Her father was Havusupai, a tribe living on the floor of the canyon many leagues downstream.

"That is most interesting. You see, my grandfather was Hernando de Alarcon, captain of the ship which sailed to the mouth of the Firebrand River as part of Coronado's auxiliary expedition by sea. One wonders if these seafarers had been able to proceed farther, a meeting might have taken place involving our forebears!" Diego was visibly exited.

"The accounts of the voyage indicate that the Firebrand was named Buena Guia by my grandfather. It means unfailing guide."

"Did the river guide your grandfather to Cibola? What happened to the cargo of supplies so badly needed by the army? It is more than likely that a contingent was formed to march into the desert from the river in the usual greedy search for gold."

Diego bristled at this insinuation. "These were honorable men. They would not have left the ships and turned the supplies to their own use!"

"Are you evading the issue? It is no wonder to me that the supplies were side tracked from their destination." Nainoma was indignant.

Sensing that a direct and complete response was needed, Diego replied in a normal tone. "Rising and ebbing tides nearly swamped the *buque veleros* but they were able to sail into the very mouth of the river and drop anchor a short distance upstream. With the help of friendly Indians, small craft loaded with supplies were towed by ropes from shore against the strong current about fifteen leagues. Two attempts were made in a strenuous effort to proceed. However, after the men hearing about the possibility of hostile tribes in the area protested going further with such a small force, the decision was made to return downstream to the ships, which had been left under the guard of a few men. Captain Alarcon was dismayed by the failure of their desperate attempts and the realization he would not reach Cibolo and the main army."

Reassured by Diego's reaction and explanation, Nainoma was both excited and pleased. "When two individuals review history together it is probably uncommon to make connections as we have. The manuscripts provide proof in writing of events crossing the paths and lives of people widely separated. Since you have access to all of this, I suggest that you write a history in book form for others to become informed."

"That thought has entered my mind. I am grateful to you for thinking that I might have the hidden talent required to accomplish such an under taking. Now, would you like to learn more about the so-called auxiliary expedition?"

"Please continue. As a desert land, mesa dweller everything about the sea is new and interesting to me." Nainoma peered directly into Diego's eyes. The now familiar blush appeared!

"Mendoza's fleet arrived from ship building facilities in Guatemala under the command of Pedro de Alvarado. Augmenting the first voyage of two buques to the Bay of Cortes, the mission of these vessels was exploration of the outer coastline to the north. They would endeavor to ascertain any information about Coronado and others in the field. At the upper end of the peninsula Juan Rodriguez Cabrillo, an accomplished navigator, disembarked to find Indians on shore who through signs indicated they knew of bearded white men with Spanish weapons about five days' journey inland. Cabrillo and his chief pilot Bortolome Ferrelo, accomplished excellent results. Sailing further along the shore line they discovered San Diego Bay. Indians of the area imitated horse men by doing a dance and were able to describe Spaniards seen inland."

"Did the ship's personnel confine themselves to the ship or did they all go ashore for exploratory trips?"

"In most locations it is probable that the ship had to be anchored off shore with the captain and a few men taking a small boat in to look about the place. While at a group of islands further north, Cabrillo went to the mainland and took formal possession in the name of the King of Spain as was also done on an island they named San Miguel. Cabrillo was stricken and died there.

"Command was taken over by Ferrelo who sailed much further north to a latitude of about forty-five degrees. The coastline was mapped as accurately as possible indicating coves, harbors and capes along the entire coast covered. The exceptional results of these explorations were indeed a consequence of Coronado's quest. Of interest was the expansion of exploration to the high seas when several ships of Villa lobos sailed across the Pacific Ocean reaching the Phillipine Islands. Our staff is scrutinizing various reports of the voyage to learn more about the natives and that part of the world!"

Nainoma thought about the jarron. "It is apparent that communications to and from the Expedition were not easily established. Messengers must surely have been waylayed in their travels through hostile territory. The courier system Mexico City and seaports to Tierra Nueva intrigues me. How did they accomplish this and keep certain documents secret?"

"Come with me to another area where many artifacts and other items are stored." Diego described and explained certain articles as they passed shelves and bins of Indian relics, seagoing gear, compasses, pieces of armor and weapons collected over the years. At the end of the storeroom a flight of steps led underground to a vault. Taking a large key from a pocket, Diego unlocked a heavy metal door which swung open on squeaking, rusty hinges. Shelves of gold and silver goblets, dinner ware and sculptured objects came into view when Diego lighted an extra lamp he carried. The interior reeked with an old, musty smell.

The cold dampness caused Nainoma to shiver as she examined a pile of miscellaneous items including a batch of jarrons of various shapes and sizes. Handling some of the vessels, Diego described their use.

"This long cylindrical metal object provides a tube-like space for such things as maps and messages of large size. The end sections screw on or snap into place. The smaller jarron usually has a flat end or partial pedestal design and opens near the center."

"Can you open the one you have in your hand? A special method of locking must have been provided, otherwise the message inside could easily fall into the wrong hands." Nainoma was eager to learn the secret of opening the vessel.

"You are right about that." Diego grasped the object with both hands. "Usually a twist of the hands and some tapping of the metal will open it. This one must have a step-lock which requires a twist, stopping at a certain position. At that point the halves are pulled and twisted allowing a lever inside to step into a groove. Another twisting motion releases the lock and the jarron opens. They are called courier jarrons and are equipped with one of several intricate mechanisms.

"Captain Tovar commanded a contingent ordered to Sonora Province in northern Mexico to quell an Indian uprising interfering with couriers. For a time, the record shows that messengers were accompanied north and south through the area by soldados. Undoubtedly, other routes had problems too."

Nainoma was persistent." Among all of the different sizes and shapes, how can you recognize a jarron having a certain lock combination?"

"At the time of manufacture, a code number is engraved at one end. See, the number appears here." Diego held the urn to the light. "Certain officers of the government, for example Viceroy Mendoza, were given a list of code numbers and instructions on how to use them. Couriers in some cases delivered a jarron carrying a number known only to the sender and recipient. The system worked well since death penalties applied to those who would wrongfully open tamper with the device."

"We have a courier jarron in our possession but are unable to open it. Can you give me a list of numbers and instructions for opening?" The request might be impertinent, she knew, but Nainoma felt it necessary to come to a conclusion.

Diego looked at her quizzically. "Even here at an important government post, we do not have such a list. A number of a specific vessel must be included with a request for instructions including the names of all parties involved."

Nainoma appeared downcast.

"I will obtain a request form to take with you, if that will help, then the answer lies with someone else with authority to grant the information required." The archivist stepped forward with arms outstretched. Lust was reflected in his eyes.

"You must not touch me. We hardly know each other." Nainoma stood fast.

At that moment the lamps went dark. Kwaahu was at her side. "Come with me, " she whispered. In an instant Nuvakwaahu and Kwaahu were soaring in the sky, northward bound, a silhouette on the Pacific moon.

* * * * * * * *

"Voyages to the Gulf of California and Great River were recorded in letters and reports by Hernando de Alarcon." Siki delved into her stacks of journals and notebooks.

"As a preface to this interesting episode, I would like to say that had Alarcon been able to proceed farther up the river, the Hopis might well have been discovered by sailors who could have arrived here ahead of Captain Tovar. It is true that destiny and history blend together to produce a final result."

Mark volunteered. "Let me read this part, if you please. Action on the sea is one of my favorite subjects!" The story unfolded.

As we entered a channel leading to a great river, the rising tide carried our small ships forward to meet the onrushing current aided by the backwash of the tidewater. The combined force smashed into the vessels which finally surged forward into the raging river. Only about six leagues were traversed by nightfall, accomplished with the help of men on shore pulling at ropes to augment rowers and sails. Encountering Indians, colored cloth, beads and other trinkets were accepted as gifts. In turn, a chief came aboard and presented a shaft inlaid with shells. This emblem was a sign of peaceful intentions.

Proceeding up the river in two launches with natives now pulling on the ropes, we came to a point where they would continue no farther apparently out of fear and recognized tribal boundaries. A tribe of sun worshipers, the Cocopas, described myself (Alarcon) as Son of the Sun, supplying food and taking to the ropes willingly and with great spirit. Farther upstream past Quicama territory we were told by a Coano chief that the tribe bordering were hostile Cumanas. We had planned to continue and disembark for an overland journey to Cibola but decided to turn back to the ships, leaving one of our men with the Coano village as an indication that we would return. Our ships had suffered some damage in the anchorage which was repaired after moving to a new mooring.

I was determined to make another attempt to join General Coronado. All available small craft were fitted with stores to be used in trading with the natives. These included assorted goods, seed grains and domestic fowl. Our voyage took us to the Coano village where our man had been well treated. From there we ventured about fifteen more leagues through high-walled canyons to the confluence of the Buena Guia and another we will call Rio Gila, where we camped and erected a large cross bearing writing to indicate I had reached this place. Possibly the general would arrive and thus would know we had been there. The date March 12, 1540 was included.

Since I could not ascertain what I needed to know, I decided to return to the ships. Two messengers from the Cumana tribe came to the camp asking for a message to give their Chief who was too far away to come himself. I advised that we tried to visit him but were now departing downstream. Further, he should try to keep and maintain peace and we would come sometime in the future. On the following day I sailed down the river.

* * * * * * * *

"I have never been much for sailing or around water, but Alarcon and his crew surely had a time of it, what with the bashing they took at the mouth of the Rio Colorado, let alone encounters with Indians. And yet in this unmapped territory they were so near to their objectives but had no way of knowing exactly where they had ventured in relation to the Expedition they sought." Cindy appeared to be dreaming momentarily about the years of exploration, passing through her mind.

"It is my turn to divulge information. Going through these notes I found a reference specifically to this letter which was later located fastened in the Herrera file and written by Isabel to Christina Blake." Cindy read the letter.

A member of the staff here advised that he had heard your brother Thomas was on an expedition into the region north of Mexico. Since that is apparently unexplored territory it would be a real challenge for the conquistadors. So many hidalgos have left this area to join the group it seems like a different place without them. Since many were from Castile, they always had good times together. One of the men, who had arrived recently from Spain, told my husband Juan that he had barely escaped being trapped into marriage by a lady of the court crowd. The lady was a daughter of the British embassy Chief of Staff by the name of Burrington. Could it be our mutual friend Elizabeth? I do not know what to think of the different versions concerning her activities and plans. One thing is certain, Elizabeth is able to take care of herself when embroiled in the quagmire of courts and people in the embassies.

Will you be coming to Mexico City after fulfilling your time at
Havana?

* * * * * * * *

Sam responded.   "It seems to be a review of previous
information and does not contain something specific concerning
your relatives. Unfortunately, with our time running out, we may
not uncover anything explicit which would pin down our expec-
tations of the revelation of pertinent events."

"You are probably right. We know my antecedents were at
Spain in the sixteenth century but have not discovered what caused
an apparent black out, or cover-up, of their activities." If Cindy was
frustrated or about to give up the search, she did not divulge a hint
of it but opened another journal to peruse.

Chapter Eighteen

THE WHITE FORTRESS

Siki searched the faces of her guests. They sat immobile, immersed in the depths of ancient Hopi culture absorbed through the enlightened narrative of the disciplined elder woman.

"You should be informed of an event which occurred during General Juan de Onate's excursion into Tierra Nueva. One that greatly disturbed our people and others throughout the Pueblo region. Since over fifty years had transpired, the story of the Coronado Expedition had been superseded by other Spanish visitors and the generations had to make judgments based on current events."

The tape recorder made a loud click. "Excuse me while I place a new cassette in the machine." Sam marked the removed cassette and sat back in his chair.

"We all appreciate your taking time for these sessions and must confess to being fascinated by your narration."

Siki nodded and smiled her 'thank you'. The story continued.

Nainoma told her father about the flight as snow eagle, Nuvakwaahu, and the Kawaahu Kachina. Aroyo listened attentively but a hint of skepticism had entered his mind.

"Your dream does indeed provide important information concerning the jarron. However, we are so far removed from the capital of New Spain, making contact with a government official might be hopeless. You may not be able to bear the disappointment in the result."

"What you say, father, is probably true. Our best hope lies in some one coming to our village who can open the jarron or can suggest some thing to be done about it. Never-the-less, the jarron seems very important to me and I will carry it to the fields and wherever I go."

* * * * * * * *

The venture of the two families, Aroyo and Pahqua, into expanded agriculture had been underway for several months. Fields were worked faith fully with abundant production evident in certain crops and little success with others. Water was involved in two ways. They had learned that since some plants required more water than others, it was evident that the crops must be segregated into workable plots and separate water flow directed to meet different needs at different times. Second, but causing much more concern, was the drawing off of precious water contained in underground pools within the rocky mesa aquifer. This source provided life sustaining water to the people and additional irrigation caused the volume of water available to recede.

Honhoya, eldest son of Aroyo and Pahqua's son Piqosha, pondered the problem at some length. In discussions with elder Hopis they learned that underground reservoirs retaining water had been excavated and enlarged by ancient inhabitants of Acoma Pueblo. These people were noted for their ability to survive through extreme periods of drought as well as having plentiful water supplies from season to season. The two young men decided to visit Acoma and study the aqua system at length, then return with information necessary to enhance facilities at the Hopi mesas.

Not having horses and desirous of traveling as light as possible, Honhoya and Piqosha ventured forth heading southward to the Little Colorado River and east to the Zuni Pueblos. Honhoya had lighter skin and was taller of the two, both at the age of nineteen were well muscled and in excellent physical condition. Carrying verbal messages from their elders and Chief of the Bear Clan, the two men were treated graciously by the Acomans at the end of their long journey. Quarters were provided and many meals were taken in the company of local officials knowledgeable in the areas of water conservation and usage, as well as pueblo construction methods. Ordinary farmers, whose experiences provided valuable information, took them to their fields.

In their instructive tours, the two Hopis learned that the huge mass of the white pueblo stood on a solid mesa base honeycombed with tunnels and cisterns, the heart and arteries of the ancient water system. Extensive connecting labyrinths were pointed out as useful in defense and dispersement of warriors in the event of attack. Politics with regard to the Spaniards was also included in an unrelated session of discussion which deeply impressed the two young Hopis.

* * * * * * *

In the preceding months Onate's army and expedition had visited several regions seeking allegiance of the inhabitants to the Spanish king and conversion to the teachings of the friars. The Hopis were not over looked. Villages on three mesas were visited but the entourage turned back upon learning that an acute shortage of water existed at the fourth mesa in the group.

Having camped at Zuni pueblos previously, the expedition passed Cibola on its way to Acoma, a pueblo of the Keres Indians. Standing on a mesa nearly four hundred feet high, the white rock walls and extraordinary size comprised of two hundred homes, made it appear almost impregnable.

They called it The Rock.

Unarmed inhabitants including Piqosha and Honhoya poured from the various pueblo entrances coming down the pathways to meet the Spaniards. They admired the soldados wearing bright metal over their bodies. Horses draped with brightly colored *caparazons* delighted them. Neighing of the horses terrified the natives. It seemed to them that the horses were talking.

Unknown to the general, two factions had polarized the occupants of The Rock, for or against the Spaniards. A plot developed by Zutacapan was underway to lure Don Juan into a kiva enabling a number of hidden warriors to kill him.

The army in full battle array impressed the Acomans who noticed the perfect lines and how well the animals were kept under control. Onate dismounted to meet the leaders and peering upward at the formidable walls of the white citadel began an ascent of the mesa with the ranks of his soldados and many Indians behind him. Upon reaching the summit a salute was fired, the smoking guns striking both wonder and terror into the minds of the natives. Some, however, noting that all commands emanated from the general, decided that if he could be eliminated, capture or destruction of the troops could easily be accomplished.

When assembled in the large plaza of the pueblo, the general was invited to observe treasures located in a kiva, mistakenly called *estufa* by the Spaniards. Making sure he was always under surveillance of his officers and troops, Don Juan agreed to go to the kiva but on arrival and peering into the dark chamber, he became suspicious and decided not to enter. Instead, he advised his host that the men in his force should first be returned to the plain below where they would establish their camp and tend to the horses.

Thus the assassination plan was nipped in the bud, so to speak.

During the night Zutacapan and his followers called upon the hydrology experts to conduct an official group into the lower area for a tour of the water cisterns, tunnels and passageways leading to upper level chambers. In these areas combat action could be taken against the Spaniards from unexpected locations. Circumstances drew the two Hopis into the meetings which were controlled by the cunning and soft spoken Zutacapan who was capable of creating great enthusiasm and brandishing of weapons to oust the enemy. The Spanish were considered to be plotting the takeover or destruction of the historical home of the Acomans.

Meanwhile Onate had received word of his appointment to the high level position of Governor of New Mexico with provincial headquarters at San Juan near the confluence of Rio Grande and Rio Chama northeast of Acoma. This was the beginning of Spanish bureaucracy in Tierra Nueva. Governor Onate lost no time the next day with his proposal that the Acomans follow the lead of other pueblos, honor the Spanish crown and give obedience to that authority. Although Zutacapan and leaders of peaceful rapport with the Spaniards, Chumpo and Purguapo, had joined with many of the people bringing gifts, water for the horses and other amenities, their outward pledge of allegiance was temporary.

The next day the new Governor departed to take up his duties at San Juan leaving Sergeant Zaldivar in charge. Ordered to return to The Rock, the sergeant and a body of men went boldly to the pueblo's ramparts. Their attempt to raise the Spanish flag - a sign of complete submission to the natives - met with violent opposition as opponents bombarded the soldados with rocks and appeared fully armed to face the Spaniards. Sergeant Zaldivar appealed to them to stop the hostile activities but Zutacapan and his followers continued, resulting in the death of Zaldivar's brother. Appearing at various balcons and openings, the Indians met the now mobilized army attempting to breach the walls of the fortress and gain positions on the approaches. A small cannon placed in action by the troops continued pounding at the walls for two days resulting in breaking the resistance and seizure of many defenders! However, capture of the great structure was obstructed by the defiance of many of the residents who barricaded themselves in kivas and hallways. Frustrated in their efforts to take the remaining warriors alive, the soldados set fire to the massive complex reducing it to a smoldering rubble.

"We have been through these catacombs so many times I have the feeling we are going in circles. Piqosha stood in the light of a small window opening. "Surely a way out of here is possible."

Honhoya was not dismayed. "I hear voices echoing from below and an occasional cry of a woman. We must join them!"

In the company of several Acoma warriors, the two Hopis made their way to several levels of the burning structure in an attempt to break out. Adversaries confronted them at every exit. Joined by Chumpo, a clan leader, and others who were attempting to surrender, they searched through compartments for survivors. Those found were cowered and frightened by the terrible conflagration. Chumpo pleaded with them to prevent further deaths by surrendering themselves. Forming small groups the inhabitants came forward in compliance but fearful that a soldado's bludgeon might await them. Somberly they struggled across debris and burned human remains mingled with corpses of the defenders of the once mighty fortress.

* * * * * * * *

"The surrender of Acoma Pueblo was so devastating that it was no doubt a significant turning point in the attitudes of the Indians and placed the Spaniards in the position of merciless conqueror. "Having previously made the necessary journals and notes available, Siki continued. "The documents I have at hand contain excerpts from the Historia de la Nueva Mexico, written by Captain Gaspar Perez de Villagra an officer with General Don Juan Onate, now recognized as the conqueror of New Mexico. Villagra's chronicles were originally written in verse after he returned to Spain in 1610 following service with Onate dating from 1598. It is apparent that he courted the praise of King Phillip and sought honors for the services he had rendered in the New World since his opening statement began with "Harken, O Mighty King, for I was a witness of all that I have to relate'."

Peering at Sam, Siki placed the volume in his hands. "The poetry has been translated and transcribed in prose, although some cantos are included in the notes. Certain passages have been earmarked, highlighting events at Acoma.."

Sam turned the pages and began to read.

I again unfurl my sails to the breeze and guide my craft back to burning Acoma, back to that frightful fire whose flames and clouds of sparks and cinders envelope the lofty houses in an awe-inspiring conflagration. Those high walls crumbled in a thousand parts engulfing the unhappy inhabitants.

Note, most worthy lord, those wretched beings who in their despair seek death by hurling themselves from those awful heights. See the savages, men and women, who with their little ones roast amid the raging flames meeting their misery and their fate.

Moved to compassion by the terrible slaughter, the sergeant Zaldivar urged Chumpo and the others to yield and cease this needless sacrifice of life, telling them on his word of honor he would spare them all. Like persons shocked by a lightening bolt, the savages moved forward sacredly viewing the mangled corpses of those who so nobly defended that haughty Rock, now bathed in their blood. Coming before the sergeant, they prostrated themselves before our banners and yielded their arms. They surrendered unconditionally in a number of about six hundred, together with their wives and children, conquered at last.

* * * * * * * *

Sam paused. "I must read a passage from Siki's notebook which portrays the grandeur of style credited to Villagra in his historia.

I sing of the glory of that mighty band,
Who nobly strive in that far distant land,

The world's most hidden regions they defy,
"Plus Ultra" is their ever battle cry.
Onward they press, nothing they will not dare,
Mid force of arms and deeds of valor rare.
To write the annals of such men,
Well needs the efforts of a mightier pen.

* * * * * * * *

Chapter Nineteen

CAPTURED

Separating themselves from the group led by Chumpo, Piqosha and Honhoya returned to the underground depths in the hope of finding a way out. As they passed a pile of half burned wooden beams and a collapsed wall of rock, muffled cries for help could be heard.

The situation called for drastic action. "We must go to the aid of these suffering people. Laying under this debris, dust and smoke they will soon suffocate." Honhoya pulled an arm of his friend.

The two men removed fallen rafters and dug into the fallen rock and mortar with bare hands. They soon cleared an opening into a small chamber where several Acomans were coughing and gasping for breath. Noting that the victims appeared to be warriors, the Hopis pulled them out of the narrow space and laid them in an adjoining room. There they were identified as resistors to the Spanish in Zutacapan's group.

A trickle of water and pieces of clothing enabled the rescuers to wash grime from each warrior's face and provide a small measure of water. Of the eight men, two had suffocated. Bows, arrows and other weapons had been broken or buried under debris leaving the men unarmed. However, a cache of firebrands was found providing torches for the darkened area.

Refreshed and strengthened by the water and respite, the men began talking about finding a way out. One of the Acomans, who had labored in the myriad of water tunnels and cisterns, claimed to know of openings in a slope on one side of the mesa strewn with large boulders. Making their way through passageways proved to be an arduous undertaking as many contained water, fallen rock and dirt collected over the years. At an intersection of subterranean tunnels the leader stopped, the men crowding around.

"These tunnels exit at two locations. At infrequent times when storage areas are filled and contain an excess of water, the overflow runs through this tunnel in which we are standing, then the two branches carry the water to the outside."

Honhoya spoke. "So the question is, which tunnel might lead to the soldados standing ready at the opening?"

"That is our situation exactly." The man scanned the faces of the grime laden followers. No one ventured an opinion. "We will all go to the right."

The group stopped when daylight could be seen a short distance ahead. "I will check the entrance to determine if a guard has been posted. Two of you follow closely behind in the event we are attacked. If an attack occurs, the rest of you run back and leave by the other opening. It is a chance we must take." The warrior grasped a large wooden fire brand to use as a weapon, as did the others.

The three warriors had exited and were advancing when set upon by a half-dozen soldados who jumped on them from the boulders. Their shouts were heard for a short time then subsided into silence.

Running back into the other diversion tunnel, the remaining five led by Piqosha and Honhoya dropped out of the opening onto a small square of ground between a growth of bushes and sparse grass. A gorge down the side of the mesa had been cut by past water flows. Through this narrow gulley the men descended, elated by the absence of soldiers. Their joy was short lived however, when emerging from the ravine at the base of the mesa they were spotted by two squads of soldados, apparently a change of the guard marching to appointed positions. Hemmed in on two sides and the steep ravine at their backs, the escapees had no choice but to meet the assault head on. Armed with bludgeons in the form of firebrands against battle axes wielded by the opposition, the Indians engaged their opponents in fierce hand-to-hand combat. One by one the Acomans were struck to the ground and bludgeoned to death. Piqosha and Honhoya were left, still standing, swinging their clubs against four of the enemy when the remaining opposing force ran over them from behind. An order was given to defer the final, death dealing blows. An army corporal approached the two Hopis who had struggled from the ground to a sitting position.

"Your attire and facial characteristics are different from the others. Who are you and what tribe do you represent?"

From bruised lips and mouth caused from repeated blows, Honhoya answered, using signs and a mixture of Spanish and native language. "That is Piqosha. I am Honhoya. We are Hopi, visiting Acoma Pueblo to observe their water system on the mesa." It was not easy to utter the words.

"Tie their hands and take them prisoner. Our captain may wish to talk to them."

The Hopis were marched under guard to the field below the still burning pueblo where many women and children and a few warriors had been impounded by the Spaniards. Resolutely, the Indians opposed Onate's army. They were determined to kill as many of the enemy as possible. Finally, fire drove them from their defensive positions resulting in the bodies of hundreds of wounded and dying warriors strewn about the macabre wreckage. Teams of soldados carried the victims by litter to the field where they were placed in rows.

Angry cries arose from the women as they pummeled a body with sticks and stones. Thinking that this might be a violation of the Indians' surrender or that the victim might be a Spaniard, the sergeant rushed men in to quell an uprising. A woman shouted.

"This is Zutacapan, the man responsible for the death of the soldados. His rash, unwarranted scheme caused the death of your countrymen and the many corpses laying in rows. Permit us to finish our vengeance as is merited by this scoundrel!"

No answer was necessary. Zutacapan's body was a gory mass as the beating continued until the women finally walked away to their assigned zone.

The scene chilled Honhoya and Piqosha to the bone as they felt a curtain of doom enveloping the area. This feeling continued when they were marched to the pueblo of Santo Domingo and brought to trial with the other captives. Charged with the death of Spaniards, several servants and failure to submit peacefully prior to the outbreak of hostilities, harsh treatment was dealt the Acomans and Hopis as well. The sentences included the severing of one foot and twenty years of service for males over twenty-five years of age; females over twelve years of age and males between twelve and twenty-five years of age were committed to twenty years of servitude. Many young girls were taken to Mexico and distributed among convents.

"Why would a fellow human, being a strutting conqueror or a neighbor, do such a thing as cut off a hand. To us it means a lifetime of pain and struggle, trying to accomplish the simple chores of farming and in the household." Lying on a deer skin mat, Honhoya grimaced as he tried to change the position of his arm, the stub of which had been seared and bandaged.

Piqosha had fared no better as both had suffered the loss of the right hand for their part in the catastrophe of war. He was philosophical about their plight.

"The sentences of some, both women and men, doomed them to nearly a lifetime of slavery. I do not understand why the Spaniards chose to cut off our hand while the others, I have heard, lost a foot. Most certainly it serves as a warning to others when we return home. At least we will be able to walk the distance."

Upon being released by the Spaniards, the two men made their way to a Zuni village where they collapsed in sheer exhaustion, unable to proceed farther. Friendly women and men took care of them, paying close attention to their slowly healing wounds and providing food and rest. When physical strength had returned and travel could be resumed, the Zunis loaned them two horses and supplied provisions. Four Zuni warriors accompanied the Hopis to Piqosha's rillage on Antelope Mesa. After a day of rest the Zunis took the horses in tow and headed back to their pueblo.

* * * * * * * *

"Mark, would you please read these writings of Villagra which appeared in his historia prior to the atrocities at Acoma. The Hopis and Zunis had received Onate's army peacefully on his earlier travels through Tierra Nueva." Siki handed over the document.

The governor left with his army, visiting the pueblos of Cibola (Zuni) and Mohoce (Hopi). When in the land of the Zuni we were met by a band of Indians Indians marching in procession and scattering flour (corn meal) over the people they met. At the pueblo the woman scattered so much meal over us that we aware obliged to take their flour sacks from them. This was not without many a scuffle accompanied by much mirth and merriment. Making peace with one another, they brought us great quantities of food and explained the significance of this ceremony, saying that it was just as impossible to live without food to sustain life as it was for us to go among them and not meet with their friendship. Seeing a cross which we had raised, they joined us in adoring this holy symbol.

Accepting an invitation to a hunt, we mounted our horses and joined and assemblage of about eight hundred Indians forming a large semicircle. At a given signal they began to close in toward the center. Our men eagerly sought to follow the many hares, rabbits and foxes darting about to escape between the horses' hooves. Nowhere are there hares larger, of better flavor, or more tender than those found in these regions.

Captain Farfan was sent to investigate certain salt lakes of which we had received great reports. He returned in a few days reporting that the deposits contained very high grade salt in immense quantities. The governor then sent him in search of rich mines said to exist in these regions. He was accompanied by eight men.

* * * * * * * *

Mark raised a concern. "I wonder why the natives and Spaniards got along so well in some areas, but in others they were adversaries."

Siki responded calmly. "By deciding in long discussions in the kivas that a peaceful approach was appropriate in meetings with the Castillians, certain pueblo people found understanding with no provocation in their dealings with the newcomers. On the other hand, it is apparent that divisive action, such as taken by the Acomans, resulted in discord and division, destroying any hope of a united front against the Spaniards. This, of course, was inflated by Onate's sergeant left in charge who was determined to wipe out any opposition, leading to a surrender disastrous to the inhabitants."

* * * * * * * *

REUNION

Since the long journey had tired the two men, word of their arrival was taken to Honhoya's family by Qomahongsi, Piqosha's sister. She excitedly described the men.

"Both my brother and Honhoya have deep lines in their faces from their long trip and wounds from an ordeal at Acoma Pueblo with the Spaniards. Many Indians were cruelly treated at that place. Honhoya wishes you to come to our home where they are resting. We can then talk about the trip and hear what they have to say about it."

Aroyo, daughter Nainoma and younger son Talowima accompanied the young woman on the return trip to Antelope Mesa.

At the sight of her brother and Piqosha, Nainoma screamed. "How can this be? Are the Spaniards obsessed with demons? These atrocities are unreasonable acts on the part of those who believe they are civilized and we are savages!" Sobbing, she embraced Piqosha and Honhoya. The others shared her anguish.

The two victims described the fine working relationship with the Acomans. "Everything was going well until the arrival of the army and expedition under Don Juan de Onate. His desire for complete submission of the people was not fulfilled as the population was divided on that subject. When the general left for San Juan to begin his new duties as Governor of New Mexico province, a Sergeant Zaldivar was placed in charge of the military. Thwarted in an effort to raise the flag of Spain at the Acoma pueblo, he began a bombardment by cannon and assaults by the soldados." Honhoya looked for Piqosha to continue.

"Fires were started to drive the residents and defenders out of the great structure with its white walls, marvelous plazas and chambers.

"Many bodies lay burned and mangled by collapsing ceilings and walls. We rescued several men caught in fallen timbers and fire. In their company we went underground and escaped through a water diversion tunnel. Unfortunately when emerging from a ravine down the side of the mesa we came up against soldados. After quite a fight we were overpowered and taken prisoner. Harsh treatment was dealt to all concerned in sentencing pronounced at a hearing convened as a trial. Many Acoma warriors suffered loss of a foot and years of service to the Spaniards. Other men and women were condemned to servitude for much of their lives. We were aware that one of the officers, Captain Villagra, arranged for several dozen young girls to be sent to Mexico for disposition by the viceroy. "Piqosha looked from one to another of the two families." The future for other pueblo tribes appears to be clouded, with not much to expect in the way of cooperation from the Spaniards."

"It seems to me that co-existence with the Spanish government is at the point of explosion. Our people have wondered for many years about the outcome of the many forays into our region by New Spain. Over the years nothing like this occurred to our knowledge. Will future armies try to wipe us off of the face of the earth?" Tears streaming down her lined face, Piqosha's mother posed the question.

Aroyo spoke. "Answers might be found if we consult the elders and discuss these problems."

Nainoma was quick to respond. "Since our families suffer as a direct result of action by the foreigners, should we not undertake our own search for a solution? The future of the Hopis is at a crossroads. We could include a few friends and leave for our ancestral home where meditation and discussion would be in seclusion. The region of the green mesa (Mesa Verde) contains homes constructed by the Hisatsinom, the Hopi people of long ago. Many of the buildings and facilities are said to be still usable. It is not too far!"

"I know about the place. The distance is about 45 leagues, a journey requiring abundant supplies and water since it is reached by crossing areas of desert land." Aroyo peered about the group, settling on the two handicapped men." Let us think about such a trip over night and discuss it further tomorrow. We could schedule our daily travel so it would not be strenuous."

Two days later the pilgrimage was underway, twenty Hopi villagers seeking a place where their deep concerns might be solved in a different environment. On the fifth day their camp was located on the approaches to the green mesa. A small sparkling creek was welcome as were the large cottonwoods providing shade from the sun's relentless heat. With meat and other foods in short supply, the group spread out to replenish their now meager stock. The men formed small groups to hunt in a wide area. Women carried baskets and animal skin bags in which to deposit roots, wild rice, berries and various edible plants.

On their return, to the dismay and surprise of all, the camp had been ransacked in their absence. No signs of intruders had been noticed but containers and pouches had been emptied, their contents strewn about with many items missing. Most of Nainoma's personal belongings were missing including the jarron. Footprints detected in grass and sand led in several directions;however, a search provided no hope in recovering the losses.

Nainoma confided to her father. "The jarron, my most precious belonging, is missing. We will probably never know what it contained."

"It is a great loss my daughter. These things happen and questions are sometimes answered later in unexpected ways. We have all suffered the loss of important personal items. Hopefully, our sojourn in the terraced houses will provide consolation, if not replacement."

Chapter Twenty

T H E   M E S S A G E

Siki peered at the Michaelsons as if waiting for one of them to speak. It had been a long session. Sam, who was about to turn off the recorder, suddenly spoke excitedly.

"The location of the Hopi camp must be at or near the same place Mark found the urn!"

Smiling, Siki was pleased. "I believe what you said is true. Those cottonwood trees have been there many, many years and the small creek comes from a spring a short distance upstream. It is and was a natural campsite and the present road to the crest of Mesa Verde follows an old trail in use over a span of probably hundreds of years.

"The odyssey of the jarron is concluded but now we must see what is inside!" Cindy showed her excitement at this prospect.

Sam removed the vessel from a brief case, turning it over in his hands. "Surely someone or someplace is located in this area, capable of opening and solving this little dilemma of ours- a metal smith, a laboratory, perhaps?" He looked questionally at Siki.

Siki, too, was pondering the problem. "Since artifacts of all kinds are handled and restored at the Northern Arizona Museum, a visit to them might be worthwhile."

"Will you go with us? We can leave for Flagstaff tomorrow morning." Sam waited for Siki to answer. "Wouldn't it be wonderful if they opened it on the spot!"

Siki was both amused and excited. "If you have room for me in your vehicle, I will go along. I appreciate your including me."

Cindy interceded. "It is certainly no trouble at all and we have lots of space in the camper. Siki, we all deeply appreciate the time you have given and your absolutely wonderful narrative. These sessions have been completely fascinating."

"It has been my pleasure. I have enjoyed addressing these events to such people as yourselves who are truly interested in our history and legends. We will meet in the morning."

Next day at the museum a van took the group a short distance to an archives building containing workshops and laboratory facilities. Greeted by professor Anthony Sportono of Northern Arizona University who served in the laboratory staff during summer months, Sam produced the jarron, relating how and where it was found. He introduced the Michaelson family and Siki.

"It is a pleasure to meet all of you. In past years I have read of your success in language and history, Siki. With much regret, I have an empty feeling of missed opportunities in not getting in touch with you previously."

"Thank you professor. We might bridge a few years today. We believe that a message is inside the vessel and hopefully it will come to light. " Siki's dark eyes twinkled as she reached for the urn.

"You see, the Michaelsons have found this artifact and worked to bring out the inscriptions on the metal case. We have put together some of the pieces but the enigma lies inside." The professor looked over the letters and numbers. "Judging by the markings, it is undoubtedly a courier jarron. It will be necessary that....."

Mark interrupted excitedly. "My Mom read some books in a library and found out where it was made. The IbIII is an artisan's hallmark in Iberia, a Province of Spain."

"Well, you have firmly established its origin. Now we must determine how to open the object. Come along this hallway to our laboratory." The professor led the way.

A robust, bearded man looked up from a microscope and came forward as the group entered a small area equipped with straight backed chairs as in a miniature waiting room. A table stood to one side with three chairs placed around it.

"Say now, what do we have here?" His eyes focussed on the urn carried by the professor.

"Let me introduce Sam and Cindy Michaelson, son Mark and Siki from Second Mesa. This is Joseph Escanada, native of Santa Fe and expert in doing things to unravel old puzzles. One of his specialties is working with metal." The vessel was placed in his hands.

"Joe, this was found by Mark at a campsite. They traced it to the proper place after covering a lot of miles. Siki provided a background and historical review as well as people involved in Coronado's time and later. In all probability a message is confined in what we believe to be a courier jarron. Can you open it?"

"It is mid-morning. This will take a little time, so why don't you go into town and have lunch. Come back about three o'clock, OK? If it can be accomplished, we will all witness the opening!" The group departed.

Escanada looked the three by eight inch vessel over carefully, placing it under a microscope to reveal any cracks or fissures. Under close scrutiny he saw the interstice. Placing the urn in a vice, he drilled a small hole on each side of the line of separation, assuming that the outer cover consisted of two layers with the upper metal a different alloy than the lower. Microscopic inspection of the metal particles drawn out by the diamond drill confirmed his original assumption. The lower encasing metal contained a portion of bronze alloy which would expand slightly when heated. Harder alloy in the upper skin would not expand at the same temperature.

Utilizing asbestos lined clamps, the innovative technician placed the jarron in a vice with the lower section exposed. Attempts at twisting the sections with bare hands proved futile. However, with the application of heat from a small gas torch and use of another clamp, a twisting motion caused the two sections to loosen and turn about one inch. A drop of fine, light oil was placed in the seam as the two sections were worked back and forth. Escanada then pulled on the lower section, simultaneously twisting to the right, again coming against a stop. A downward pull and turn to the left allowed the section to disengage. Joseph, however, having solved the locking system did not fully open the urn, desiring to defer that event for the finders to observe.

About mid-afternoon the Michaelson family and Siki returned, again accompanied by Professor Sportono. The laboratory entry room was bare.

Joseph Escanada came forward from the laboratory carrying a polished wooden box in which the jarron had been placed. "Greetings again. It is such a fine day, I had chairs and the table moved to our patio. It will be more comfortable." He led the group outside. A pitcher of iced lemonade and glasses had been placed on the table.

"This is truly a beautiful setting. Your facilities nestled here among the evergreens with the sounds of squirrels and birds- we appreciate your thoughtfulness and hospitality." Sam grinned broadly.

Professor Sportono eyed the box. " Come on Joe, what have you discovered about the urn?"

"Now hold on, Tony. An artifact of this magnitude deserves to be on stage. A little show-biz is well deserved. We will try to accomplish it without an orchestra or kleig lights but with maybe a little fanfare, at least a proper setting." Joe strode to the table and placed the box at the center. The audience, now filled with anticipation, sat in a semi circle of chairs facing the table.

"To quicken your pulse, I now announce that the jarron has been unlocked. However, it has not been opened as that occasion is for all to see!" With obvious delight, Escanada opened the box, removed the vessel and held it at arms length. Brightly polished, it reflected the sun.

"A type of step-lock has held this urn tightly together for over four hundred years. The mechanism requires an initial turn to the right to a stop; then pulling down on the lower section another twist to the left, contacting another stop. A steady pull while again turning to the left follows a groove inside, allowing the sections - upper and lower- to disengage." Escanada carefully accomplished each move, then paused as if a magical trance had descended on everyone.

"Now for a look inside. " He slowly divided the jarron exposing a cream colored material tightly rolled to fit in the inner space. Laying the top of the receptacle on the table, he deftly removed a scroll, consisting of two sheets, then placed the lower part of the urn on the table.

"Come forward for a closer look." Escanada waited for the spellbound onlookers to circle the table. "I want to make sure that this parchment is still pliable and capable of being unrolled without falling apart like a dry leaf." On the table top he pulled the scroll downward while simultaneously holding the top edge flat by pressing it with a ruler. The first words appeared, together with a date. "The lettering is in old Spanish. I will try to translate the message for you."

November 18, 1540
Zuni Village
Province of New Spain

My Dear Honmana:
The dreary road I have traveled the past few months now seems like a dream as my thoughts were only of you and a void exists since our parting at Oraibi. Very vivid are the events that occurred at the mesas of your homeland. We were together in a world seemingly separate from ordinary life on planet Earth. It is a world to which I wish to return when it is possible.

My assignments have taken me to other regions in the vast expanse of Tierra Nueva. Sonora Province, which lies at your southwestern border, is a wretched place with much hostility between the native people and the army. Keeping the road open for government couriers serving headquarters several thousand miles apart is quite a task. A stopover here at the Zuni village is brief since we must now catch up with the main army on its way East.

My whole being is with you and comes with this letter.

You may use the jarron for an answer which I will look forward to receive even though delays may occur.   Please tender my best regards to your grandmother, a wonderful lady for whom I hold deep respect.   To you - the flower of all pueblo land and my truelove- I send prayers for safety, well being and happiness.

Yours forever,
Pedro de Tovar

A stunned silence pervaded the group, particularly the Michaelsons and Siki. They again seated themselves. The fact that a message would be forthcoming from such an artifact after four hundred years was one thing, but knowing the story of the people affected was itself humbling and thought provoking.

The silence was broken by the beating of wings. Siki rose and pointed to a large fir tree close by.   Pulsations translated into motion as a large snow white eagle swooped down over Siki as if to seize the scroll. Some thing white, a copy perhaps, clung from its claws.   The great bird accompanied by another of regular plumage flew off into the brilliant blue sky. From a great height they soared in a circle over the earth people, undoubtedly as a signal acknowledgement of a communication. Their circling flight ended abruptly as they flew north toward the San Francisco Peaks.

In the mystic mountains beyond the realm of Earth stood a stately figure in pure white, her arms outstretched to receive the snow eagle Nuvakwaahu-Nainoma and the eagle Kwaahu- Kachina.

Delivery of the divine tidings had been portended by a Deity of love and great power. Honmana's long wait was over.

* * * * * * * *

Joseph Escaneda, the astute technician, watched as the impact of the event impressed his audience. All were seated except for Siki who continued to stand and gaze skyward.

"The kachina messengers have completed their journey. Concluded also is the saga of Honmana, Captain Tovar and the generations they created. A legend of the Bear Clan has become very real and can now be shared by all." Siki looked at Cindy, Sam and Mark, then took her seat.

"This has been traumatic and I can appreciate your feelings. However, one page of the message remains." Escaneda grasped the sheet and held it up for the group to view. "The writing appears to be from a different hand. I will read it, translating as I proceed."

San Geronimo
Sonora Province
July 10, 1549

Dear Honmana:

I must explain why my writing is included in this jarron. Having lain in an obscure place in the Zuni village of Hawikuh for several years, it came into the possession of Kalisomi, a local resident who decided it should be turned over to the Spaniards for its disposition. An Indian courier delivered it to my command at the fort. The vessel was opened by me. Since I wished to advise you of existing circumstances, my message was included when the jarron was relocked and sent by native courier to Hawikuh in the hope that it would then be forwarded to you.

In the intervening years since Captain Tovar sent the message he became alcalde Mayor of Culiacan. Undoubtedly he sent several messages to you but they may have met the same fate as this one. With the withdrawal of the army from Tierra Nueva no method was available to guarantee delivery as courier service was limited to the confines of New Spain except in isolated instances where native residents to the north participated.

Don Pedro is now married to Dona Francisca de Guzman, the daughter of a former Governor of Cuba, Nuno de Guzman. She is a lady of high quality and virtue with great beauty and Christian fervor. They have two children, a son and daughter.

My sister Christina, who was born when our father and family resided in the British embassy compound at Madrid, Spain, advised in correspondence of an item of interest. It seems that Glendora, the oldest daughter of British ambassador Clayton Burrington, became involved and produced a child with a Spanish nobleman, the same Nuno de Guzman. Shortly after the birth he was transferred to Havana to serve his appointment as Governor of Cuba. He supported the mother and child for two years then arranged to have the governess take the young girl to the governor's residence in Havana. The mother was left in Spain. The child was Dona Francisca. Together with her father and stepmother, she arrived later in Mexico City where Guzman had been commissioned commander of an army delegated to conquer the region from the capital city to the Pacific Ocean and the northern province of Sonora.

After a series of fierce battles with the native population, Guzman established headquarters at an outpost on the west coast which became Culiacan, now a city of fair size.

I do not wish to cause you distress. It is my prayer that you are living a full life of your own and that your people are happy and at peace.

With my highest esteem and respect,

Tomas Blaque

An aura of expectation, tinged with a certain tenseness, permeated the atmosphere. Cindy was visibly shocked by the revelation. "No wonder our family tree had a broken branch in the sequence. Clayton Burrington knew of the sixteenth century disgrace at the King's court but did not reveal it in England. The resulting scandal would have upset the family and had demeaning results at home. " She looked thoughtfully at Siki for a few moments, then her face lit up. "But in all of this we have discovered something else! We are related!"

Siki and the other members of the Michaelson family appeared to be momentarily bewildered at this statement. Sam spoke. "I know that you have something figured out, but who is related to whom?"

Cindy responded eagerly. "All right, consider this. In fact, maybe you should write it down as it may be a bit complicated."

Sam complied, ready with pencil and paper.

"Dona Francisca was the daughter of Nuno de Guzman. She married Pedro de Tovar and they had two children, at the time

301

Tomas Blaque wrote his letter. Now, Aroyo's father was also Don Pedro and his mother, of course, Honmana. Therefore, Aroyo had a half brother and half sister, all three had the same parent, the father. Right? Moreover, Siki is directly related to Honmana and her descendants.

"So far, so good. The blood line might be a little thin four hundred fifty years later, but since a relative of mine, Glendora Burrington, was the mother of Dona Francisca, that becomes the tie that binds us together!" Cindy sat back in her chair.

Sam read his notes aloud, going slowly over each detail. "The genealogy comes out all right. We have found a full four hundred and fifty year history of pedigrees! It is really amazing to me that such a finding could result from these days of research, Siki's narrative and the jarron!"

Siki had risen from her chair. Cindy leaped to her feet and turned to the smiling Hopi lady, embracing her in a friendly hug. Sam and Mark also came to express their feelings,

"Well, I suppose we will have to continue our investigation to determine more about Tovar's lineage." Cindy smiled as her eyes twinkled.

Mark answered. "I am for that, all right. But how about taking a break for a few weeks before getting into it? Dad has to return to work and school will soon be starting!"

* * * * * * * *

EPILOGUE

Chapter Twenty One

THE NARRATIVE CONTINUES

Light blue moonlight drenched the landscape as the Michaelson camper traveled Highway 160 on the return trip from Flagstaff to Shongopovi, Second Mesa. Sitting beside his dad in a bucket seat Mark, whose chin had been drooping to his chest in a momentary nap, suddenly jerked upright and turned to ask a question.

"It bothers me to think of the Hopis, persuaded by Onate's over whelming presence to submit to the authority of the King and forced to change their life style. What happened when the army left?"

"Well, son, that is a good question. Let's ask Siki about it when we arrive at the village." Cindy and Siki were comfortably seated at the rear of the vehicle. Sam hummed a popular tune as they turned at Tuba City on the last few miles to the ancient mesa.

At their destination Siki thanked Sam and Cindy, expressing appreciation for being included in the day's events. When Sam relayed Mark's question about the Hopis, she put off further discussion.

"This has been a wonderful, yet arduous day. We will all feel brighter and rested tomorrow. I am inviting you to breakfast at eight thirty in the visitor center. We will begin the day with pika bread, corn cakes with syrup, homemade wild-game sausage, eggs and hot coffee."

Sam responded. "We will join you. Can't pass up an invitation like that!" The others agreed.

Following breakfast the next morning, the group moved from the small dining room adjacent to a kitchen, to what they called "our room" where all of the previous meetings and discussions had taken place.

Siki spoke to the younger Michaelson. "Mark, your interest in the aftermath of Spanish intrusions of the Hopis is gratifying to me. An understanding of our culture and that of other Indians is surely necessary for this bright new generation."

She sat calmly at the table. Although reference journals lay before her, they remained unopened as she continued her narrative relaying Hopi history as it had been told to her and retold by many previous generations.

The arrival of Juan de Onate with a great militant entourage in 1598 had resulted in an announcement that the Hopi villages had submitted in the name of the King of Spain. The report was issued by the chronicler of the expedition but Hopis discounted its effect on the people. They continued with ancient ceremonies, festivities and self governing free from outside influence. In this environment the young residents, with the aid of the elders, of course, became more intensely involved in Hopi religion, culture, legends and their unique way of life on the high mesas.

During these years Nainoma became married to Piqosha with three young ones, two sons and a daughter, filling the family household. Aroyo, as grandfather, took great pleasure in observing the children at games with others and in telling them stories based on his exploits of earlier years. His son Honhoya, noted for outstanding knowledge and abilities related to irrigation and farming, enjoyed life with his wife and four children, two girls and two boys.

The tranquility was destined to end. In the year 1629 at a family gathering, Honhoya revealed what he had heard that day. "A friend from Antelope Mesa advised the elders in a meeting at the kiva that three friars had come into Awatovi accompanied by ten soldiers."

Nainoma was startled. "What will they try to do? Why are soldiers necessary if it is a peaceful visit." The others shared her disbelief.

"It is not a visit. They are missionaries and have already announced their intention to build a church and establish their religion. " Honhoya looked around the group as he spoke.

"Now that they have come to our land we must be careful to watch what they are doing. If possible we must plan ways to resist, as they will surely expand to other mesas and villages." Piqosha rose from the mat he was sitting on, unable to mask the anxiety of his countenance. Groups of people from the Santa Fe area have arrived in various locations looking for places where they could avoid the Castillas. Severe punishment has been inflicted at Pueblo villages which have resisted the Spanish."

"This is truly a problem. At various times recently, Myovis and villagers of the Rio Grande pueblos have been accepted on our mesas and live in small communities along with Acomans, Payupkis, and Lagunas. Some of them are on Antelope Mesa and others on Black Mesa." Hunumoma, mother of Honhoya's children was obviously concerned. "Women and men have spoken of the harsh treatment and penalties dealt to them by the Castillas, They are happy to get away and raise their families in a new place."

It was decided that Piqosha, Honhoya and two other men would travel to Antelope Mesa and there observe the missionaries. "People have been made to carry materials, logs and stones to a site where a mission building is under construction." Honhoya reported.

A year later another report was received confirming that San Bernardino Mission at Awatovi had been completed and many Hopis were converted. Further, after the passage of three more years one of the priests, Padre Francisco Porras, was reportedly poisoned. However, the work of the church continued.

An uneasy feeling infected the people throughout the mesas when word of the conversion of many Awatovi citizens to the Spanish religion was received. At clan meetings and among family gatherings Nainoma summed up the situation.

"The missionaries have no respect for our cultural, ancient religious ceremonies or way of life. They seem to be determined to change everything to their way, disregarding the fact that we trace our roots back to the Hisatsimon who lived here before their religion was born. Friends who have moved here from Awatovi say that nothing of ours is worth saving according to the priests. They say our inner spirits are worth saving if we accept their ceremony, called baptism, and do what they command. We lose the freedom to think for ourselves and that is too high a price to pay."

The isolation of the Hopis and primarily, unrest among the Rio Grande pueblos were factors in suppressing extensive missionary effort in the mesas for a period of about twenty years. Nainoma's son, Yuclima and Honhoya's son, Honowaitiva had grown to adulthood and had families of their own. Siki shifted in her chair as the narrative continued.

Spanish priests arrived at Oraibi asking for a meeting with the elders. Yuclima attended the meeting held in a kiva. Although Castillians and Hopis had been killed in confrontations in previous times, over the years they came to tolerate one another on relatively peaceful terms.

Yuclima reported the event to his family and a group of friends.

"The priests were amiable and somewhat humble as they requested permission to erect a structure in which they could live. Nothing concerning missionary effort was discussed. Within a few minutes the elders granted the request assigning land farther north on the mesa away from the village. A consensus was reached by the group after a light discussion that no harm could come from the action of the elders. However, Nainoma had previously expressed her views to many of the same gathering and inwardly felt the elders had been too lax in dealing with the Spaniards.

With help from the local villagers, the residence house was soon completed with the resolute priests working from dawn to nightfall. The activity then progressed into construction of a meeting place or mission.

Honowaitiva worked in the labor force a few days as a form of surveillance. He confided in his friend Yuclima. "The friars are making the laborers work longer each day and compelling them to bring more adult men and friends to raise the heavy wall and ceiling supports and go out and obtain more construction materials. "

"They are certainly going beyond building a place to live. What materials are required? The new building must be one of large size."

"It needs plenty of stone for walls and long, thick logs for high ceiling beams." Honowaitiva grew solemn. "Our people must haul stone that has fallen from the mesa slopes to the desert floor. Available stone from atop the mesa has been virtually used up. But that isn't all. Our people are treated like slaves as they have dragged many logs from the Kisiwu area about twenty five leagues northeast of here. The trip to and from the San Francisco Mountains to obtain very large logs for roof beams is one that should not be forced on our people. The ends of so many big trees scraping across the weathered, surface stone of the mesa have caused ruts right up to the location where they are to be used. Many families are unable to produce their crops of maize as so much time is taken in working for the priests. The building is being called the slave church by the townspeople."

Large bells sent from Santa Fe were installed in the square tower of the completed church. The Hopis took note of this. They thought the Castillas would be satisfied and not bother the people. The friars had other ideas, demanding attention when the bells were rung for church services or some new tasks. The Oraibis were expected to be baptized.

Complaining that the water at Oraibi was unclean, the priests sent villagers to other areas for water. It was carried as much as fifteen leagues from Moencopi where the friars said the water was holy and fit for church services. Becoming tired of the tedious trip, the carriers obtained water from nearby springs, staying out overnight to indicate they had made a long trip. The water was indeed satisfactory until the priests discovered what the men were doing and punished them.

Yuclima's daughter, Kywonqa, came to him one afternoon. "Father, I have learned from the girls sharing our cooking and sewing classes that the friars have been out among other villages. The are forcing the young girls to spend time with them against their will. Many are afraid to tell their parents and are frightened that they might be severely punished."

"I am grateful that you came forward with this news, my daughter. The elders will be told about this. Something must be done by the people." Soon after, an event happened which added extreme resentment to the undercurrent in the Hopi village. A story handed down from Oraibi through the years states that Friar Salvador de Guerra intercepted a Hopi in "an act of idolatry". In the presence of the villagers, the man was thrashed until covered in blood, then drenched in burning turpentine.

Visibly shaken by the repeating of this event, Siki reached for a journal before her and passed it across the table to Sam. "Would you please read some of the particulars concerning the effect of this constant harassment on the people and mention the recorded names of the missionaries?"

"I am sorry that these recollections have upset you, Siki. It is evident that deep feelings of empathy for the people involved still linger in present generations even though over four centuries have passed." Sam opened the journal and turned the pages. He began to read at a page designated by a red marker.

The village of Awatovi on Antelope Mesa where the conquistadors had first discovered the Hopis in 1540, also received the first missionaries, namely; Andres Gutierrez, Francisco Porras and Cristobal de la Concepcion. With most pueblo tribes in the Rio Grande region under domination of the priests, religious conversion effort spread to the remaining Hopi mesas. As expected, the Hopis at Oraibi witnessed the advent of Augustine de Santa Maria and Padre Figueroa with attendants. Construction was started immediately, recruiting the local residents. In record time the San Miguel Mission at Oraibi, the San Bartolome Mission at Shongopovi and visitante facilities at Walpi and Mishongovi were established and completed by 1674.

Village life was interrupted by constant demands for food offerings causing many families to relinquish shares of squash, corn and melons. In addition to demanding that the Hopis regularly attend meetings at the mission each Sunday, the priests attempted to force cessation of kiva ceremonies by disrupting the gatherings. The people were told to stop kachina dances and to have nothing to do with kachinas as they were devils not accepted by God. The friars threatened the villagers and removed their prayer feathers from hallowed places and sacred objects.

In secret meetings, the elders observed that crops had withered in the fields, rain had become more scarce each year and the people were very discouraged with the way things were going. In a bold decision kachina dances were restored in the village plazas, kivas again became the centers for religious ceremonies and prayer feathers appeared in abundance in homes and at shrines. The more durable of the Hopis at Oraibi planned a regular midsummer Niman Kachina ceremony specifically designed to produce rain. It was secretly conducted at a small isolated clearing among the mesa cliffs. Within four days, clouds gathered and rains fell on the parched land. The Hopis had proof that their ancient rituals brought the rain and the foreign religion of the Castillians was not valid for them.

THE PUEBLO REVOLT

Siki had regained her composure and continued her narrative. Meeting in the kivas, the elders became convinced that the time had come to take action against the missionaries but realized that such a course could not be accomplished without the backing of other Pueblo tribes. They sent emissaries east of the mountains to learn what was happening in other villages. Named to represent Oraibi were Honowaitiva, a tall handsome man with lighter than average hair and skin and a lithe, wiry frame. The other was close friend Yuclima of stocky, average height, black trimmed hair and a muscular build. Representatives were also selected from Shongopovi, Walpi-Koechaptevela and Awatovi.

At Acoma, Zuni and Laguna as well as pueblos in the Rio Grande area, lengthy discussions took place. After all Hopi emissaries had expressed their views, Honowaitiva was designated as spokesman and coordinator in order to arrive at a consensus.

"What we have found here is typical of other villages of the Pueblo people. All, including some who have been baptized by the Castillas, are unhappy and distressed by the conditions under which they have been forced to live. The underlying restlessness, very much in evidence, points to one thing, we must plan now to find a way to get rid of our oppressors!" Honowaitiva was speaking at a meeting in Laguna pueblo.

"A young man from a local clan rose to speak excitedly. "A plan is already in the making! It is said that a Tewa man named Popay has arranged meetings and is attempting to bring the tribes together in a revolt against the Spanish."

"Where can this man Popay be located?"

"He is from the San Juan Pueblo on the Rio Grande and is now supposed to be in Taos."

"Yuclima and I will go there and learn of his plans. The Hopis, like you who live in this region, desire to lift the oppression of the Castillas." Honowaitiva's remarks were met by cheers of support.

Two days later, the two Hopis met with Popay at a secret meeting place buzzing with activity. The Tewa confided in them. "Since you have come a great distance it is evident that your people wish to join in our rebellion. The heavy yoke of the Castillas will be removed forever! The Rio Grande people and those who live close to New Spain headquarters in Santa Fe are ready. Others, who have helped organize the revolt are waiting, as tight as bow strings!"

Honowaitiva felt the excitement and strength radiated by this man. "The land of the pueblos is so vast, how will all the tribes be able to act together? Has a certain date been decided upon?"

Popay explained. "Final details were concluded earlier today. Clan chiefs and tribal representatives at the meeting returned to their pueblos and trustworthy runners were dispatched to other areas. You see, each village will be given a length of animal skin with a certain number of knots tied at intervals. Each knot represents a day and when the final knot is reached, the rebellion will begin that day. "

The Hopis headed for home carrying their thong of deer hide on which a knot was untied each day of the journey. Several extra knotted cords had been supplied which were given out starting at Awatovi where the chief was told about the plan, the number of knots remaining and asked to provide the information to smaller villages. In this manner the chiefs at Walpi -Koechaptevela, Shongopovi and lastly Oraibi were informed resulting in coverage of all villages on and near the mesas.

Siki continued. As might be expected, such a widespread "secret" was revealed in advance to the Castillas at a Rio Grande pueblo. Popay moved at once against the Spaniards on August 10, 1680, three days ahead of the scheduled August 13.

At Oraibi the clans joined together for a discussion in secret as far as the local priests were concerned. Yuclima and Honowaitiva were called in to explain again all that they knew about the planned revolt which, unknown to them, was already underway.

"It is the contention of Popay and others that caution must be taken in the initial assaults to protect the identity of those involved and that the finest warriors take part." Honowaitiva paused for reflection of that statement.

Only a few moments were required. The Badger Clan leader, who was also the kalatakmongwi, or warrior chief, proclaimed; "Our Badger Warriors are ready. We will take to the front of the attack and destroy the priests and soldiers guarding them. Since we are related to the Kachina Clan we will use the Kachina masks and dress."

The assemblage agreed with the Warrior Chief but insisted that members of other clans wear the kachina costumes and participate along side the Badger warriors. Two of the strongest Badger men wearing the masks of the warrior kachina were designated to lead to attack groups; Hapeeya,to gain access to the priests quarters and Chavayo, to dispatch the sentry at the entrance to the building.

The final knot was untied in the black of night. Preparations for the assault were completed. Kachina masks and costumes were donned. The call of a screech owl greeted the dawn, signaling the attack.

Yuclima paired with Chavayo, who thrust a short spear through the sentry, then the two rushed the door backed by members of all clans. In the onslaught, all soldiers were killed.

Since the heavy wooden doors to the priests quarters had been barricaded, the warriors aided by townspeople began battering holes through the roof. Haneeya, joined by Honowaitiva, dropped inside the room and seized the two priests throwing them to the floor. A door burst open and the incoming warriors overpowered several native assistants who were dragged outside along with the priests and flung to the ground. All were killed. Remaining soldiers were apprehended in their billet and brought outside where they met the same fate. As it happened, only two of the priests were at the mission the others having gone south to Zuni for supplies.

Dragged by their legs to the rim of the mesa, the corpses were thrown into a gulch below. An avalanche of stones hurled by the clans men buried the bodies. The friars trappings and ceremonial objects were disposed of in the same manner.

Yuclima later explained what followed. "By daylight many villagers had gathered near the mission. When the warriors beckoned, they made a thorough search through the storage rooms gathering food supplies of great quantities contributed by the townspeople. These items, plus cattle and sheep from the corrals were segregated for distribution among the clans."

Honowaitiva expanded. "I heard a loud clanging sound and looked up to see the mission bell tumble down the roof and hit the ground. Workmen had pried it from its bearings. Afterwards, the bell, weapons and armor of the soldiers were sealed in a cave.

Stone by stone the buildings were demolished. Large poles and support beams which had been carried and dragged all the way from the San Francisco Peaks area years prior, were salvaged and stockpiled for future use."

The actions of the people in other villages were similar. Spanish priests were killed and missions were razed. Included were Padre Jose de Trujillo at Shongopovi, Padre Augustin de Santa Maria and Jose de Espeleta of Walpi and Oraibi and Padre Jose de Figuroa at Awatovi.

* * * * * * * *

Cindy questioned Siki. "Were any signs of remorse evident among the people?"

"Legends reflect attitudes of the people who suffered years of persecution and harassment. Since this was inflicted by the Castillas and priests, the villagers' embedded resentment forestalled any feelings of remorse for what had been done to escape from this oppressive yoke. Remember, all of the pueblo people were involved in the uprising.

"Markings on a large rock in the eastern pueblo region have been identified and other documented evidence indicate that the townspeople suffered many casualties in that area as well as the Rio Grande valley. An estimated five hundred Castillians were killed in the revolt which drove the Spaniards from Santa Fe, New Mexico Province and south into Mexico."

Sam was reflective. "Were the pueblo people able to sustain the independence they had won?"

"In the aftermath of the rebellion, although individual pueblo tribes were autonomous, Popay and others were unable to establish an effective governing group at Santa Fe which had become an important supply point and a crossroads of trade and commerce. Settlers from across the border came to the community and Rio Grande Valley. In about a dozen years the army returned, re-occupying Santa Fe, spreading their influence and again bringing missionaries and government emissaries from New Spain."

Siki continued her narrative.

The Province of Tusayan, with Hopis living in a cluster of small villages scattered among the arroyos on the edge of the desert and atop the mesas, was remote from the more heavily populated eastern pueblo region. The immediate period following the revolt was one of apprehension that a Castillian army would soon appear over the horizon. This proved to be a stimulant for vigilance and preparation. Measures were taken to defend themselves in order to prevent the return of the overlords. Hopis not living on the mesas moved their villages for re-location along the rims where they could be more readily defended.

Refugees from the Rio Grande pueblos had arrived in large numbers. An offer of sanctuary to the newcomers formed a bond with the Hopis which produced a union of interests and strength to repulse attempts at colonization by the Spaniards. Chief organizer and leader of the grand plan of resistance was Francisco de Espeleta, who became a Hopi hero.

A festering sore in the movement was the belief by a group of Christianized residents that a restoration of Spanish missions would prevent warfare. In time, two missionaries arrived and were welcomed at Awatovi, only to be threatened and provoked by members of other villages who expressed their hostility. As a result the priests abandoned the project but let the people know that they planned to return.

With the missionaries out of the way, Francisco de Espeleta gathered a militant, anti-Spanish group for an assault on Awatovi. In a series of forays the known mission supporters were killed, as were any men who resisted the onslaught. The village was then methodically destroyed and Awatovi no longer existed. Women and children were divided among the other mesa communities. These events proved the reality of the Hopis quest for freedom. Documents indicate that Spanish rule was never formally installed nor did Christian missionaries venture into Tusayan Province over a period of a century and a half.

The Michaelsons, Sam, Cindy and Mark sat solemnly in their chairs at the table over which so much history and events had passed. Each retained his own reflections on culture, religion and the unique way of life of the Hopis as well as other ancient pueblo dwellers.

Siki, who bore lighter skin and was taller than the average Hopi woman, sat erect and yes, stately in her accustomed place. Her shining black hair, now showing signs of gray, belied her three-score and ten years. She spoke again.

"The dream of the Hopis was and is the same as the dream of any free people. Those early years in the end served to strengthen their dream - one where they are not stripped of their culture, their mesa land or their spiritual freedom. It is more than a dream. It is a prayer."

* * * * * * * *

GLOSSARY AND PRONUNCIATION GUIDE - HOPI

ANASAZI (AH-nah-sah-zee) - The ancient ones.

AWTAS (AW-tahs) - Bows.

HALIKSAI (hah-LEEK-sah-ee) - Listen.

HAWA (HAH-wa) - Abode, house (Havasupai)

HISATSINOM (hee-SAHT- see-nom) - People of long ago.

HONO (HO-no) - Bear.

HORNO (HOR-no) - open hearth for cooking and heating.

HOOHUS (HO-o-hus) - Arrows.

HOPI TUTSKWA (toots-KWA) - Hopi country.

I'PAAVA (ee-PAH-ah-vah) - My older brother.

I'MAANA (ee-MAH-ah-nah) - My daughter.

KACHADA (kah-CHA-dah) - White man.

KAKLEHTAKA (kah-kleh-TAH-kah) - Warrior.

KIIHO (KEE-ee-ho) - My house.

KIIKI (KEE-ee-kee) - House or village.

KIIKIINUMTO (KEE-ee-Kee-um-to) - Come visit.

KOKOB (KO-kob) - Burrowing Owl(Clan).

KWAAHU (kwah-AH-hu) - Eagle.

KWAATSI (kwa-AHT-see) -Friend.

KWITAMUH (kwee-TAH-muh) - Renegades, roughnecks.

KWIDI (KWEE-dee) - Orion, the constellation.

MAANA (MAH-ah-nah) - Girl.

MANAWYA (MAH-nah-yah) - Little girl.

MANTA (MAHN-tah) - Cloak, heavy shawl, blanket.

MOOHA (MO-o-hah) - Yucca.

NOOSIQWA (no-o-SEE-qah) - Food, groceries.

NUVAKWAAHU (nu-vahk-wah-AH-hu) - Snow Eagle.

OVEKNIOLWI (OVAYK-nee-ol-wee) - Picnics.

PAHANA (PAH-hah-nah) - The lost white brother.

PI-YO (PEE-yo) - Purple yucca fruit.

PIKA - (PEE-kah) - Baked corn meal.

POYO - (PO-yo) - Knife.

PUUMPI (poo-OOM-pee) - Bed.

QOYANTA (qoy-AHN-tah) - Killing.

SOMIVIKI (SOM-ee-vee-kee) - Corn meal dough wrapped in husk and boiled .

TAAQA (TAH-ah-ka) - Man .

TAPUAT (TAH-poo-aht) -Mother and Child.

TAWA (TAH-wah) or TAOIWA (TAh-o-ee-wah) - The (Great) Sun Spirit.

TSOMO (TSOH-mo) -Hill.

TUMPOVAGE (tum-po-VAH-jay) - Over the cliff.

TUMPOVI (tum-POH-vee) - Edge of the mesa.

TUVA (TU-vah) - Pine Nuts.

TUWITA (tu-WEE-tah) - Know, understand.

WIKWAKNA (week-WAHK-nah) - Rope.

* * * * * * * *

<u>Author's</u> <u>Note</u>: The Hopis had no written language. It is not known who first began to write Hopi. Early missionaries possibly could have delved into the language structure searching for letters and words to express the lingual form. Hopi word lists were compiled in the 1890's by Henry Voth who issued a Hopi/Engliah dictionary. Other studies

followed but scholars still do not agree on a single orthography. No one, accepted way of writing Hopi exists today.

GLOSSARY- SPANISH

ABISMO - abyss
ALCALDE MAYOR- mayor with judicial powers
ARROYOS - arroyo - water course, gully
BALCON- balcony
BARBA- beard
BARRANCA- gorge
BATTALA POSICION- battle position
BIGOTE - mustache
BUQUE VELEROS- sailing vessel
CABALLISTA- horsemen
CABALLEROS - noblemen, horsemen
CABALLOS - horses
CACIQUE - native chief
el CAPITAN - a captain , (the)
CASTELLANOS - Castillians , Spaniards
CASTILLA - Spaniard, Castile
CESACION - cessation, suspension
COCINA- cooking, kitchen
COLUMNA - column
COMIDA- food
COMPARAZONES- horse blankets
CONQISTADORES - conquerors

DESTACAMIENTO - detachment
ESCUADRON - squadron
ESPOSAS - handcuffs, manacles
ESTAR el VIVAQUE - to be bivouacked
ESTUFA - steamroom
FERVOZ - intense emotion, fervor
GENTE - people
HIDALGOS - noblemen
HIERBA - grass
INGREDIENTE - ingrediente
JARRON - urn, vase
MALEVOLO - malevolent, vindictive, violence
OBILESCO - dagger
el PACIFICO OCEANO - the Pacific Ocean
PANADERO - baker
PANTALONES - pants
PRINCESA - princess
RIO COLORADO CHIQUITA - Little Colorado River
RUEGA PLUMA - prayer feather
SERVIENTE - servant
SOLDADOS - soldiers
TENIENTE - lieutenant
TERRAZA - terrace
TIERRA NUEVA - New Territory
TUSAYAN - Hopi Country
UNA JOURNADO de MUERTO - one journey to death
VESTIBULO - lobby, vestibule
VIGILANTE - guard, watchman

REFERENCES - ARCHIVES

Museum of Northern Arizona, research center, publications of Northern Arizona Society of Science and Art and PLATEAU, Flagstaff.

> How Don Pedro Tovar Discovered the Hopi and Don Garcia Lopez de Cardenas Saw the Grand Canyon, Katherine Bartlett, PLATEAU
> Vol. 12 No. 3, Flagstaff 1940.
> Hopi Agriculture and Food, Issue No. 5, 1954.

University of Northern Arizona, library, Flagstaff.

> Hopi Language, Walter Hough.
> Hopi Proper Names, Voth.
> Vargas Letters, J. M. Espinosa.
> History of Hawikuh, Frederick W. Hodge, 1937.
> Havasupai and Walapai, L. L. Hargrove, 1930-35.
> Lessons in Hopi (language), Milo Kalectaca 1978.
> Indians of Old Oraibi, Titier, diaries 1933.

University of Denver, library, Denver, Colorado.

> The Human Adventure - An Introduction to Anthropology, textbook by G. Pelto and P. Pelto, 1976.

Heard Museum of Anthropology and Ancient Art, Phoenix, Arizona.

> Hopi Tricentennial, exhibits, 1980
> Notes on Exposition.
> Publication, Phoenix 1971.

Hopi Cultural Center

> Second Mesa, Arizona
> Pictorial presentations , historical tribal events.
> Interviews.

BIBLIOGRAPHY

Arribas, Antonio, The Iberians, forging weapons and traditional cinerary uns and vases. Praeger Publisher, N. Y. 1964.

Bandelier, Adolph Francis (1840-1914), The Delight Makers. Dodd, Mead Publisher, N. Y. 1947.

Final Report of Investigation-Indians of the Southwest. Archae ological Institute of America, Cambridge, Mass. Printed by Wilson and Son 1892.

Bancroft, Hubert H. , History of Arizona and New Mexico, Vol. 17. The History Company, San Francisco 1889.

Beaglehole, Ernest and Pearl, Hopis of the Second Mesa. The American Anthropological Assoc. Menasha, Wisconsin 1935.

Benedict, Ruth, Zuni Indians Patterns of Culture. Houghton Miflin Co. 1934.

Bolton, Herbert Eugene, Coronado Knight of Pueblos and Plains. University of New Mexico Press, 1949, 1974.

Bourke, John Gregory, The Snake Dance of the Moquis of Arizona, reproduction of 1884 Edition. Rio Grande Press, Chicago 1962.

Chapman, Abraham, editor, Literature of American Indians, with Hopi lullaby and ritual recordings by Natalie Curtis. Published by New American Library New York, 1975.

Courlander, Harold, People of the Short Blue Corn. Harcourt Brace Jovanovich. Inc. N. Y. 1970.

The Fourth World of the Hopis. Crown Publishers, N. Y. 1971.

Hopi Voices, University of New Mexico Press, Albuquerque 1908.

Crampton, Charles G. , The Zunis of Cibola. University of Utah Press, 1977.

323

Dorsey, George Amos and H. R. Voth. The Mishongnovi, ceremonies, and The Stanley McCormick Hopi Expedition, Chicago 1902.

Dozier, Edward P. , The Hopi-Tewa of Arizona. University of California Press, Berkeley 1954.

Euter and Dobbyns, The Hopi People. Published by Indian Tribal Series, Phoenix 1971.

Gordon, Suzanne, Black Mesa-The Angel of Death. John Day Co. N. Y. 1973.

Gumerman, George J. , Black Mesa Survey and Excavation in Northeast Arizona. Prescott College Press, Prescott 1970 .

Hallenbeck, Cleve, Land of the Conquistadores. The Caxton Printers, Ltd. Caldwell, Idaho 1950.

Hirst, Stephen, Life is a Narrow Place, Havasupai villages. Published by David McKay Co. N. Y. 1976.

Hughes, J. Donald, American Indians In Colorado. University of Denver, Department of History, published by Pruett Publishing Co. , Boulder, Colorado 1977.

James, Harry C. , Pages From Hopi History. University of Arizona Press, Tucson 1974.

Jaramillo, Nash, Civilization and Culture of the Southwest. Distributed by Lavilla Real, Santa Fe, 1973.

Jones Oakah L. , Pueblo Warriers and Spanish Conquest. University of Oklahoma Press, Norman, 1966.

Lowie, Robert H. , Notes on Hopi Clans, Vol XXX, Part VI. Printed by the American Museum of Natural History, N. Y. 1929,

Lockett, Hattie Greene, The Unwritten Literature of the Hopi, marriage ceremony included. University of Arizona, Tucson 1933.

Neithammer, Carolyn, Daughters of the Earth, Hopi culture. Collier Book Division of Macmillan Publishing Company, Inc. N. Y.

1977.

Nequatewa, Edmund, Truth of the Hopi and Other Clan Stories of Shongopovi. Northern Arizona Society of Science and Art, Flagstaff 1936.

O'Kane, Walter Collins, The Hopis and Sun in the Sky and The Hopis Portrait of a Desert People. University of Oklahoma Press, Norman 1953.
Don Juan de Onate Colonizer of New Mexico 1595-1628, edit. George P. Hammond, University of California. Coronado Cuarto Centennial Publication 1540-1940, Vol. V, VI, The University of New Mexico Press 1953.

Pierson, Dixon, The Iberians of Spain, silversmiths and metal working. Oxford University Press, London 1940.

Powell, Major J. W. , The Hopi Villages - Ancient Province of Tusayan. Filter Press, Palmer Lake, Colorado 1972.

Qoyawayma, Polingaysi, (Elizabeth Q. White), No Turning Back (Hopi). University of New Mexico Press, Albuquerque 1964.

Sando, Joe S., The Pueblo Indians. The Indian Historian Press, San Francisco 1976.

Schwartz, D. , Havasupai Pre-History - Thirteen Centuries of Cultural Development. Dissertation for degree of Doctor of Philosophy, Yale 1955.

Stanislowski, Michael Barr, Hopi Indian Antiquity - Wupatki Pueblo. University of Arizona Press, Tuscan 1963.

Titier, Mischa, Old Oraibi, a Study of the Hopi Indians of the Third Mesa. Cambridge, Mass. , The Museum 1949.

Villagra, Gaspar Perez de, Historia de la Nueva Mexico. Pub. in Spain 1610.

Translated by Gilberto Espinosa, Quivira Society Publication,
No. 4 Los Angeles 1933. Printed and Manufactured by Johnson
Pub. Boulder, CO 1962.

Vivelo, Frank Robert and Jaqueline;Gloria Levitas, American Indian
Prose and Poetry. Published by George P. Putnam's Sons
Capricon Books, N. Y. 1974.

Voth, Henry R., Four Hopi Tales and Miscellaneous Notes From Hopi
Papers. Bound in book, Chicago 1912.

Waters, Frank, Book of the Hopi. Viking Press, N. Y. 1964.

Weaver, Thomas, Indians of Arizona. University of Arizona
Press, Tucson 1974.

Winship, George Parker, The Journey of Coronado. A. G. Barnes and
Co. N. Y. 1904. The Coronado Expedition, Orig. Publication
1896.
Translation of Castaneda, Rio Grande Press, Chicago 1964.

Whiting, A. F. Ethnobotany of the Hopis. Published by Northern
Arizona Society of Science and Art, Flagstaff 1939.

Wright, Barton, and Evelyn Roat, Hopi Kachina. Museum of Northern
Arizona, Flagstaff 1939.

* * * * * * * *

CHRONICLERS OF THE EXPEDITIONS

Pedro de Castaneda
Don Garcia Lopez Cardenas
Franciscans
Antonio de Espejo
Juan de Onate
Hernando de Alarcon